The Genealogists:

On Holy Ground

by

Jane Lawry

This book is dedicated to
The Legend of The Wandering Jew

Story by Jane & Joel Lawry

Special Thanks to Joel Lawry
Story Co-creator
My son, my friend and my muse

Additional Thanks to

My husband Kenny "The Great One" Lawry

For cooking lots of dinners when the writing process

couldn't stop long enough for me to get to the kitchen

Linda Chapman

Darlene Healey

Brandi Lawry

Robyn Owen

For helping catch our blunders

All the wonderful people on Authonomy for their constructive
comments and encouraging words! Thanks Authonomites!

And

Thank You Authonomy for helping writers become Authors

Prologue

AD 30: Valley of Gehenna, Judea

Evening shades of reddened orange, darkened in bent waves, forming elongated fingers reaching to touch the earth. Shadows cast from the ancient tree limbs crept over the horrific scene. Silence intensified the fiery crimson spectacle.

Using his forearm to wipe beads of sweat from his brow, the repulsed worker kicked the sheep's bloody leg off the dead man's face. The worker's affronted, ebony eyes, at once transfixed, on the corpses' empty eyes staring back at him.

The worker's accomplice, a short uncaring man, followed his companion's vexed gaze, then lifted his arm and elbowed him.

"Let's go," the short one said. "Our work is finished. The buzzards will feast when we're gone. Soon he'll have no eyes."

The short man then nodded toward the blood-soaked corpse. He shook blood from his own hands and observed thick red droplets splash upon the lifeless face of the staring man.

Disgusted by the sweet stink of death and gruesome sight before them, the men began backing away as if to make sure they weren't followed. Beneath their feet, the field trembled angrily. A body part changing position thumped against the parched, cracked ground. At once on guard and prepared for an impending attack, the men held fast, anticipating the emergence of a new devil rising fiendishly from an unforgivable death. Other than a ragged piece of cloth tossed by a single gust of air, nothing stirred. Conscious of the dead eyes following them, and not entirely aware they were doing so, they watched for movement before feeling confident enough to turn and face their new direction, heading to inform their employer of their completed task.

Left alone on the bloody field, surrounded by increasing darkness, the rotting bodies silently waited …

Chapter 1

Maria finished filling her supply cart and rolled it into the narrow hallway. One wheel consistently jammed, too often forcing her to push harder than normal. Today was the third day of her new job, and although thrilled to find work north of the Mexican border, she regretted being financially unable to explore the nearby sights of this new country. Nursing school amounted to a lot more than she had anticipated, and it would take awhile before she saved enough to think about going.

She maneuvered her body between the cart and the door and pushed backward, feeling instant bright warmth on her back. It didn't matter which country you were in, the sun always felt the same. Well, maybe not quite. Here it was warm, not the scorching hot of Mexico where just crossing the road made you sweat.

Pushing the cart toward the rooms marked for her to clean, she stopped and let her eyes scan the parking lot. Several cars still remained. Wanda, the other housekeeper, had informed Maria that most guests were gone by ten o'clock, and she had plenty to do between now and then.

Maria pursed her lips when one wheel of her cart rolled over the edge of the sidewalk. Hurrying to the cart's tipped front, she lifted it up, pushing it back onto the concrete walkway just as the door to Room 112 opened. The man coming through the doorway came to an abrupt halt, waiting for her to roll the cantankerous cart past him. Nodding in her direction, he touched one hand to his hat.

"Buenos días," he said.

Preferring to return her greeting in English, Maria politely nodded back and said, "Good morning."

The words were becoming more natural to her tongue. Upon her arrival in America, she inwardly pledged to resort to her native language only when making her weekly call home.

Determined to fluently learn her new country's language, the bold decision made her stand a little straighter.

When she stopped to reorganize her disarrayed assortment of cleaners, the departing guest walked to the trunk of his older mid-sized sedan and tossed his bag inside. In the blink of an eye, he jerked his face up toward the heavens and froze. Startled by his movement, Maria's eyes darted toward the sky, searching the wild blue yonder for some approaching horror. She twisted her head in every direction, examining the deep blue heavens until she was at last sure and very relieved to see the sky wasn't falling. Seeing nothing out of the ordinary, her initial scare turned to a mild passing wonder at his behavior, and she looked back at the frozen man. In the short time it had taken her to scan overhead, he had unfrozen and was casually inserting his key into the car door's lock.

When I'm a nurse, I want a car that beeps when I unlock the door, she thought and then smiled at the silly notion.

As the man's vehicle pulled from the curb, Maria saw a scrap of paper lying on the sidewalk beneath the back bumper. Retrieving the unsightly litter, she unfolded it and panicked when she discovered it was a map and at once knew it belonged to the odd man. Being concerned he might need the map to locate his destination, Maria dashed into the parking lot, holding the wrinkled yellowing paper high in the air. Other than a blue jay sitting on the motel's eave spout, there was no one to notice. The past two days had taught Maria that many guests checked out at the office before leaving the motel, so she pushed her stubborn cart to the side and ran in that direction in hopes of catching the lone traveler.

Hank, the desk clerk on duty, looked pleased when Maria entered the main lobby. But then, according to Wanda, Hank was always glad to see *any* woman ... especially those he thought were beneath him. Figuring Hank must have overslept since he had again arrived late to work, Maria overlooked his rumpled appearance and pretended not to see when he spit in his hand and tried to smooth an unruly clump of hair into place.

"*Buenos días,* little gal," Hank said. "You look like you could use a little hug to wipe that frown off your pretty little Mexican face. Come on over here and let ol' Hank fix you right up. I got just what you need to put that smile back in place."

Maria turned and walked out of the office. Worry about Hank's possible reaction didn't set in until she was outside. Regardless, not wanting to create a scene by running like a scared rabbit, she only got a few feet when the door behind her opened and Hank yelled, "Hey, you come back here when I'm talking to you!"

Her rising fear mounted in time with the red flush surfacing on her cheeks, but she refused to look back at the messy man. Keeping her eyes straight ahead, she caught sight of the elderly couple from Room 110 leaving at that very moment, and, as luck would have it, *they* stopped at the office. Chancing a look back when they climbed out of their packed auto, she heard an infuriated Hank mumble something inaudible under his breath before going back inside the office with the couple.

Maria raised her eyes toward the sky, uttering a clearly American, "Thank you," while tracing the sign of the cross across her breast.

Noting the number 112 on her cleaning list, she returned to the room and knocked before using her passkey. As she expected, the room was vacant, and she decided to begin her cleaning with the empty room in hopes the man would return. Locking the door's deadbolt, she worked diligently, all the while listening for the return of the beep-less automobile or, at the very worst, the vile desk clerk. Neither showed up.

The nightstand between the queen-sized beds was last to be cleaned. Removing the phone book and the Gideons Bible, she wiped inside the drawer and returned the phone book. Reaching into her pocket, she withdrew the map and placed it at the back of the Bible. She made sure the Bible was straight when she put it on top of the phone book, then closed the drawer.

Finished with her tasks, she locked Room 112, continuing on her way until each room was spick-and-span and her day was complete. Before going to sleep that night, Maria thought about the map and felt content, confident it was now in God's hands.

Chapter 2

He stared out the broken window of the vacant warehouse located on the city's south side—the industrial side of the city where houses of those less fortunate bordered the abandoned warehouses. The location of the building, however, was of no significance to him. He had a vague idea where he was, but couldn't have cared less if he hadn't known at all. His eyes were focused on the light shining from the house across the alley. If someone had witnessed his observation, they would have thought he was staking out the house. He wasn't. He didn't know or care about staking out a house. He wasn't thinking. He was feeling. And what he was feeling at that particular moment was the way the woman's throat had felt when he strangled her to near death.

She had been the one to lead him to the warehouse. Stupid, mundane, mortal human that she was, she'd believed she had seduced and led him to the building for sex, after which he would be expected to return payment for her services. What did he care about sex? Sex was only a tool to get what was really important. Didn't these simple humans know blood was what sustained life? Blood. Blood was what he needed. Blood would make him live forever. He knew this to be true. After all, he had been using blood to sustain his life for almost two thousand years. He was no vampire, though. A vampire at least has some human elements, a memory of a previous life for instance, ... of which he had none. His first memory was waking in a field filled with bloody and decaying animal carcasses, having their blood matted to his body. When he'd stood to better view the field of beasts, he swallowed after tasting remnants of blood, and soon felt the mixture of saliva and blood course through his body, giving him strength. Overcome with the need for more blood, he drank what he could from the lifeless bodies until the ashen color of his skin changed to a darker tan. Later standing knee deep in a nearby pool of water while washing the blood from his body, he saw a reflection and knew it belonged to him. For whatever reason, his body, which had lain on the blood-soaked ground in the midst of the beasts, had been given life. His birthplace, in his memory, was a field of blood.

His only human element was his appearance. Fairly tall, his dark handsome looks often came in handy when his need for blood surfaced. Because his brownish-red eyes, which easily adjusted to light or dark, exposed his lack of emotions, he found it simpler to use the nighttime's cover of darkness to mask that missing quality.

The woman's moaning and slight movement forced his attention on her. Picking up a metal pipe from the dirty floor, he hit her across the head. Not hard enough to kill her, but hard enough to knock her out for a bit longer. He looked for an object he could use to catch her blood flow and soon found an unbroken glass light globe. One thing he had come to know was blood tasted better from clean glass containers. Plastic containers permitted lingering tastes of previous occupants of the container to mix with the blood, and although his body could absorb the dirt, he didn't care for the gritty taste.

His black boots made a clanging sound when they scraped the metal stair rail as he leapt over it to land at the bottom of the fire escape. Not an extraordinary feat since it was only one landing. He had decided it was easier to leap over the rail rather than walk through the debris cluttering the stairway. Looking right, under the building's downspout, he saw a rusted barrel filled with rainwater. Thrusting the light globe deep in the water, he used his fingers to wash all traces of dirt from the glass. Last, for no particular reason, he breathed deep of the fresh air. Satisfied, his stride quickened as he eagerly returned to his task on the second floor.

His need for blood was not daily. It depended on the quality of the blood he drank. Some humans' blood kept his body strong for up to a year or more, while others left him feeling weak after just a few days. He hadn't determined the reason for this, but when he drank the blood that preserved him longer, he tasted something different—a kind of clean, sweet, airy taste. The breath of fresh air he'd breathed in minutes earlier reminded him of the taste. It seemed the taste of dirt wasn't present in the long-preserving blood.

While he was thinking on this, he slit the woman's wrist and held the clean globe under the fresh wound. After several ounces, he tipped the globe to his mouth to taste the blood before gulping it down. Disappointed, he knew he would need more. The blood had the taste of dirt, but it would sustain him for several days. Long enough for the woman to renew her blood supply and satisfy him many more times before he would get rid of her. While he drank, he held the wound tight to keep the fresh cut from spurting blood everywhere. Then, placing the light globe on the floor, he seared the wound with the knife he had been heating in the fire burning in a discarded metal trashcan, afterward wrapping the wound with a strip of cloth he tore from a sleeve of the woman's soiled blouse.

Knowing the woman would not awaken for several hours, he picked up the light globe from the floor and, returning to the fire escape stairway, again leapt over the railing. Once outside, he went back to the barrel of rainwater and stripped himself of his clothing, washing his body as best he could. Stretching and flexing his taut muscles in the moonlight, he eyed his physique in admiration and enjoyed the regenerating rush of the woman's blood coursing through his vessels. Although her blood was not as good as the quality of some, he realized it was better than he originally thought as he witnessed his skin's already younger appearance.

Before dressing, he picked up the bloodied light globe and dipped it in the water only enough to allow water to flow in the top. Removing the globe, he swished the bloody mixture around, tossing it afterward into a thin patch of grass. He repeated this process three times before daring to dip the globe in far enough to give it a thorough washing.

Not caring to walk back upstairs, he set the light globe inside the fire exit door and left to walk the streets of the city. Although unfamiliar with his whereabouts, his instincts were keen, and he knew he would have no trouble locating the warehouse again.

Passing beneath the window of the house where the single light still shone, he listened to two men quarrel. Their voices grew louder until he suddenly heard a loud bump against the wall of the house. He knew someone had just won an argument, and he absently nodded his approval of silencing the weaker opponent.

Tempted to enter the house to view its occupants, he strode to the front of the building, where he came in contact with two full-grown rottweilers chained to the front-porch railing, both coming to attention when he drew near the porch. The simultaneous growl of the dogs was rebuked by a low snarl, causing both animals to back closer to the house's doorway. Neither, it became apparent, was trying to protect the door's entrance but instead attempting to gain entry for their own protection. Greatly disapproving of the cowering dogs, he reproachfully dismissed them. Continuing to the street, he soon disappeared into the darkness.

Chapter 3

Rich shades of green generously spread across, rolling, meadows came into view. The fertile landscape was a welcome change from the monotony of the dry barren terrain they had been driving through. The lush scenery made him think of an oasis, transporting him inside an image. Shutting his eyes, he watched himself sit under an oak tree beside a small pool of sunlit water. Further releasing his mental boundaries, the tranquil vision grew, invariably relaxing his tight muscles. From deep within his mind, a gravestone sprang up on the far side of the envisioned water. Startled, a look of mild distress appeared on his face. Even so, the pounding in his head lessened.

/////

Cassandra Elliott, dubbed "Casper" by school chums deciding her pale complexion too closely resembled that of the friendly ghost, glanced sideways at Shade. She knew they needed to eat soon. His face looked drawn. She wished they had stopped at the small diner they passed earlier, and she admonished herself for letting her desire to reach the cemetery silence her better judgment. They were close, however, and if they were ever going to find any of Jack's relatives, these trips would be necessary.

At least one good thing had happened during those last few months of Jack's life: Shade had come home. Shade and his sister Brianna, or Breeze as most called her, had both been there to wrap their arms around their father and say good-bye. For that, Casper would be forever grateful. After Jack's death, Shade stayed. He confided in her of his drug use and asked her for help.

Casper was determined to help, and this trip away from the city—from the temptations and the trappings of familiar surroundings, as far as she was concerned—was just what the doctor ordered. She promised herself the next stop would be quick. Then they would get some food and keep his feet planted firmly in the real world.

"There's the turnoff, Mom," Shade said. "Turn left. It's a gravel road, but it can't be any worse than this one."

Within minutes, Casper pulled the car to the side of the road and turned off the engine. Shade shot out of the car, visibly reinvigorated by his rush of freedom. After stretching his legs, he dashed smoothly toward the top of the hill as if gravity had not been present on that particular swath of land. Casper held a hand above her eyes, shielding them from the blinding sunlight, and watched his private race. A group of trees caught her attention when a gust of wind bent their branches, sweeping them up and down, appearing to wave in a beckoning gesture. Sparked by the positive imagery, she yelled out and rooted him on as he raced upward.

Once he reached the top, she was ready to get moving and started up the hill. After witnessing Shade's speedy performance, she refused to stop to rest and surprised herself by making the climb in a respectable time.

"Not bad, Mom. I thought I'd be waiting for at least another ten minutes."

"Hey, mister! I still have some vavoom left in my tank," she said through ragged intakes of air. Turning full circle to take in the view, her breathing gradually evened, and she said, "Nice scenery. Except for those trees on the right, you can see in every direction. Who would expect to find a cemetery here? It's a nice location but certainly off the beaten path. Have you looked around yet?"

"Just a bit. Not much. I was waiting for you," he answered and walked a few feet to kick a crumbling headstone.

"Shade Elliott!" Casper said. "A cemetery's a person's final resting place. When a headstone is destroyed, the person buried could become lost forever. We—*the living*—are responsible to ensure their graves are respected."

"Sorry, Mom. I wasn't thinking. I won't do that again."

In an instant, Shade's face lost all expression, and Casper felt sure he was thinking about his father buried beneath a headstone of his own. With that look, she knew any further reprimands would not be necessary.

"Okay. I'm off to have a look around. Why don't you find an older headstone that looks intriguing?" she said. "When we get home, you can do some research of your own: find out who they were, where they came from, and how they ended up here, in such an out-of-the-way cemetery. What do you think? Want to give it a try?"

After a rather lengthy pause, he mumbled, "I'll think about it," just after his face took on a bewildered expression.

Leaving him alone to mull over the idea, Casper disappeared post-haste behind a large gravestone. As she smothered her chuckles, his bewilderment wasn't lost on her, and she peeked back to see him bending to touch the stone he had nonchalantly kicked a minute earlier. His softly spoken "Sorry" was drowned out when she tripped on a rock meant to mark a grave. Forgetting her son, she turned her thoughts on her deceased husband's missing relatives.

Other than their names, she knew very little about Jack's parents. They had severed all family ties not long after they were married, moving across the country to distance themselves from their interfering families. Three months after Jack was born, it was all over: both of them killed in a boating accident.

With no way of locating Jack's grandparents, their new friend Dan took Jack in and raised him as his own. Dan, an orphan himself, knew how cruel the system could be. Unfortunately he was older and died when Jack was twenty-two. After his death, Jack found a letter his mother had started but died before completing. Neatly printed on the outside of the letter's envelope was the name *Conrad Elliott*—no address, only the name.

Conrad was who she was looking for today. After

visiting the courthouse, she already knew the Conrad she came to find was not a match for Jack's grandfather, but she still couldn't resist checking area cemeteries wherever she traveled on her research excursions. Regardless, eyeing the old stones, she didn't feel she would find Conrad here, either.

It was sheer coincidence they even knew about the cemetery. She'd found the crude map at the back of the Bible inside the nightstand's drawer in their motel room. If she hadn't been looking for cemeteries in the phone book, she wouldn't have picked up the book lying on top of it. While holding the Bible, she saw a piece of paper sticking out the back and, pulling it from the book, was dumbstruck to see a map leading to a cemetery. Wanting to believe it had been put there for her to find, she delayed their return home to visit the graveyard. Now she realized her foolishness.

Giving the cemetery a last look, she called out to Shade. Not seeing him among the gravestones, she looked toward the car and spotted him. Looming larger than life next to him was a gigantic, dimly lit shadow. The human-shaped shadow made Shade appear ten times his normal size. Shade waved an outstretched hand, and his shadow's arm lifted, thrusting a sword toward the sky. A drifting cloud, filled with the sun's rays, burst at the seams, spilling streams of light and erased his eerie shadow from view. Waving back, she began her trek back down the hill.

The hill was easier to navigate on the way down. Thankful to find gravity had not been left from that particular piece of ground, she appreciated its downward assistance. At one uneven spot, she was more than a little concerned, however, that her head might beat the rest of her to the bottom, so she grabbed the nearest bush to keep from falling head over heels. Minutes later, she reached the foot of the hill and was soon standing in front of her son.

"Did you find an interesting headstone to research?" she

asked.

She noticed his eyebrows contort before his gaze dropped to the ground.

"No," he said.

"Shade, I know this is not what you prefer doing. I'm only trying to help you keep your mind busy while you're adjusting and making changes in your life. Please … *help* me to help you." Casper paused, considering her next words: "I took several pictures, and I found an unusual marking on a grave by the grove of trees. Would you consider looking at them and possibly give it a try?" Casper asked, bending her head at an odd angle in an attempt to catch sight of Shade's eyes as they continued to stare at the ground.

"I'm not going to like researching dead people, Mom."

"I know … and that's okay. This is only a temporary hobby until your mind and spirit are able to heal. The healing process takes time, and if it helps you to know this, we're both in need of healing. Without my new hobby, I think most of my day would be spent crying and feeling sorry for myself … and I don't want that for either of us. Give it a try, okay?"

Casper was ready for whatever answer he gave, but her heart leapt for joy when his "Okay" was heard.

"If I'm going to pick out a headstone from one of your pictures, then I guess I should take a real look while we're here," Shade said. "Wait here. I'll be right back."

With that, Shade again sprinted up the hill. This time, he didn't stop to kick at any of the headstones but went straight to the grove of trees.

Casper watched when he stopped, first before the headstone with the unusual marking. Then, moving to one of the nearby trees, he ran his hands over the bark. After several minutes, he turned and began his descent. Instead of his usual rush, he paused to look directly at each stone he passed. The sun had already dipped behind the hill, and a beautiful golden glow shone directly above the cemetery. While she watched, the glow settled on Shade. Her breath caught when barely visible tentacles of light shot out in all directions around him as he walked through the midst of the cemetery, silhouetted by the sun's setting light. Bursts of light sprang from the granite meshed with the rock of the headstones. The effect was mesmerizing, and in that moment, somehow she knew his healing had begun.

/////

The sun had faded into the moon and stars. The rubber tires rolled once again over the rough and rugged highway. Casper looked over at her sleeping son. Dinner at the small diner had been more than adequate. The sign read *Home Cooking,* and neither had been disappointed.

At the cash register, she bought some fruit and picked up some chips for snacks. Returning to their car, each agreed to return for breakfast before beginning the long drive home. Soon they would be back in their own environment. Her intuition, however, told her this trip would be repeated.

Chapter 4

Patty slowly opened her eyes and tried to focus on her surroundings. Nothing was coming into view. Gradually she realized she was surrounded by total darkness. She sat up, confused, looking for the glow from the city's streetlights. When she moved her arm to better support herself, excruciating pain shot through her wrist. She fell back and hit her head on the hard surface behind her. Beginning to panic, she used her good arm to feel the area around her and, determining its shape, realized she was in a bathtub. That explained it. Miles must have given her something and she had passed out in the bathtub sometime afterward. From the way her head ached, she must have done a nosedive into the tub, she thought, tenderly rubbing a knot on her skull.

Unalarmed now, she lay back and rested her head again on the tub's hard enamel, remembering her first meeting with Miles. A friend told her Miles could help her earn the money she needed for the university's tuition payments. At first, she balked when she learned of the activity required to earn the money. Miles, on the other hand, had obviously witnessed the tentative look on his applicants' faces before and was prepared for any hesitation from his newer female staff members.

Shushing her with a finger on her lips, he'd placed an arm around her and led her to an empty room where he whispered of her beauty. He it seemed, wanted to get to know her better and, over the next two weeks, took her to the finest dining establishments and bought her expensive jewels. Later, she discovered the jewels were fakes, bought at the local pawnshop.

Her introduction to drugs happened during the latter part of the second week when he slipped her a molly. By the third week, she was turning tricks and handing him the money. As long as she performed her services to his clients, all was well:

her tuition paid on time, books purchased when she needed them, and a new outfit on a regular basis. Oddly Miles and Patty had never had sex. Once he'd learned of her virginal state, he refused to take advantage of her, or so he said. A few months later, she learned a virgin was worth more—much more.

Recently in an effort to keep her from attending classes, he had been refusing to give her the Ritalin she needed. She didn't have ADHD; the Ritalin simply increased her ability to study. Her grades had improved a full grade point since Miles introduced her to the drug. At first, after his refusal to give her the study aid, she had been angry—until walking past a church, when she had been stricken with extreme remorse and then entered through the church's heavy wooden doors. The silence in the church was intimidating, increasing her feelings of unworthiness. Alone on a wooden pew near the center of the saintly room used by the regular worshipers, tears streamed down her face. She gazed in silent respect at the stunning statues, the stained-glass saints and angels decorating the windows of the holy place of worship. Timidly walking to the altar, she knelt and sincerely asked God's forgiveness for her sins. A calming peace descended upon her, and her tears began to dry. Unfamiliar with God's forgiveness, she begged Him to talk to her until she finally gave up and walked away in despair, never understanding that God had forgiven her when she first asked.

Climbing the steps of a nearby bus, she'd ridden to the city's south side. She had been to the house where Miles got his drugs several times. Before going inside, though, she desperately needed to make some money. That was her last clear memory. Searching inside her bruised head for what happened next, a man's dark, blurred, face began forming in her mind's eye. A choking bout interrupted the mental image. Coughing violently to catch her breath, the yet unrecognizable face faded away before she was able to identify the man. Once the uncontrollable fit ended, the lost image returned, clearly visible. She sat forward in the tub, recognizing the unmistakable face of Miles. That had to be it. Miles must have found her, and now she was being punished for her disobedience.

Listening, she could hear him moving in the next room, and she called his name but was too weak to make her voice heard. Leaning back, she closed her eyes and succumbed to the darkness.

/////

In the room next to the woman, he sat with his back to the steps inside the opening in the wall. He knew the woman had awakened and listened carefully for her movements. The woman calling to someone named Miles alerted him to the possibility of someone searching for her. His concern was minimal, knowing his whereabouts were well concealed.

After his return a few nights earlier, he had scoured the warehouse. Apparently the previous owner of the warehouse had a few secrets of his own. Concealed behind a sliding fake-paneled wall on the top floor of the warehouse was a small apartment, complete with a small combined kitchen and living-room area, and an even smaller bedroom with a bathroom. Even though the electric and plumbing were of no use, the apartment's furniture remained. He was even able to gain access to the roof from a louvered furnace door. Once opened, the door exposed four steps leading to an opening in the roof. An empty heat pump shell covered the opening. After unlatching the phony covering, he removed it to breathe the night air instead of the apartment's dusty interior. The toilet, although dirty, looked unused, but knowing sewer gases could be deadly to humans, he carried buckets of water to flush and fill the toilet bowl before carrying the woman up the flights of stairs and dropping her in the tub. Slightly stuffy, the windowless bathroom remained cool due to the seasonal weather. The bedroom door, when opened fully, fit against the side of the bathroom's door handle. Since the bathroom door opened out instead of in, it created a perfect cell for his newest blood donor. Yes, he felt the owner of the warehouse had secrets—secrets he would like to have known.

With the bathroom silent again, he slid open the concealed paneled wall to step out of the apartment. Sliding the wall back in place, he trudged through the darkened warehouse until he was outside in the cool night breeze. It would rain tonight. He could smell the fresh dampness in the air. When thunder rumbled in the distance, he stopped to listen to the warning rumbles, staring in the direction of the nearing sounds before proceeding to his destination.

Twenty minutes later, he returned, carrying a paper sack. Re-entering the hidden apartment, he placed the sack on the small kitchen counter and removed some of its contents, carrying the rest to the imprisoned bathroom. Moving the bedroom door to open the bathroom, he looked through the darkness at the sleeping figure in the tub. Seeing no movement, he set some of the sack's items on the black-and-white vinyl flooring and afterward lit a candle, placing it on the back of the toilet's tank top. Lastly he returned with a bucket of water and set it beside the tub. Satisfied nothing more was needed, he closed the doors to recreate the cell's barricade.

Back in the small kitchen and living-room area, his eyes scanned the room's interior before heading to the steps leading up to the roof. While ascending the steps, he observed the night sky before stepping onto the rooftop. Crossing to the ledge atop the waist-high wall surrounding the roof, he merely glanced in the direction of the house across the parking lot and alley. Due to the moon's disappearance behind the threatening rain clouds, his figure, should someone look in his direction, would be hidden by the darkness.

Finding the door used ordinarily for access to the roof, he descended the warehouse stairs until he found an upturned barrel similar to the rain barrel on the side of the building. After inspecting the insides, he carried it to the roof and positioned it in one of the roof's adjoining corners. It sat about six inches beneath the top of the ledge, which sloped inward. Going back inside the warehouse, he returned moments later with a large piece of tin and wedged it to fit inside the barrel. He bent the tin and angled it to catch any water pouring off the ledge. He finished just as the first drops of rain began to fall.

Going back inside the apartment, he headed straight to the kitchen sink and opened the cabinet beneath it. He found an almost full bottle of dish detergent and brought it back with him into the living room, setting it on one of the steps inside the exposed opening. He shed his clothes, tossing them haphazardly on the room's armchair.

Returning to the rooftop, he pushed the empty heat pump covering over the concrete lip surrounding the opening, to keep the rain out of the apartment. The metal scraped the concrete, making a high-pitched screeching sound. A loud boom of thunder drowned out the noise when the winds gusted and picked up speed. His hair, although not long, lifted from the back of his neck and blew sporadically. The rain had not yet fully started, only dampening his body. Popping the top of the dish detergent bottle, he squirted the soap all over his body and then set the bottle down. Methodically he began scrubbing himself with both hands. His hair, which had blown wild earlier, now lay in suds on his head. His eyes remained open as he scrubbed the dirt and grime from his face. The rain came harder, pelting his body and splashing violently on the roof around him. Within minutes, he stood ankle deep in its depth. The rain accumulated on the surface until it ran through one of the concrete's minute cracks and streamed rapidly below.

Lightning flashed, illuminating the man washing from head to toe. He lifted his head and held his face resolutely toward the black sky, letting the raging rain pound him. An average man would have found it difficult to keep his balance in the high winds of the storm. He remained unmoved, as though his feet were planted in the roof's concrete. He observed when the detergent bottle blew against the side of the ledge's wall, only to float violently back seconds later.

/////

Inside the bathtub, Patty woke to the sound of thunder and, seeing the lit candle, thought the electric was out. She called out to Miles again but was still too weak to make her voice heard, even more so now over the rumbling thunder. She had soiled herself and, climbing from the tub, weakly removed her jeans and underwear. Sitting on the toilet, she emptied her bladder, afterward using the cheap, scratchy tissue from the half roll on the holder. Her gaze fell to the material wrapped around her wrist, and removing the cloth bandage, she gasped at the wound. Had she tried to kill herself, she wondered? Why wasn't she in a hospital? She realized immediately Miles would never take her to a hospital. This, she thought, is exactly what he would do to one of his girls who tried to off herself. Reaching behind, she pushed the toilet's handle. When the toilet wouldn't flush, she decided, in her confused state, it was because of the power outage.

Looking down, she noticed a small paper sack on the floor with a tiny spider crawling across it. She grabbed one of her shoes next to the toilet and knocked the spider off the bag, smashing it on the floor, then cautiously opened the sack. Inside, she found a sandwich wrapped in plastic, a carton of milk, and an apple. She was hungry but too weak to eat very much. After a few bites, she rewrapped the remainder of the sandwich and placed it and the unopened milk back in the bag with the untouched apple. Despite not being able to eat, she was thirsty. Grabbing the edge of the sink, she pulled herself to stand, then reached to turn the faucet handle as she lowered her head to drink before discovering the faucet wouldn't work. Confusion at the inconvenience gave way to anger when she realized Miles must have shut the water off.

Pissed, she grabbed the bathroom's doorknob and pushed but couldn't open the door. Rattling the handle back and forth proved useless. Frustrated, she softly slapped her hand against the door's surface and sighed. Too weak to pound on the door and fight with Miles, she crossed the room to the tub and tried the spigot, with the same outcome as the sink's faucet. She gave up and lowered herself back to the floor and, forming a cup with her hands, dipped them in the bucket of water and drank the water from her hands, all the while wondering where the hell Miles had her locked up.

Temporarily defeated, she crawled back across the floor to the sink and opened the cabinet beneath it. She was relieved to find a couple of towels and washcloths. Dipping one of the washcloths in the bucket of water, she stretched her arm to the sink top and felt until she found a used bar of soap. She partially cleaned herself before realizing she didn't dare rinse the washcloth out in the bucket of water in case she needed a drink later. With no other options available, she continued using the dirty washcloth until there were no clean spots left to use, then threw it and her dirty underwear in the sink. In her weakened condition, the bucket was too heavy to lift to pour water in the sink, but she tried. Finally, wrapping a towel around her waist, she lay down on the floor between the sink and the tub. Exhausted, she fell back to sleep.

/////

Finishing his exhilarating outdoor shower, he stretched his hands to the sky. A brilliant flash of lightning struck a nearby tree and was instantly followed by a thunderous boom that shook the warehouse. He remained unmoved. Oblivious to heaven's powerful display, he turned slowly around to rinse the last of the soap off his body.

Satisfied all traces of soap were gone, he bent over to pick up the floating dish detergent bottle from the water flooding the rooftop and then sauntered to the apartment's camouflaged entrance. Lifting the heat pump shell to descend the steps hidden beneath, he stopped to re-latch the covering before entering the rooms below.

Inside the apartment, he realized he had forgotten to get one of the towels from the cabinet in the bathroom so made do with a much too small T-shirt from one of the bedroom's dresser drawers to dry himself. With his body mostly dry, he ripped the blankets from the bed before lying down. He rarely slept, but tonight he would rest. The storm's fury continued, and the closed furnace door did little to mute the sound. Listening to the rain pounding on the metal covering, he did not hear the woman, nor did he listen for her at all during the night.

Chapter 5

Shade faked running right then dodged left, skimming the side of the armchair. He crossed the room at breakneck speed, spun backward, and tiptoed sideways to avoid running into the wall. Jumping and spinning in midair, he flew across the coffee table to land backside first on the sofa. His opponent stopped his forward progress as soon as he witnessed Shade's landing. His sorrowful brown eyes looked at his master as if to say, "How could you? That's my seat." Instead his woeful "Arf" was his only audible response.

"Sorry, Charlie, I beat you fair and square," Shade told his dog.

Charlie let out a loud sigh in protest but plopped down on the floor in front of the sofa. Reaching down, Shade patted his furry body, then picked him up and put him on the couch beside him. It was a common scene in the Elliott household, with Shade more often than not the winner. In his younger years, Charlie had been a formidable foe and often outran Shade to their favorite spot in front of the living room's television. Occasionally Shade would still let him win the game. Shade's homecoming had helped restore some of Charlie's youthful antics. He had even returned to sleeping in Shade's room, letting the household know just *who* was Charlie's favorite member of the Elliott family.

"Shade, I left my camera on the desk in the den for you to download the pictures from our trip," his mom said, coming into the room. "I'm driving into the city to meet Brianna for lunch and do a little shopping. I'd invite you to join us, but I have the distinct feeling today is girl talk. I can't decide if she's having school problems or if there's a new boyfriend on the horizon. Either way, only female Elliotts are permitted on this trip. But I can drop you off at the library if you'd like."

"Not today, Mom. Charlie and I have our day mapped out. After we have our walk and visit with that fine little poodle the Jeffersons brought home, I'm going to jump on the computer and find some perfectly good dead guy to chat with. I'm hoping he'll share some wisdom about life on the dead side. You know, like, do you just use your finger to brush your teeth? And what's it like to have your hair keep growing without a comb around?"

"Okay, smart guy. I want a full report on the dead guy's teeth and hair when I get back, and while you're at it, find out what kind of clothes they prefer; more importantly, should I wear tennis shoes or heels?" Mom asked.

"Have fun and tell Breeze just because now she's one of those preppy intellectuals doesn't mean she can't drop by and visit her lesser intelligent big brother."

"Shade, you are not less intelligent. You'll know that when you re-enroll in school next spring."

Shade lost sight of her halfway through her sentence when she sped off to the next room. The quick closing of the door to the garage let him know she was determined to have the last word on the subject.

"Huh? Next spring? How does she always manage to do that, Charlie?"

He waited a full five minutes after his mom left before jumping up to find Charlie's brush. After brushing all the kinks out of the dog's wavy coat, he dug through the shelf in the coat closet for the bow tie the family had bought for the dog one year while caught up in the spirit of Christmas. Spotting the red plaid bow on the top shelf, he slipped it over Charlie's head and around his neck then stepped back to look at him. Something was still missing. He needed a hat. He didn't know if Charlie had a hat, so he found an old favorite of his own. Charlie, nevertheless, kept shaking it off. Snapping his fingers, Shade ran upstairs to his mother's bedroom to look for some bobby pins. Pulling open her dresser drawer, his hands froze when he spied an almost full bottle of Oxycontin. His heart began beating faster, and he couldn't stop himself from staring at the bottle containing the addictive pain pills. Picking the bottle up to look on the side, he read his father's name. His hands trembled as he continued hunting for the bobby pins, and even though he told himself he wouldn't take any of the pills, he still held the bottle when he closed the drawer.

He stopped by his bedroom and slipped the bottle of pills in the pocket of a jacket hanging in his closet before returning to Charlie. He consoled himself with the theft by reasoning the pills were only in case of emergency.

The bobby pins did just the trick, and after clipping on Charlie's leash, they were out the door and, within minutes, passing the Jeffersons' house where the new poodle was bouncing in and out of a pile of leaves in her front lawn.

Charlie promptly sat, refusing to budge from his spot on the sidewalk. The Jefferson poodle approached the fence and rested on her belly. Soon she stuck her nose through the narrow opening between the slats, prompting Charlie to do the same. After a couple of getting-to-know-you sniffs, the poodle snatched Charlie's hat, pulling it through the slats to her side of the fence, heading at once back to her pile of leaves. A light tug on the leash alerted Shade that Charlie was ready to go, and the two continued their walk around the block.

Shade eyed the fluffy poodle lying on her belly and watching their progress with the hat tucked possessively under her front legs. He made a mental note not to dress Charlie in a hat ever again when walking past the young dog's house. He was glad the bow tie was fastened securely in place.

After their brisk walk, Shade was ready to get to work. Plugging the camera into the iMac computer, he uploaded the pictures without a hitch. There were more than he expected, and he shook his head wondering how they'd managed to take so many on such a short trip. With his sister away at college, his mother seldom wanted to be far from home for very long. Since Jack Elliott's death, she worried and always wanted to be available in case of any emergency, making it necessary to shorten her trips, research or not.

The pictures were sharp and very clear. He needed to remember to compliment his mother on the camera she had purchased for the trip. One particular photo caught his eye and caused him to linger on it. It was a picture of him near the center of the cemetery. At first, he couldn't account for the strange, faint lights cast around him, the lights appearing to extend from his body. Thinking back, he remembered the reflective, phosphorescent shirt he wore that day. The picture's eerie glowing lights made him look mystical and one with his surroundings. Normally that would have pleased him, but being one with a cemetery didn't exactly fit in with his mystical ideas. Although, if someone were going to be mystical, he supposed a cemetery might be the place to give it a try.

Still in front of the computer, he typed in the word "mysticism" on the Safari browser and was surprised to learn mysticism basically meant having a conscious awareness of a direct communication or *personal* experience with a supreme being … for him, God. He hadn't felt any direct experience with God, but he had to admit, standing in the cemetery, he had felt something. What it was, he didn't know, and he shook his head at his inability to translate the experience into words. Flapping his arms about, he began mouthing *doo-doo-doo-doo, doo-doo-doo-doo* to the tune from the theme of *The Twilight Zone* before returning to the task at hand.

"Okay, whom shall I raise from the dead for a chat?" he asked out loud while browsing through the pictures in search of his research subject.

The pictures fully refreshed his memory of the cemetery visit. His mother's words, when she'd rejoined him at the car, convinced him to return to the graveyard to take a closer look at the headstones. Once he heard her spoken need to heal, the urge to help his mother had been almost overwhelming.

His eyes, it seemed, had developed tunnel vision when they instantaneously targeted the headstone near the grove of trees. A visual memory standing in front of the headstone with the odd marking flashed in his mind, and the word "mystical," involuntarily this time, whispered inside his head. Standing at the grave in front of the trees, he remembered the dizziness he'd experienced—dizzy to the point he felt lightheaded and weak, and needed to clutch the nearby trees to keep from falling.

At the time, he thought he was having a flashback from his drug use and was alarmed. Then, for no reason, he was overcome with a sense of peace, and the dizziness cleared. Was this the mystical "God experience" the Internet site wrote of? He didn't think so. He rationalized that the peace he experienced came from making the right choice to return to view the headstones. God only knew how few of those he had made in the past two years. The dizziness, he decided, probably stemmed from hunger, remembering how they'd waited to eat until after the cemetery visit. Realizing researching the stone would be the only way he could be sure of his assessment, his decision was made, and at once, he felt calm. He couldn't help but wonder if this was the calm before the storm. Regardless, his mind was made up and would not be changed.

When his decision became final, he printed out the picture of the oddly marked headstone. Hovering over the photo, he used a magnifying glass to enlarge the marking and the lettering on the stone. The details were partially hidden beneath green moss stains randomly covering the stone. He wished there was a way of power-washing the years of dirt and grime away.

After several minutes, he was able to determine that the marking on the stone was a symbol of some kind he had never seen before. Only rough partial indentations in the first letters of the name were visible, but after several more minutes of examining the picture, he was able to make out *AMIN* as the last part of the deceased's first name. Regardless, it wasn't enough to identify the name. The last name was totally unrecognizable, making it impossible to know who was buried beneath the headstone. Maybe his first step should be finding out the name of the cemetery. Then, with any luck, he could find a list of names of those buried there. Locating a map, he began his quest.

Chapter 6

For the most part, the morning commuters had already arrived at their destination before Casper began her drive into the city. In spite of being used to the slower speeds of her small town's streets, she drove often enough into the metropolis to be used to the speedier, crowded freeway traffic. Exiting the freeway, nevertheless, was always a welcome relief.

She planned to meet Breeze at one of the university's trendy street cafés close to the city's downtown district. Casper would have preferred to meet Breeze at her dormitory, but she had insisted on meeting at the café. With a sigh, she realized it was time to loosen her hold on her daughter, but she couldn't help being concerned for her safety in the big looming city.

Just ahead, a car pulled out from an on-street parking space within sight of the café. Casper's confidence with her parallel-parking abilities wavered just a little when she pulled beside the car in front of the space and backed smoothly into it as though it was an everyday occurrence.

It's going to be a good day she thought as she bravoed her parking success.

The meter still had thirty minutes left, but she added coins until she couldn't add any more. She didn't want their lunch interrupted by needing to hurry back to the meter before they were ready to leave.

The café, in spite of having a studious atmosphere, felt cheery. Finding a small round table with a maroon-colored vase holding bookmarks instead of flowers, she pulled off her light jacket and hung it on the back of the chair. The sun was so warm and irresistible that she closed her eyes and lifted her face toward its rays. The warming sensation relaxed her and for some reason made her feel part of the group of students with open books and laptops, studying at the various tables.

A city bus pulled to the curb, and Casper was delighted

to see Breeze step from its interior when the doors opened to release its passengers to the streets. Casper raised her arm when her daughter's eyes swept over the busy restaurant's group of patrons. Her visual scan shifted in the direction of the upraised arm, and Breeze grinned in recognition when she spotted her mother. Her lithe body twined through the tables, and with Breeze's huge smile still in place, mother and daughter hugged warmly.

"Since when did you start riding a bus?" Casper inquired.

"Since I decided to learn my way around the city. Mom, it's great! I've only gotten on the wrong bus once and now can pretty much get around anywhere," Breeze said.

"Brianna, some parts of the city can be rough. You have to be careful. I don't think it's a good idea to travel alone. The daytime might be safe, but definitely not at night."

"Don't worry, Mom. I'm being careful—and this is my first trip alone. Can we talk about it after we eat? I'm starving. If you know what you want, I'll go inside and put in our order."

Casper reached inside her purse and handed Breeze some money. "Decide for me," she said. "You know what's good here. I trust you."

It wasn't long before they were eating chicken gyro sandwiches and sharing a plate of calamari, followed by large cappuccinos and nonstop chat to catch up on events.

Casper was enjoying the café's youthful atmosphere, and her daughter's choice of food not on her normal diet was an added treat.

"I almost forgot! How was your trip?" Breeze said once they were caught up on the news.

"Very pleasant, but unfortunately, except for the unusual cemetery we visited, uneventful," she said, knowing her face looked somber as she thought of her recent trip with Shade.

"Mom, I wouldn't know what to do if you did find Dad's

relatives. Your family is all we've ever known … and they're plenty for me."

Casper nodded, seeing that Breeze's face reflected her true feelings of the statement.

"I know," Casper said, "and I admit we may never find them, but for now, I'm going to keep looking. I'm glad you still have my parents to call Grandpa and Grandma, but your dad may have aunts or uncles still living, and if he does, you may have relatives you've never met."

"Okay, I just don't want you to be disappointed if you don't find them." Breeze paused before saying, "So what was unusual about the cemetery you visited?" She squinted her eyes as she finished her question: "A hand didn't reach up from a grave and grab you, did it?"

Casper chuckled. "No, nothing so dramatic. I guess it was just the odd way of finding the cemetery," she said, then briefed her daughter on the map's discovery. "We left a note of thanks and a little something at the back of the Bible when we put the map back at the motel. A lottery ticket isn't sacrilegious if you put it in a Bible, is it?"

Breeze looked thoughtful before answering, "Mom, it would only be sacrilegious if you placed it there with sacrilegious thoughts. That makes me think of a Bible verse I learned in Sunday school. I can't remember the words exactly, but they're something like, God makes all things work together for good for those who love Him. That lottery ticket is right where it's supposed to be: in God's hands."

"You sound so grown-up. College agrees with you. How are things on campus?" Casper said.

"Good. I'm keeping my grades up," Breeze answered. "I have some terrific friends. My roommate and I make great study partners. She even likes to run. It's too bad our classes aren't always on the same schedule. Lately we've had to run more in the evenings, and since it's getting dark earlier, we feel safer running together."

"Don't be running late, Breeze, and stay in well-lit areas. Please be safe, sweetie. Running here in the city isn't like running on our streets at home."

"I won't … and I will. Ha! How's that?" Breeze's face changed to a serious expression and she said, "There is one thing at school, but I don't think it's anything to worry about. One of the older girls in our dormitory has been missing for a couple of days. Her roommate thinks she might have gone off with her boyfriend. Apparently she's been spending a lot of time with him lately, but her roommate doesn't know where he lives. All she knows is his first name: Miles, I think. Rumor has it she's been having some problems paying for her classes, and I hear she was ready to drop out and might have left with him."

"I certainly hope she turns up soon. Keep me posted, Brianna. I want to know if this turns out to be more than what it sounds like now," Casper said, feeling mild concern. "Speaking of money …" She reached inside her purse and pulled out a somewhat puffy envelope, then handed it to Breeze. "This should get you through until the next time I see you. Spend it wisely, please. Money doesn't grow on trees."

"Thanks, Mom. I'm thinking about getting a job so you won't need to give me money."

"No, Brianna, not yet," Casper spoke softly. "Your father made some good investments. Unless we squander the money, we should be fine. I want you to concentrate on your schoolwork, so when you join the work force, you'll be well prepared. That's how your father and I planned it, and if it's alright with you, I'd like to see that dream through."

Breeze crossed the distance between them and bent to hug Casper.

"Would you like to go shopping with me?" Casper asked. "I happen to know you're finished with classes today."

"Only if you promise not to spend any more money on

me," Breeze answered.

"Now where's the fun in that?" Casper laughed.

They reached the parking meter just as it clicked and the *Expired* sign popped into view.

It is a good day! Casper thought.

The next two and a half hours were spent shopping. Casper bought herself a pair of tennis shoes, Shade some jeans, Charlie a bone, and unbeknownst to Breeze, a bright green, reflective running jacket. Opening the trunk of the car, she handed the bag containing the jacket to her daughter and smiled while Breeze looked at her in amazement, never suspecting the gift.

"Mom, you weren't supposed to buy me anything!" Breeze exclaimed.

"It's to keep you safe when you run in the evenings and it gets dark. Wear it, please?" Casper requested.

"Thanks, Mom," Breeze said. "I love you."

"I love you too, Brianna. It's been a fun day! Keep up the good grades. I'm very proud of you. Now, though, I've got to get going if I'm going to beat the evening's rush-hour traffic."

And with a final hug, Casper got back into her car and put down the window.

"Tell Shade 'Hi,' I love him, and I'll see him when I come home for the holidays. Bye, Mom."

"Bye, Brianna!"

/////

Breeze waved to her mom as she pulled from the dormitory's parking lot, and she continued watching until her mother turned the corner and was out of sight.

Smiling, Breeze ran to the dormitory and dashed up the stairs, taking them two at a time, slowing only when she reached her room on the third floor. She pulled the new running jacket from the shopping bag and tossed the bag on her bed. Slipping on the jacket, she was still admiring it in her closet door's inside mirror when her roommate returned from her last class. It was decided at once that a very long run would be required to break in the jacket.

Chapter 7

Shade spent the afternoon and early evening hours searching for the name of the cemetery in hopes of locating a list of people buried there. After checking numerous online maps and making countless phone calls, he was no further than when he began. He even called the county's courthouse, where he was transferred four times before politely being informed there wasn't a cemetery at the location he had given them. Knowing the county had to be the correct one, but without any other ideas, he called all of the surrounding counties and gave them the cemetery's location. He was told he had the wrong county every time. He wished they would have copied the map, or, he thought, *Why didn't we bring the map home?* Surely whoever had left the map wouldn't be returning to the motel for it.

Out of ideas, he sat staring at the computer with his chin propped in the palm of his hand. His position remained unchanged when his mom arrived home just as rush-hour traffic was beginning on the nearby freeway.

"Were you able to find any information about your dead guy's teeth and hair?" Mom asked.

"Not about his teeth or hair, but I found out he's buried in a cemetery that doesn't exist," Shade answered.

"What do you mean?" she asked, looking baffled by his gloomy comment.

Shade told her about his day's work and gave her the location of the cemetery he had given to the county courthouse.

"That sounds right," she said. "The gravel road didn't have a sign with the road's name. Maybe that's part of the confusion. You may have to research one of the names on another headstone, and maybe when you find him, his burial location will be listed. Then you'll have the name of the cemetery."

Shade jerked back to life at the suggestion. "Why didn't

I think of that?" he said to himself. "Anyway, how's Breeze?" he asked, his dilemma all at once forgotten.

"She's fine. School seems to agree with her." His mom kicked off her shoes and gave him a condensed account of their day. When she finished, she tossed him one of her shopping bags.

He opened the bag and pulled out a new pair of jeans. "Mom, thanks, but don't spend your money on me. You've already done too much for me. I'll find a job soon."

"Oh, you sound like Breeze. Can't I buy my children a little something now and then? Oh, wait, something else … a girl is missing from Breeze's dormitory."

"What? Who? Did she tell you her name?" Shade asked.

As Shade folded and shoved his new jeans back into the shopping bag, he saw his mom's brow furrow, then she looked down at the floor. He understood the look all too well and waited while she searched her memory for the correct details.

"No," she said at last. "No, I don't remember Breeze saying her name. The only name I remember her saying was Miles."

Shade swallowed at the mention of the name but said nothing.

"Yes, Miles was the name of her boyfriend," his mom said. "She said the missing girl was having trouble paying her tuition and thought she might have gone off with her boyfriend Miles."

"Well … she'll probably turn up soon. I doubt it's anything to worry about."

"Yes, that's what I told Breeze too. She's supposed to let me know if they don't find the girl, though. I'll give her a call in a couple of days to check in case she forgets. Oh … I'm fixing meatloaf for dinner. Okay with you?" she asked.

"Sounds fine, Mom. I was so busy researching I forgot to eat. Thanks for reminding me *I'm hungry*!" Shade exaggerated his sudden hunger realization, and then paused before asking, "Since I'm having trouble finding information on the cemetery, could I borrow the car to go to the library tomorrow?"

Casper stopped walking toward the kitchen and looked at him. It was evident she didn't like the idea of him going into the city—where he began his drug use.

"You're worried about me meeting my old 'friends,'" he said, flexing two fingers on each hand to form mock quotation marks around the word "friends."

His mom just looked at him.

"I promise, Mom, I am not planning to buy or use any drugs. I need someone in the library's genealogy department to point me in the right direction to research the cemetery and headstones," he said.

Casper paused before she spoke: "Okay, but I want you to take my cell phone, and you are to call me every hour. I want to know where you are at all times. If you see any of your old 'friends,'" she said, imitating his gesture, "you are not to socialize with them. You are not ready to be around anything or anyone that reminds you or tempts you to return to using drugs. I want you home before dark," she said. "You are accountable to me for every move you make tomorrow," she finished and headed to the kitchen.

"Thanks, Mom. I won't disappoint you," Shade said then turned back to the computer.

He printed out the pictures of headstones with legible names, placing them in a folder with the photo of the headstone he had researched earlier. When he finished, he leaned back in his chair but reconsidered and changed direction, pushing forward so quick that he was rocketed from the seat. His urgent mission led him up the stairs to his room and straight to his jacket. Removing the Oxycontin, he returned the bottle to his mother's dresser drawer. He was proud of himself afterward, but his pride was mixed with feelings of guilt for taking the bottle of pills in the first place. Once the pills were back where he'd found them, he hustled down to the kitchen and got two plates from the cabinet to set the table.

Casper glanced up when he got out the dishes and lifted her arm to use the sleeve of her blouse to wipe tears off her face. "These onions," she said, "are making me cry."

Noticing her red eyes, he hoped that was the real reason for her tears but admitted to himself his upcoming venture into the city might have more to do with them than the onions.

Setting the table, the name "Miles" came unwelcomed, but necessary, back into Shade's thoughts. The Miles he knew was known in the criminal world as Mile Marker—the nickname stemming from his placement of his less classy female employees at several well-known established locations on the city streets. In addition to his lucrative prostitution business, Miles was also a notorious drug dealer running the house on the city's south side where, at one time, Shade had been a frequent visitor. He had met Miles on a variety of occasions. He hoped the girl hadn't gotten mixed up with him. Those who knew Miles knew he used his newest, prettiest girls to satisfy the appetites of his wealthier clientele. Once the girls were either too hooked on drugs or their looks were gone, they were placed on the streets to satisfy the perversions of whoever happened to come along that night.

It has to be a coincidence, Shade thought.

He shook his head as if to shake the unwelcome thoughts from his brain. Maybe he would visit Breeze and say hello while he was in the city and find out if the girl had returned. If nothing else, he would warn her about the Miles he knew.

An hour later, he and his mother sat across from each other at the dinner table. Charlie lay beside the table gnawing on a new bone. When Shade cut into his meatloaf, he said, "I hate meatloaf." And realizing his blunder, he rushed to add, "But yours is great, Mom."

His mom's fork stopped in front of her open mouth. "It is not. I make horrible meatloaf. I only made it because I thought you liked it."

"Well, don't do it again," he said, and both laughed. The leftovers never made it to the refrigerator.

After dinner, Shade cleaned the kitchen while his mother took Charlie on a walk around the block. When she returned, she commented about a knit cap hanging on the Jeffersons' fence post—one that looked a lot like an old one he used to have.

"Humph," was all he said in reply.

With his mind stuck between the missing girl and the pimp/dealer Miles, constant cravings crept in and out Shade's thoughts. The Oxycontin called to him over and over again. That night, his mind was in constant turmoil, fighting a relentless desire to use. Every time he was ready to give in to his addiction, his mother's tear-stained face, as she cut the onions, flashed in his mind and filled him with shame. The guilt-inducing visual aid strengthened his resolve. Regardless, mentally and physically exhausted by the battle warring inside of him, he called it a night earlier than usual. His body and mind, however, couldn't relax, and it was several hours later that he went to sleep.

Chapter 8

The church meeting proved a success. Several of the leaders
stayed to discuss church politics while the distant traveler met
privately with a handful of higher leaders. He was quick to
enlighten them on his recent travels and any new discoveries
abroad. He had been instrumental with several of the discoveries
himself, albeit his name was never written on any documents.
His privacy was well protected. Any required information
associated with his new revelations was given to the church
leaders, who proceeded with the work involved with the
discovery. As a benefit, they handled all of his financial needs
without question and were quick to give him total support.

Although during his visits in the United States he visited
churches throughout the country, the church that held this
meeting was the one he depended on entirely for his needs while
in America. He partook in events when younger members moved
to the inner sanctum and befriended them with elderly advice or
spiritual aid while he better acquainted himself with them. The
older seasoned members had always realized the necessity of
sharing their knowledge to those following in their footsteps.

He left early the third morning. His good-byes had been
said the night before. He liked driving during the early morning
hours before traffic began flooding the highways. This morning,
fog slowed his progress. Staring at the thick white mist, his mind
drifted back through time. Reflecting on his life, he couldn't help
thinking what an amazing life his was. At one time profitable
and respected by his peers, then suddenly a cursed man.
Foolishly, he had laughed at the curse and ridiculed the man he
thought a madman when he spoke the inconceivable words.
Later when he watched his loved ones die, eventually leaving
him alone in the world, his fortune lost, he became a broken
man. He had considered suicide but found that wasn't an option
for him. He wandered through life aimlessly, hungry, and

homeless until he could take it no more, and, falling upon his knees, begged God for the curse to be taken from him. His life, however, remained unchanged.

It wasn't until Jesus came into his heart that things changed. Repenting, he bowed down and asked for forgiveness, accepting Him into his life. It wasn't that his life changed. It was his heart that changed. The lack of money or a home were no longer important, and he believed with all his heart that he would one day see his loved ones again when he went home to heaven. All the same, his heavenly reunion would have to wait. His work on earth was just beginning. He now understood that even though the curse had closed the doors, God had opened a window. He wasn't sure he could ever forgive himself, but if God chose to use him to do his work, then he was more than willing to try his utmost to help in whatever way he could.

Finally the diner's inviting neon light flashed through the lifting fog, and feeling a little hungry, he decided to stop and have a light breakfast before going on to the motel where he had dropped the map. He wasn't worried. The map would be waiting for him, although he was unsure where exactly. He didn't know why he was supposed to drop the map, but once the voice had spoken inside his head, he obediently dropped it from his hand. He, after all, didn't need the map to find the cemetery and wouldn't, in fact, be traveling to the cemetery until later in his trip. He had only gotten the map from his bag to make sure of its whereabouts and was planning to put it in the glove compartment of his car.

Still too early for many customers, his simple breakfast consisting of two eggs and toast was soon placed in front of him. He had never acquired a taste for coffee and asked for hot tea instead. Sitting beside one of the diner's windows, he watched two semi trucks pull into the restaurant's lot and drive behind the building. A few minutes later, two men, apparently the drivers of the large trucks, entered and sat at the counter. Without asking, the waitress promptly set coffee in front of each of the men and continued her duties without a word to either. Regular customers, he assumed with a passing interest.

While on the road, he seldom had spare time, making it necessary to use his time wisely. Finished eating, he counted out his tip. Due to his meager budget, he couldn't afford much, but he knew restaurant employees depended on their tips and made sure to leave a fifteen-percent gratuity. If he could afford to eat, then he would show his appreciation for the service, bad or good.

While paying his check at the cash register, a car parked in the space beside his sedan. Without any worldly reason why, his senses intensified and he shifted into high alert. He paid rapt attention to the driver and passenger getting out of their vehicle, and kept his eyes glued on them when they headed toward the diner's entrance. Pocketing his change, he reached for the door and held it open for the two to enter. He tipped his hat to the woman then looked past her. Tunnel vision took over, and he locked eyes with her younger companion. The young man's head turned toward him before they were able to break eye contact.

Once they were through the door, he continued on his way out but overheard the woman say the boy's name before the door closed. "Shade," she called him when asking where he wanted to sit. Needing no explanation, he fully understood the spiritually arranged meeting and made it a point to read the state and county of the license plate on the car parked next to his—the car belonging to the woman and young Shade. Now he knew the location of his real destination in the United States. Shade was about to learn about the spiritual world, the hard way … and he would be his teacher.

Driving to the motel, he thought about the young man. He knew the boy had experienced an inner recognition of souls. All the same, the boy wouldn't have understood those terms. He could have returned to explain it to him but knew the young man would never believe him.

Patience, he thought, *the proper time will come.*

Now he needed to retrieve the map to help him understand and convince the boy when the time came. He understood now Shade was the reason the map had been left at the motel. He knew they had been to the cemetery. All the same, he was sure the young man didn't know there was an aura around him—an aura you can only get from standing on holy ground ... and the map had led him to just that ground.

Arriving at the motel, the traveler pulled to the office just as one of the housekeepers was backing out of the office hallway's side door with her supply cart. He reached her in time to hold the door open for her.

Turning, she said, "Thank you," just before her face broke into a jubilant expression. "I find your map. I run to catch," the housekeeper said and then stopped in mid sentence. Slowing her speech, she began again, "I found your map. I tried to run after you, but I couldn't catch you."

"*You* found the map. Now I'm sure it was in safe hands," he replied with a smile.

"Yes, follow me," she said and, continuing to push her cart, led him to Room 112. There was not a *Do Not Disturb* sign hanging on the handle and the housekeeper took a quick look at the empty parking space in front of the room before knocking on the door then used her passkey when no one answered. Unlocking the door, she went straight to the nightstand and removed the Gideons Bible from the drawer.

The traveler waited at the open door until she returned. When she opened the Bible to the last page, her face broke into a wide grin. Lifting the map from the book, she handed it to the traveler.

Beneath the map, though, was a sealed envelope with the words: *To whoever placed the map in the Bible.* Looking puzzled, the housekeeper removed the envelope and handed it to the traveler, who held up the palm of his hand toward her.

"No," he said. "It says to whoever placed the map in the bible. That belongs to you."

"But … it's your map,"

"I have my map. If you'd like, miss, why don't you open it? Then we'll decide," the traveler replied.

"Maria, my name is Maria," she said. "Okay, I'll open it."

She nodded and proceeded to open the envelope containing a handwritten note saying only *Thank you*, paper-clipped to a lottery ticket.

Maria held the ticket out toward the traveler, who took a step backward. "No, it belongs to you."

"Thank you! Maybe I'll win enough for my nursing school tuition!" Maria said and placed it in her pocket.

The traveler looked at Maria when he spoke. "Thank you, Maria, for taking care of the map. I have a long trip ahead of me. May I say a blessing over you before I leave?"

"Yes, please," she replied.

Clasping her hands together, Maria bowed her head and closed her eyes.

"Father in heaven," he said. "Your wisdom is beyond all understanding. We know all things work together for the good of those that love You. Bless this woman, Maria. Keep her safe from harm. We ask this in the name of Jesus Christ, Your Son. We give You thanks and praise Your name, Father God. Amen."

With his prayer ended, he again told her, "Thank you, Maria," and left to return to his car in front of the motel's office. Nearing the corner, he turned back to see her watching him and waved before disappearing around the corner.

Driving away, he glanced in his rearview mirror and saw the motel sign displaying *No Vacancy,* come on. It seemed early in the day for the sign's display, but he reasoned the motel wasn't open to new guests until the rooms had been cleaned, and he dismissed the thought.

He liked the girl Maria. He trusted his ability to read people and, through their brief conversation, believed she had a good heart. He hoped she continued learning the English language. It was difficult learning another language. From personal experience, he found languages were easier to learn when you spoke with the inhabitants of the country. He had learned several languages throughout his lifetime. It was only after conversing with those native to the country that the languages at last clicked.

His facial expression changed to puzzlement when he wondered why the lottery ticket was with the map but, trusting God, left the win-lose decision to Him. Amusement at once replaced the puzzled look, as he recalled how the map had been kept safe in the Bible, and he laughed out loud at the thought of it. He should have already known where it would be found.

Glancing at his watch, he sighed before stepping harder on the gas pedal and watched the speedometer needle climb to the speed limit. He had a long way to travel and positioned himself to get comfortable.

/////

Maria smiled and waved back at the traveler as he turned the corner. She was glad the map was in the possession of its owner. She glanced at the ground as soon as he left, making sure nothing else had been lost. Relieved to seeing nothing on the concrete, she remembered the Bible clutched in her hands and went back inside the room to return it to the nightstand.

Once it was back inside the drawer, her anticipation was too much, and she dug inside her apron pocket for the lottery ticket. After reading its directions, she retrieved a dime from her pocket and began scratching the silver film from the individual blocks to find several matching fruits. Now she was supposed to see how much money she won under another silver block that matched the number of fruits. A bit impatient, she wondered while she was scratching the new block's silver film off why it didn't tell her the first time. Her eyes grew large when she read *$10,000.*

I must have it wrong, she thought, and read the directions again.

"It's ... right! It can't be right? It is! I win! I win! I can go to school!" she said with excitement and was about to jump up when she heard the door to the room close.

She spun around and saw Hank's eyes glued on her, with one hand reaching behind him and turning the room door's dead bolt.

"I saw you with that Arab," he said in an accusing tone. "He didn't stick around long now, did he? I guess he got what he wanted and vamoosed. The boss won't be too happy to hear you're selling your wares to his customers. I'm feeling charitable today, though, and I think we can work out a deal." His hands began unfastening his belt buckle while he continued speaking: "Now you and me are going to get to know one another ... and I promise you're going to like knowing this part of me, little gal. Like I told you before, I can put that smile back on your pretty little face. Ol' Hank's gonna show you what being with a real man is like."

As Hank's intentions became clear, Maria looked for a way around him, only to have him block the pathway to the door.

"Let me introduce you to what you're going to be riding on soon."

Hank grabbed her arm and began forcing her down while unzipping his jeans, ignoring Maria's pleading.

"No, please! Let me go!" she shouted as she struggled to free herself from Hank's grip.

After forcing Maria to one knee, he suddenly stopped. Maria's panic-filled eyes registered what her mind couldn't when she saw him looking at the lottery ticket in her hand. Hank stopped unzipping his pants to grab it from the hand of the arm he held.

"What are you doing with a lottery ticket?" he sneered, eyeing the ticket. "Is that how these boys are paying you? With lottery tickets?" he asked, never taking his eyes off the ticket. His eyes grew round as saucers when, just above a whisper, he spoke: "$10,000."

He turned it over twice to read the instructions and back again to check the scratched blocks.

"HELL YES! IT'S ABOUT TIME! LAS VEGAS, HERE I COME!" he yelled, then turned and ran out the door.

Maria, still frightened from Hank's attack, couldn't move for several seconds. When she recovered enough to start to think again, she ran to the door just in time to see Hank's car pulling from the parking lot. She began shaking. Her mind raced, struggling to grasp the events that had just transpired.

Wanda, the other maid, was standing on the balcony of the floor above Maria, and leaning over the railing, she asked, "Where's Hank going? He's supposed to be in the office."

Distraught, Maria barely heard Wanda. Wanda raised her voice to call Maria's name, then waited to hear a response before repeating the question.

Maria, remembering she was in a strange country and knowing what happened to the people who contacted the police in her country, looked at the street where Hank's car had vanished.

Maria lowered her head, staring back at the ground, trying hard to control her voice before she answered, "He had a lottery ticket and said, 'Las Vegas, here I come.' I guess he must have won." She steadied her voice and wiped a tear from her face.

"What? He must be crazy! Are you sure?" Wanda asked.

"Yes ... that's what he said." Maria bit her lip to keep her voice from cracking.

"Well, I'd better call the boss and let him know he needs to get someone over here to cover the front desk." Wanda headed down the stairs. "Just what is Hank thinking?" she said, shaking her head.

Maria walked back inside Room 112 and locked the door. She sat on the side of the bed and cried for several minutes. She thought about the man's prayer and looked up when she realized the prayer had asked God to keep her safe from harm. Maria felt embarrassed and ashamed, but she hadn't been physically harmed. Without the lottery ticket in her hand, only God knew what would have happened.

Wiping the tears away, she washed her face and was thankful that Hank was no longer a threat in her life—*At least for a few days*, she thought.

"Dear God," she prayed aloud, "let him win a lot of money in Las Vegas so he'll never want to come back. Amen."

Then she began cleaning Room 112. While she cleaned, she wondered whether or not she should return to her homeland. Remembering the rapes and murders that occurred regularly throughout her country, the question didn't remain in her mind long.

All the same, before she went to bed that night, although it wasn't time for her scheduled weekly call, she broke a rule and chose to call home to say "Hello" and tell her family she loved them.

Nearing the end of the conversation, her mother, no doubt sensing something was wrong, rightfully asked if anything was the matter.

In her native tongue, Maria replied, "I'm just feeling a little nostalgic. I love you, Mom. Bye."

Chapter 9

At the library, Shade placed his third call to his mom before beginning research on the next name photographed on the headstone. He had been able to find information on one of the names but still hadn't found the name of the cemetery. Searching for another half hour, he sat back and rubbed his eyes. Having no luck finding information on his latest subject, he yawned and placed the photo at the back of the folder.

Singling out the librarian in charge of the genealogy department, he briefed her on his quest and listened in frustrated silence to her already tried suggestion of calling the county where the cemetery was located. She looked baffled when he informed her of his recent call to said county and asked him to give her the cemetery's location. Jotting down all the information, she wanted to photocopy the pictures to do some research of her own at a more convenient time. Since the photographs were still on his home computer, he instead wrote his name and phone number inside the cover of the folder containing the photos and handed the folder to her.

After thanking her, she in return assured him she would call within forty-eight hours to give him the results of her efforts. He was grateful to leave the confounding task with her, allowing him time to see Breeze before returning home.

Outside in the warm sunshine, an older man sat alone on one of the library's concrete benches feeding a squirrel from a brown lunch sack. Enjoying the picturesque scene, Shade watched the man reach inside the bag, pull out a peanut, and toss it to the nearby squirrel. The squirrel scampered with brief periodic pauses to the peanut, then froze on his hind feet to look at the man before snatching the nut and scampering back to his preferred distance.

There was something vaguely familiar about the man. On his way past, Shade looked down in hopes of catching a glimpse of his face. He was a bit disappointed when the man chose that particular moment to search inside his sack to select the next staple food for the waiting squirrel, and as a result, he kept his face hidden. Preferring not to disturb the scene, Shade decided he probably didn't know him anyway and dismissed the man from his thoughts.

At the street's sidewalk, he turned right to go to Breeze's dormitory. He viewed the familiar surroundings with mixed feelings, remembering his misspent years in the campus area.

College, in the beginning, had been a new and exciting adventure. His 3.8 GPA had been achieved with very little studying during his first year. Near the end of his second year, though, he and a couple of his college buddies ventured off campus in search of more excitement than what the campus activities offered. Not long after, Shade's off-campus activities increased, and he began skipping classes, resulting in slipping grades. After a while, he didn't show up for classes at all, preferring to stay with his new companions in the boarded-up building they illegally inhabited. Unless a neighborhood complaint was issued, the city's police force forgot about the shuttered buildings, knowing their inhabitants would just relocate.

Shade lived among the various building members for almost two years after he left school, his whereabouts known only to those who inhabited the drug dens. Through the grapevine, he heard about his family's search for him, but other than a phone call home to let them know he was okay, he chose to ignore them. Otherwise he knew they would force him to leave his new friends … and he couldn't let that happen.

Shade felt his face flush from the shame-filled memories of those days he could never leave far enough in the past.

It was only after one of the female house members overdosed and died in the building that he woke up to his pathetic drug-induced state and realized what he was doing to his life.

No one knew how long the girl had lain motionless before anyone attempted to stir her. When she wouldn't wake up, several members went back to their needles, rocks, and crystal meth without any further effort. He and two of his fellow addicts sat staring at the girl for what seemed an eternity before deciding to do something; anything was better than doing nothing.

Even in their drugged state, they could tell she was dead when they carried her outside.

Unable to carry the dead girl the four blocks to the neighborhood clinic, they looked around until they found a wheelbarrow behind one of the neighboring houses and then put her inside. Each of them took turns pushing it the four blocks to the clinic with her body bouncing up and down the entire way. When they arrived at the clinic, they were coherent enough to confiscate a wheelchair from the waiting room and placed her in the chair before deciding which of them would push her inside. The majority decision was to leave her sitting in the wheelchair outside the door.

Abandoning and walking away from the girl's body, propped stiffly in the wheelchair like somebody's useless discarded dummy, Shade looked back and felt such remorse he rashly ran, grabbed the wheelchair, and pushed it to the clinic's front desk. His two comrades watched in disbelief and cowardly raced away down the street, pushing the empty wheelbarrow. The busy staff saw the girl's lifeless body and rushed to her side, relieving Shade of his task. He slipped unnoticed out the clinic doors from whence he came.

Nevertheless, he was back two days later and began the clinic's free methadone treatment program. Two weeks later, he called home and learned of his father's illness.

He'd cut his own hair, donned clean clothes from the Salvation Army, and returned home, keeping his recovering drug addiction from his gravely ill father. He tried to be strong for the sake of his parents, but after his father died, he knew he needed to confide in his mother about the past two years of his life. He not only owed her that much but needed her help to leave that part of his life in the past. The short counseling sessions he attended at the clinic cautioned him not to try going through rehabilitation alone. Together he and his mother drove into the city to attend meetings, while, at times, she waited outside for him and, other times, attended meetings of her own to help her understand his addiction.

When Breeze's dormitory was within sight, Shade looked at his watch and called his mom. She was pleased to hear he planned to visit his sister and, after a quick "talk to you soon," hung up before he reached the dormitory. He sped up his pace the last few yards to the housing facility where several female students were sitting at picnic tables on the building's front lawn with books open studying for their classes. None of the young women spoke to him, although some looked up with interest when he passed by them. Once inside, he approached a girl sitting alone by the stairway and asked if Brianna Elliott had returned from classes. Her answer to wait while she checked was given through a burst of giggles before running upstairs.

Two minutes later, the giggling girl returned with a girl dressed in running attire, introducing herself as Susan, Breeze's roommate. According to Susan, Breeze was expected anytime.

"You going for a run?" Shade asked, noting that Susan was graced with a runner's build.

"Yes," Susan replied and told Shade about plans to run when Breeze got back from class. "Unless, of course, you and Breeze have other plans."

"No, I'm just here for a quick visit," he said just as Breeze came rushing through the front door and skidded to a halt, changing directions when she spotted Shade. She ran to throw her arms around his neck and hugged him tight while the other girls watched with a few whispering behind cupped hands.

It wasn't until she released her hold on Shade that she realized they were the center of attention, and, apparently, became aware of the flirtatious looks several of the girls were giving Shade. With a mischievous glint, she grabbed Shade and Susan by their arms and headed back out the dormitory's doors with her book bag still on her back. The picnic tables were all occupied, but the threesome spied a shaded grassy spot under one of the yard's big elm trees. Still clutching their arms, Breeze pulled them toward the tree.

Susan blushed when Shade grasped her hand to shake it after being properly introduced.

The first several minutes were spent in casual conversation involving Breeze's life at college and experiences at her new school. She even volunteered having a secret crush on one of her professors.

Susan's total surprise was expressed when she blurted out, "Who?"

"Mr. Monroe," Breeze exclaimed through giggles sounding much like the previous giggling girl.

"Oh yeaaah. He's cute!" Susan said with her own set of giggles.

Shade chuckled at their secret admissions. He was filled with instant regret, knowing he needed to burden their light hearts with the dirtier aspects of life. His need to know that Breeze and Susan stayed away from Mile Marker, nonetheless, outweighed his sadness. He was careful choosing his words when he broached the subject.

"Mom told me a girl was missing from your dormitory. Has she come back yet?" he asked.

"No, not that I've heard. Have you heard anything, Susan?" Breeze asked, ending her giggling.

"No," Susan answered. "Our dorm supervisor called Patty's parents, but they haven't seen or heard from her, either."

"Patty? What's her last name?" Shade asked sounding

more concerned than he intended.

"Uh … Chandler … yes, Patty Chandler," Susan replied.

"What's going on, Shade? I can tell by your voice something's wrong. Do you know her?" Breeze asked.

"No. I don't know *her,* but I'm wondering if I know Miles. Do you know anything about her boyfriend, this Miles?" he asked.

"I saw him once, but I've never met him," Susan responded.

"What does he look like?" Shade asked.

"Good looking, but something wasn't right about him. He gave me a … creepy feeling," Susan said. "About your height and size … dark brown hair—*perfect hair,* actually … not a strand out of place. He was immaculate. Like he never ran or did anything that would mess him up. He was just too perfect. His clothes looked expensive too. Some of us were wondering what he did for a living. We figured his parents must be rich for him to dress the way he did. You weren't back from class when he picked Patty up," she said, glancing at Breeze. "That was a few weeks ago. I never saw him again. We must have been out running or studying and missed him."

"Did he wear any jewelry?" Shade asked, remembering the flashy rings and wristwatch Miles liked to show off.

"Mmm, yes," Susan said. "He had on a really nice ring with a pretty red stone, maybe a ruby. I noticed it when he reached to smooth Patty's hair when they were leaving. And his watch looked expensive. So … do you think you know him?"

"I'm not sure … but maybe. He sounds like a man who's known as 'Mile Marker'—and both of you steer clear of him. He's not your type. You don't want to get mixed up with him," Shade said and told them about the Miles he knew.

Both girls appeared shocked by the Miles he described. Their concern for Patty was evident by their frowns and the creases deepening around their eyes as they listened to him talk about the corrupt man.

"Don't start worrying needlessly," Shade said. "It may be nothing. I'll do some checking and see if Mile Marker knows Patty or has anything to do with her disappearance, and then let you know what I find out."

"How are you going to do that, Shade?" Breeze asked.

"I'm not sure yet. I'll make some phone calls. I have to come back into the city in a day or two. I'll let you know what I find out then," Shade said. Recognizing his sister's worried look, he knew she was thinking about his troubled past. Taking her hands in his, he tried to reassure her: "Don't worry. Everything's okay."

She gave him a slight nod and paused before saying, "Well ... I hate to cut our visit short," she said, "but," and turning to Susan, finished her sentence, "if we're going to run before dark, I'd better get dressed."

Shade stood and offered a hand to each of the girls, pulling the two from their grassy seats. "I need to go too. I promised I'd be home before dark."

"Let us know if you find out anything. If you think Patty is with Miles, we'll talk to our dorm supervisor so you can stay out of it. No matter what, I don't want you involved with someone like the Mile Marker you told us about. We'll let the authorities handle it," Breeze said and gave her brother a tight hug.

"Alright, I'll let you know when I know something for sure. It was nice to meet you, Susan," Shade said.

"Nice to meet you too. See you in a couple of days," she said, and the two girls hurried back inside the dormitory.

Shade retraced his steps back to the library. Upon his arrival, he noted the time and pulled out his cell phone to call his mom. Lost in thought, he forgot the earlier man feeding the squirrel and didn't notice his absence on the now empty benches.

"Yes," he told his mom, "I had a nice chat with Breeze

and her roommate, but they wanted to run before dark, so we cut our visit short. I'm going back to the library for a little while and then I'll be home."

"Before dark," Mom said.

"Before dark, like I promised. Talk to you soon," he replied.

His mind raced trying to think how to contact Mile Marker without journeying throughout the city. He didn't have time for that today. He had to find someone who could help him. Realizing he needed some phone numbers, he went straight to one of the library's computers and entered switchboard.com, the website known to list existing landline numbers. He entered his only two friends from the past who knew Miles and hoped they were still in the city. Encouraged when he found both names, he wrote their phone numbers on the pre-cut squares of note paper the library left for its patrons and hurried out of the building. He practically loped to his mother's car in the building's parking lot and wasted no time hopping inside. Preoccupied with his mission investigating the girl's disappearance and the need to get home before dark, he was unaware of the vehicle that pulled out right after him. The library's side street soon joined the main street where it was necessary to turn right to get onto the freeway's entrance ramp. Joining the heavy northbound traffic, Shade didn't see the sedan that continued following his route home.

Half an hour later, Shade placed his last phone call to his mother: "The next time I talk to you will be in person."

"Good," she said. "Dinner's almost ready."

/////

Breeze threw her book bag on her bed and hastily changed into running clothes. The new jacket was a must. She made sure her bus fare was in the jacket's small zippered pocket. The run the day before had been a blast, and they planned to repeat a similar run today.

The girls figured if they rode one of the city's buses a

certain mileage from the dormitory, then they would be forced to run the entire distance back. To ensure the success of their run, they refused to take extra money, thereby guaranteeing their triumphant outcome. Instead of the usual three miles, yesterday's run had been increased to five miles. They planned to continue increasing the mileage until they had enough endurance to run a full ten miles.

The driver of the last bus had been a saint, making sure he let them off in a safe area and giving them instructions for the best route home. They made sure to remember his bus when traveling in the northern direction of the city.

In order to avoid boredom, they preferred to choose different routes, agreeing to travel in different directions until they found their favorite route to run. Today they would be running east, tomorrow south, and the next day west. Then they would start the process over.

Finishing their five-mile run yesterday, it was not yet dusk when they arrived back at the dormitory, and after a short rest, they still had plenty of time to study before bedtime. They were confident that even after adding a couple more miles, they would still safely make it back by dark.

Dressed in minutes, Breeze hurried to join Susan downstairs. As soon as Susan saw the bright green jacket on the stairway, she said, "Gotta run," which brought immediate groans from her small group of friends.

Exiting the building, neither said a word on their way to the bus stop to wait for the bus that would drop them off on the east side of the city. Their silent reverie continued until their bus came into sight when together they said, "Seven." Once the new mileage was established, the girls climbed aboard the bus, anxious to reach their destination and begin the challenging run before them.

/////

Bored, he left the warehouse to walk the city streets. On his way out of the apartment, he did a quick check of the barricaded bathroom to make sure the woman wouldn't escape.

The late-afternoon sun was bright, making it necessary to wear his sunglasses in case anyone passing too close took notice of his less-than-human eyes. It wasn't long before he was strolling through one of the city's older historic sections not far from the large bustling university.

Chapter 10

The stained glass of the church's windows was not lost on him. It looked to be an older church but not near as old as those from the country of his origin. He was keenly aware the church was more than a structure, although few knew of the life force housed within the building.

He beheld the eyes of the saints portrayed in the stained-glass windows peering in his direction, seeming to fasten on him. He felt they were watching him. He removed his sunglasses to stare directly into their watchful eyes and witnessed the look of recognition enter their gaze. His eyes mirrored their recognition. Neither respect nor contempt was evident in either's eyes. It was simply an acknowledgement of the recognized presence of the other. It was the same in every church in every country. They always knew him. He, of course, knew them after seeing their statues, paintings, and created likenesses in various churches throughout the world. He supposed their recognition of him was the result of his continual presence throughout the centuries. He had grown curious throughout his lifetime and learned the names of all the saints. Peter the Rock, Paul the Missionary, and Luke the Doctor were the ones currently watching while he peered back at their luminous regard. It was apparent to him the humans didn't see their watchful eyes and understand the intelligence behind their bloodless faces.

He longed to drink their blood, often wishing he could find their earthly bodies. The thought of it made him forget their watchful gaze while he lusted for the feeling of their blood coursing through his body. Without knowing how, he knew their blood would have that clean, airy taste he craved. Their blood, he instinctively knew, would enable him to last many years without the need to hunt the lesser beings in the world.

Replacing his sunglasses, he entered the heavy wooden doors of the church and crossed the marble entrance to enter the inner sanctuary. Not a soul was present in the massive room. His footsteps were muffled on the carpeted aisle leading to the thick wooden altar where the figure of the man hanging on the cross stared at him from behind a pulpit sitting a couple of feet above the altar. Removing his glasses, he stared at the man's face and watched when tears began to flow from His sculptured eyes.

He had grown used to seeing tears fall from the eyes of this man called Jesus and cocked his head while considering the pain the man must feel. A thought formed on the edge of his mind but disappeared before it could surface to his consciousness where it could be analyzed. Staring at the floor without seeing it, he tried to retrieve the thought and felt pressure building in his temples from the force of his internal quest. Whatever the thought had been, it would not resurface from his sheer will. Whenever he was near this man, it seemed the same unknown thought would begin to materialize, only to disappear in the black depths of his mind without disclosing the wisdom of the thought.

Walking closer to the figure, he raised his hand to touch the man's feet. He relished the sensation when a vibration of electricity shot into his hand and, from there, traveled to the rest of his body. Life was in this man. If only he could drink His blood. His blood would be better than all of the others. The thought had crossed his mind many times in the past, causing him to be unable to resist entering the churches to see the man whom, he sensed, had the blood he needed to live forever. Removing his tingling hand, he continued to let his mind dwell on the man for several minutes.

Just when he was prepared to leave, the sound of the heavy wooden doors echoed inside the empty sanctuary. He moved back to stand in front of the altar, continuing to stare up at the man hanging on the cross. He heard light footsteps walking on the carpeted aisle behind him, followed by the creaking of wood when the newcomer apparently sat in one of the empty pews. Immediately, without the repeated creaking of wood, the sound of the footsteps returned until they were centered behind him before moving to his left.

Using his peripheral vision, he witnessed a slight figure in a bright green jacket kneel at the altar. The girl glanced in his direction before she began praying. Although he was planning to leave, he stayed, listening to her whispered prayer asking for the safe return of a girl named Patty, who, according to her prayer, had gone missing from her school.

The woman in the warehouse? Could she be praying for the promiscuous woman? No, he thought, *not likely.* But all the same, he still wasn't sure and considered the possibility while the girl prayed.

He chanced an inquisitive look in the girl's direction and then looked back up at the man on the cross. The air inside the room became irresistible. A carnal instinct caused him to breathe deep and take in the sweet, clean, airy scent he associated with the taste he craved.

Within minutes, the small figure stood and softly retraced her steps. The sound of creaking wood returned when her footsteps neared the back of the room. He turned in time to see the green-jacketed figure leave the sanctuary with a similar figure by her side. Watching the girls leave, he felt eyes watching him. He returned his gaze to the figures in the stained-glass windows and shrugged his shoulders. Choosing to ignore their stares, he focused once more on the crucified Jesus. With a curious gesture, he nodded his head once toward the figure, then turned and sauntered from the church.

Outside, the growing shadows made it unnecessary to replace his sunglasses. Glimpsing the green jacket now diagonally across the street, he journeyed in the same direction. It wasn't long before the girls turned a corner and, after a short distance, headed toward a well-lit building with picnic tables in the front yard. He saw several girls coming and going from the building and got closer to get a better view. Two women looked up when he walked past where they sat at a nearby picnic table. He recognized their flirtatious stares and knew he could persuade either of them to accompany him to wherever he might wander, but he wasn't interested in their lustful desires. His need for more blood still wouldn't be for a few days. Until then, he would wait in hopes of finding the clean, airy blood he now related to the scent that had filled his nostrils in the church's massive sanctuary. He wondered if the girl in the green jacket had such blood or would at least lead him to the hunted blood.

/////

Outside the church, the girls congratulated themselves on their successful run. A decision was made to take the next day off to rest their bodies.

While walking the short distance from the church to their dormitory, Breeze confided to Susan about her discomfort approaching the altar to pray for Patty's safety. Kneeling in front of the altar, she'd glanced at the man standing to her right and, for some strange reason, felt threatened for her safety. She couldn't explain why, and if not for the man who entered the church with them, believed she would have left the sanctuary. During her prayer, her fear of the man was forgotten until she rose to leave and caught herself looking at the profile of the forbidding man. His eyes were closed in prayer, and seeing his devout posture, she scolded herself and dismissed her thoughts as foolish.

When they were crossing the marble foyer on their way out, she spotted the older man who had come inside the church with them. He smiled at her then entered another room through a side door in the foyer. She guessed the door led to offices within the facility and was comforted by the thought that he belonged in the church.

The unaccountable feelings of apprehension were forgotten when the girls neared their dormitory and changed the subject to their homework assignments, preparing themselves for their evening studies.

Arriving at the dormitory, Breeze reached the entrance first and held the door open for Susan. She glanced back as her friend passed through the doorway. A chill she couldn't account for passed through her, compelling her to look at the scene in the front yard, seeking the reason for the unexplained sensation. Seeing nothing unusual, she blamed the chill on the night air and shook her head at the foolish, unwarranted, spooked feeling.

"Twice in one night," she scolded herself.

Turning back to the doorway, she didn't see the tall dark man step from behind the elm tree with eyes fixed upon her. Once the building's door closed behind her, his whereabouts were lost in the growing darkness.

Chapter 11

Shade's determination was at risk. He woke to Charlie tugging the covers from his face.

"Charlie, stop! What do you want?" he said, then sighed with marginal annoyance during the brief tug-of-war.

Capturing his furry friend, Shade tucked him beneath the covers, telling the aging cocker spaniel his doubts about locating the name of the cemetery and, therefore, any information about its deceased inhabitants. Rambling on further, he confided to the attentive animal his increasing skepticism about unearthing any information about the girl missing from Breeze's dormitory.

Charlie's answer was to squirm from under the covers and stand on all four feet. Able to move about freely, he licked his master's face several times before Shade could stop him.

"Okay, okay, I'm up," Shade told his pesky pet. "Do you want to go for a walk this morning?" he asked, then yawned.

Charlie leapt from the bed, barking in midair before landing with a thump on the carpet. He raced back and forth between the door and the bed, displaying his answer.

Pulling on sweatpants and a T-shirt, Shade made his way downstairs with Charlie at his side. Shade found his mother in the den shuffling through a pile of papers.

"Good morning, Shade. Hungry?" she asked and then put several of the papers inside a folder.

"No, not yet. Charlie wants to go for a walk, and I'd like to visit Dad for a little while this morning," Shade said.

"Your dad would like that. He'll enjoy your visit," she said.

Shade hadn't told his father of his drug use before his death. As a result, he avoided visiting his dad's grave. The morning air was crisp, and Shade was glad he'd grabbed his hooded jacket on his way out the door. Charlie stayed close to his side, seemingly aware of Shade's troubled thoughts. The grass was still wet from the morning dew when they reached the gravestone Shade recognized belonging to his father. He sat beside the granite grave marker and gingerly touched the cold hard surface.

"Hi, Dad. I'm sorry I've taken so long to come." He paused before continuing. "I've been ashamed of something, and I need—no, I *want* to tell you about it."

The words began spilling from him when he told his father about the two years of his drug-addicted life. He left nothing out when he spoke. He told his father things that he could not tell his mother, knowing how it would alarm her. When he finished, tears overflowed his eyes.

"I miss you, Dad."

The sun chose that moment to shine through the limbs of the trees and warm his face. When he finished telling his father of his guilt-ridden past, he began talking about his new activities and the difficulty he was having with his current challenges. Although he wasn't ready to give up, Shade confessed that he needed help.

Last, he comforted his father with the knowledge of his mother's well being: "She misses you, Dad," he told him, "but she's doing okay."

When he finished talking, his heart felt lighter. There were no lightning bolts or voices from the sky, but the memory of pride in his father's voice when he spoke about "my son, the soon-to-be college graduate" the day he left for college, now surfaced in his mind. His head lifted when the sudden realization registered that although those dreams might take longer, they could—no, they *would* still be fulfilled.

"Thanks, Dad," Shade said, forgetting he was in a cemetery and there wasn't a real physical presence beside him, but glad he and his father had the conversation.

Charlie stood, making Shade again wonder how a dog could be so smart.

"Which way, Charlie?" he asked.

Charlie eyed him then took off scampering down the street leading to the Jeffersons' street to go past the little hat-thief poodle's home.

The slack in the leash tightened when the dog saw the Jeffersons' house. Coming to a stop by the fence post where the filched hat hung, the furry pet observed his master expectantly. Shade, taking his cue, lifted the hat from the post and put it in his pocket, afterward bending to scratch Charlie.

"Sorry, boy, it looks like she's not outside today."

"Woof, woof, woof," was Charlie's reply. Keeping his eyes on the house, his tail jerked in a wag.

Following his pet's unyielding gaze, Shade saw a curtain move just before a little white fluffy head peered out the house's front window. Barking from within the house continued until the front door opened and the excited dog ran outside.

Sticking his nose in Shade's pocket, Charlie snatched the hat before his owner had a chance to stand.

"Hi, Shade," Mrs. Jefferson called out.

"Hi, Mrs. Jefferson," Shade said, waving at the woman. "Charlie seems quite taken with your new poodle."

"Jasmine—we named her Jasmine. Was that your hat on the fence?" Mrs. Jefferson asked.

At that precise moment, Charlie held the hat near one of the slat's openings and released his bite when Jasmine pulled it through, backing away protectively after reclaiming it.

"Well, it was, but it looks like Charlie wants Jasmine to have it," he told her.

"I'll get you a new one," she told Shade.

"No, it was an old one I gave to Charlie. I don't think he liked wearing it anyway," Shade said, accepting that his hat now belonged to Jasmine.

"It looks as though they're going to be great friends. You and Charlie come by anytime," she said, waving good-bye.

Releasing the tension in the leash, Shade sat in the grass between the sidewalk and the street to let Charlie and Jasmine bark and get to know one another. He was surprised when Charlie, evidently deciding not to overstay his welcome, joined him in the grass. With a quick lift of his head, he licked Shade's face, walked away and, tugging on his leash, signaled he was ready to go. Shade slid his hand sideways though the fence's slats to scratch the top of the poodle's fluffy head. Charlie barked his approval of the forgiving gesture. When they left, Jasmine walked on her side of the fence with them until she reached the side-yard fence's barricade, where she sat to observe their onward progress up the block.

With renewed energy, Shade and his childhood pet returned home. Shade unfastened Charlie's leash, closed the front door, and headed to the kitchen.

"I'm starved," he said and gave his mom a hug. "I love you, Mom."

"I love you too, Shade," his mom said.

She didn't pry, though. He and his father had always had private talks in life, and he appreciated that she would let them have their private talks now, too.

"I'll start your breakfast, but you'll have to finish it. I'm going to the town's historical society to see if I can get some ideas and help on figuring out where and how to find Dad's roots. I don't want to give up," Mom said.

"Go, Mom. I can handle breakfast," Shade said, impressed by his mother's willpower. Her determination made him think of his waking doubts and also realize he still had avenues to explore while his mother's chances of success were slim.

"No, I'm going to start breakfast so I know you'll eat something hot. I've got time."

She took a bag of hash browns from the freezer and bacon from the refrigerator. When they were nearing completion, she cracked two eggs and dropped them in the skillet, afterward pushing the toaster lever down.

"All yours," she said.

"Wow, you left me a lot to do," Shade said. "Good luck!"

Sure that he could flip the fried eggs in the skillet without using a spatula, Shade was glad his mother left before witnessing one egg smash onto the side of the frying pan before plopping into the hash browns, where it ended up scrambled with the potatoes.

Breakfast fueled his thoughts. Anxious to get started with the missing girl's investigation, he forced himself to clean up the dishes first. As soon as he finished, he retrieved the phone numbers he had found on the landline website on the library's computer and sat down to phone his old buddies. Guilt washed over him when he admitted to himself he was glad his mother was gone because he didn't want her overhearing the calls. He overlooked the guilt, though, knowing she would be worrying for no reason since the calls had nothing to do with going back to his old life but were, he hoped, to save someone's life from a similar self-destructive path.

His stomach did a crazy flip-flop when the first phone number began ringing. Two rings later, despair crept in when a female voice answered, all the while doubting that his old buddy would want to speak to him.

"Hi," Shade said, "I'm trying to reach Dave. I'm an old college acquaintance. Does he still live at this number?" Shade's stomach did another wild flip-flop.

"Yes, let me see if I can catch him. He's on his way out the door. Hold on," the girl's hurried voice replied.

Shade heard the sound of rushing footsteps and the woman calling Dave's name. A moment later, his one-time comrade's familiar deep voice greeted his ears.

"Dave, it's Shade Elliott. Do you remember me?" Shade

asked.

"Shade? Shade … Elliott? … Of course I remember you. How are you? Where are you? Are you okay?" Dave asked.

"Yes, I'm fine. I'm living at home again. It's a long story, but I'm out of the old life and planning to re-enroll at school next spring," Shade answered, a grin widening with each word, relieved his friend sounded glad to hear from him.

"Oh man, that's great news. I've tried finding you. Man, it's my fault you got mixed up with that crowd. I'm glad you got out of there. You're clean? You're … okay?" Dave asked.

"Yes, I've been clean for several months and don't plan on ever going back to that life," he told him, and all at once he heard his own words and felt really good.

"What a relief! Shade, I want to talk but I can't right now. I'm on my way to class. Give me your number and I'll call you back and we'll get together," Dave said.

"Yes, let's do that, but real quick, I need some information. Mile Marker … have you seen him? My sister has a dorm mate missing, and I hear her boyfriend is a Miles somebody. I'm almost sure he's Mile Marker," Shade said.

"Are you talking about Patty Chandler?"

"Yes, that's her."

"Yeah, I heard about her. You're right: she's one of his girls … but Miles is looking for her too. It seems she just disappeared. Maybe she took off to get away from him. The only place I know to find him is the house on the south side. You know the place. I haven't been there in over a year, but I've heard through the grapevine it's still in business. Give me your number and I'll let you know if I hear anymore," Dave said.

Shade rattled off his phone number and told Dave about his plans to call their other friend Trevor, too.

"No, don't bother calling him. He transferred out to a seminary. We got together last summer when he was home, and he's doing great. I'll tell you more when I see you. Gotta run, buddy. I'll see you soon, though," Dave said and hung up before saying good-bye.

Shade hung the phone up with mixed feelings. He was glad to talk to his old friend and was glad to hear Patty wasn't with Mile Marker—or was it a trick Miles was using to turn suspicion away from him and his illegal activities?

There was one way to know the answer, and it would involve traveling to the one house he hoped never to see again. Now he wondered how he was going to get to the illegal drugstore.

Chapter 12

Watching from the rooftop, he saw the short unkempt man pull the small figure from the car. The child had a blindfold over her eyes and a gag in her mouth. Her hands were tied behind her back. He was amused to realize he would have a chance to meet the owner of the concealed apartment after all. For the first time, his movements quickened to re-enter the apartment, where he strode straight to the bathroom door and yanked opened the makeshift cell.

The woman spoke at once: "Miles, why are you doing this? Please turn on a light. I can't see. I promise I'll be good. Where are you?"

Walking to the tub, he punched her in her face with his fist. The blow knocked her head against the back of the tub, knocking her unconscious. She slumped deeper in the tub when he closed the door and returned to the rooftop. He made it back to the roof in time to catch a glimpse of the little man dragging the child inside the fire exit door to begin the trek up the cluttered stairway. Hidden behind the furnace's louvered door, he waited several minutes before he heard the door sliding back to expose the hidden apartment.

/////

The apartment's truant owner shined the flashlight around the room. In the dim light, his vision was limited, but already confident the apartment's whereabouts had remained undiscovered he was soon satisfied and pulled the bound and gagged child toward the bedroom. Through the flashlight's small circle of light, he saw he had left the bedroom door in his crafty engineered locked position and started to pull the door away to free the bathroom. Annoyed by the muffled crying coming from the scared child, he smacked the whimpering girl, knocking her to the floor beneath his feet. Using one foot, he shoved the child, forcing her out of the way. The frightened girl tried to get up, so he stepped on her back, holding her down while he pulled the bedroom door out of the way.

/////

Patty came to a few minutes after being hit. Dazed, she lay still until she could force herself to think more clearly. The brutal attack from Miles came slowly back to her memory. She had no idea how long she had lain unconscious from the blow. Why the hell had Miles struck her so violently, she wondered?

Listening, she began hearing sliding sounds coming from outside the room and very quietly rose from the tub, feeling her way until she was able to press her ear against the bathroom's door. Sounds of a child's muffled crying reached her ears, adding to her dazed confusion.

The door jiggled against her ear, and she realized it was being opened. She spun around in an instant. Forgetting the burned-out candle, she knocked it from the top of the toilet's tank when she lifted the tank top with both hands. A loud thump sounded outside the bathroom door, masking the soft thud of the candle's landing when it hit the floor.

A soft glow of light illuminated the doorway when the door cracked open. Forcing herself to remain perfectly still, she waited for the door to open farther. Filled with anger from her previous attack, Patty, clutching the toilet top with both hands, swung the heavy top with all her might in the direction of her suspected assailant's head ... not caring if she *killed* Miles. A feeling of triumph washed over her body when her hands felt the reverberation from the blow and she knew she had hit her target. Her eyes had closed when she swung the tank's top, re-opening a millisecond before the booming thud of the intruder's landing body reached her ears.

Upon impact, the man staggered backward and stumbled. Abruptly, his arms jerked awkwardly forward, reaching out blindly. The forward motion changed his momentum, forcing him to fall facedown with his head landing inside the bathroom. He dropped the flashlight during his fall and shined the beam directly on his unseeing face, spotlighting the blood oozing from his nose and mouth.

Patty's confusion and disbelief turned to pure shock when she realized her jailer had not been Miles. Her head jerked up at a frightening muffled sound of high-pitched screaming.

What? Where's the screaming coming from?

Panic ensued but was replaced by unselfish actions when the dim light exposed the quick shadowy movement of small hands waving erratically under the odd-looking man's legs, and Patty remembered the earlier sounds of a child crying. Using what was left of her strength, she pushed the little man on his side, freeing the small hysterical girl. Grasping the terrified child by her small arms, the two ran from the darkened apartment.

"It's okay, it's okay, you're safe now," Patty kept repeating to the child, lifting and leading her through the clutter down the dim moonlit stairway.

Patty stopped for an all-too-long second to remove the gag from the girl's mouth and pull off the dirty cloth covering her eyes, but without enough light, she couldn't untie her hands. She wished she had gotten the flashlight, but in her frightened state, she'd left it shining on the little man's bloodied face. Sure she heard noises behind her, she did not dare stop to listen for fear the man would catch them. After what seemed longer than any human could endure, she made her way to the fire exit door and the only house she knew in the area.

/////

Watching the scene from his concealed hideaway, he crept into the apartment from the louvered furnace door when the little man entered the bedroom. From a darkened corner, he witnessed the captive girl hit the vile man in the head and run from the room with the child. Recapturing the fleeing twosome was not considered. The girl had fought for her freedom and rescued the child, along with herself. He felt a strange regard from within himself that closely resembled respect and admiration as he silently cheered her stamina.

Once the escaping girls were out of the apartment, he hunched over the still man, dabbing a finger in the blood dripping down the man's face and afterward touching the red liquid to his tongue. He was at once disgusted by the foul taste and spat it back onto the man. There was nothing good in the blood, only a dirty taste that repulsed him. With deadly intent, he lifted his booted foot over the man's head, deciding to satisfy himself with the apartment owner's death. Just before impact, the little man opened his uncomprehending eyes for the last time and saw the dirty bottom of a boot just before it smashed his brains onto the bathroom's vinyl floor.

Eyeing the dead man and the scattered objects in the bathroom, he gauged the scene. Grabbing an empty sack from the kitchen, he tossed all of the girl's items into the bag. Then, lifting the little man by one arm, he tossed him over his shoulder and carried his load to a windowless bathroom on the third floor. He positioned the man in nearly the identical position he had been in the concealed apartment. During the process, he dropped the girl's purse, spilling its contents. Among the scattered items was a driver's license, and for the first time, he read her name: *Patty Chandler*. A vivid picture of the green-jacketed girl praying for a girl named Patty flashed in his mind.

Before leaving, he positioned the current bathroom's toilet tank top on the floor near the dead man. It was a last-second decision that made him stop to add one final touch to the not yet grisly enough scene. Using his booted foot, he stomped down on the dead man's head, again squishing more brains on the previously bloodless floor.

It took two trips before he felt confident the scene would be accepted as the prison cell and death place of Patty's supposed assailant. He piled more items on several stairs to make them even more difficult to climb.

His improvised death scene was accomplished in a matter of minutes, allowing him time to pile objects on the last stairway, making it nearly impossible to reach the top floor.

His keen ears listened until he heard the sound of barking dogs and several voices becoming more distinct as they approached the building. The owners of the voices entered the building just after he slid the apartment's paneled wall partly closed, leaving only enough room for him to fit sideways through the opening. He remained crouched outside the apartment near the barricaded stairway, listening to the exchange of voices coming from the floors below.

"Where? Show us where you left him," one of the voices shouted over the rest. "Spread out and find him. Let the dogs loose. They'll take care of this sucker."

"Can't let the dogs loose, Miles. It's hard tellin' what they'll do. He ain't goin' nowhere. If she hit him hard as she says she did, he would'na been movin' fast. Besides, his car's still here. We'll find him," a male voice said before taunting loudly: "Ya hear me, ya piece of crap? We're coming for ya."

Thrashing sounds from the men searching the ground floor continued for several minutes.

"Nothing down here unless he's hiding in one of these trash cans," a voice said just before several loud metallic bangs rang throughout the building when the man apparently kicked over the cans in question.

"Let's go upstairs. This way … follow the dogs," a different voice said.

"Yes, stairs. I remember stairs," said a female voice he recognized as Patty's. "I can't go back up there again. I'm too weak … there's too much stuff piled on the stairs. I just can't, Miles."

"Stay here," said the man called Miles. "We'll get him. Somebody stay with Patty until we catch this creep."

Loud banging could be heard from objects being thrown

off the stairway to allow access to the second floor. "Damn, I dropped my flashlight. Anybody see anything?" a voice asked.

"Somebody take one of these dogs! I can't hold both of them and climb through this junk. They're dragging me through this garbage," a disgruntled man yelled.

Sounds of the warehouse remains being tossed and pushed aside, continued as the group searched the vacant building. The men's voices became muffled when the search traveled to the far side of the second floor only to be heard clear again when they returned to the stairwell after failing to find anyone hidden among the abandoned rubbish.

"Nothin' on the second floor. Goin' to have to throw some more trash off the other stairs to go on up. How'd Patty get through this crap? She musta been havin' one of those rushes," yet another voice said.

"Adrenaline rush," said the voice belonging to Miles. "Why can't the dogs find him? They ought to be able to smell the creep by now."

"They're not bloodhounds, Miles. They're for protection and keepin' people away. Remember?" the owner of one of the previous voices answered.

"No, they just need somethin' of his to smell," another voice said.

Sounds of more rubbish being thrown from the third-floor stairway could be heard as the men climbed the next flight of stairs. "What's all this junk doin' here?"

"Maybe the perv didn't want no visitors," a voice answered.

"Oh yeah," the earlier voice said. "Hey, perv! You got company."

Just then, the dogs began to bark.

"Somebody shine a flashlight over there! The dogs 're pulling me over toward the other side of the room. There, look … what's that?" the voice near the barking dogs asked.

"Looks like somethin' laying on the floor over there … hold on a minute."

Several sets of footsteps echoed across the third floor.

"Damn, girl!" one of the men shouted. "You done smashed this man's brain's all over the floor. Wha'd ya hit him with? Man … You did that? Whoa! … Remind me not ta mess with you!"

"Is he dead? Did I kill him?" Patty yelled up the stairs. "I didn't mean to kill him. I can't go to jail! I don't want to go to jail, Miles!"

"Don't worry, girl. We're gonna take care of it. We ain't gonna have no police comin' here. Police don't even care about no perv. You done did 'im a favor, woman."

"Get the dogs back to the house. We don't need 'em anymore. We'll be there soon as we get this mess cleaned up," a voice spoke with authority. "Tory, Steve, pick him up and put him in his car. Wait—check his pockets for his keys." The voice paused … a faint metallic jingling soon followed. "Got 'em," he continued. " Good. See to it he has an accident."

"Sure thing. Gotta great cliff I've been wantin' to see somebody go flying off. The perv's gonna have a front-row seat," either Tory or Steve said.

"My purse, do you see my purse up there?" Patty yelled, her voice echoing up the stairs.

"We got it all. Can't tell nobody was even here," one of the previous voices said. "Can't even see those brains he left on the floor. Dogs ate 'em. Bloodstains blended right into the floor with the dirt. Anybody see 'em, they'd just think a cat got a rat. Hey, maybe that's what happened. You be the cat and he be the rat," the voice said.

Groans of feigned laughter lightened the mood of the skilled crew as they eliminated the last of the evidence of the murder of the city's longest sought serial killer.

Music from Mile Marker's cell phone blared over the

laughter. "Yeah, everything go okay? You waited until she got inside? Good. We're finished here. Get back soon as you can; I've got business to take care of," Miles said, then shoved the phone back in his jacket pocket and returned to the first floor. "The little girl got dropped outside the police station across town," he said to Patty and any others within earshot. "She doesn't have any idea where she was, and the police will be looking on that side of the city. They won't look long—and you keep quiet unless you want them to know about tonight's events. Here, take this; it'll calm your nerves." He handed Patty a small round tablet with a smiley face on it. "Let's go home where I can take proper care of you. Don't worry, baby. I'll take care of everything. Are we finished here?" he called to the remaining few descending from the third floor.

"We're done. Nothin' to see here. Damn, girl. You nailed that john!" were the last words echoed inside the warehouse.

Impressed with the precision the small group worked, he retired to the apartment where he could watch the final procedures from the rooftop. Seconds later, the dead man's car pulled from the warehouse lot and stopped, waiting until a second car pulled behind it. Subsequently both cars pulled from the alley and turned left on the street, heading south. Wasting no time, they sped away, and soon both vehicles were out of sight.

A minute later, Patty and the man he figured was Miles ducked into the backseat of a more expensive-looking car pulling in not long after the first two cars disappeared. All was quiet in the now empty alleyway.

Re-entering the apartment from the rooftop, he exited by the sliding door and jumped the stair rail to land on the floor below, returning to see the tidied-up death scene. Except for a small smear of blood he rubbed out with his booted foot, nothing was left to tell of the crime committed. Aware they might come back in the daylight to make sure all the evidence had been removed, he left the blockade on the last stairway to discourage anyone attempting to access the top floor where his apartment was hidden.

Returning to his rooms, he lay on the bed, mulling over the unanticipated events. The disruption to his routine was minimal in comparison to the excitement the unscripted event aroused in him. The unexpected visit from the depraved apartment owner brought him out of his boredom. Nevertheless, his loss of control of a situation was rare, and his usual confidence in his own abilities had been challenged. In order to regain control of his bruised ego, a daring change in tactics was now a crucial requirement. After much deliberation, he decided his next move would have to be made during daylight hours instead of his usual cautious cover of darkness.

His thoughts turned to his escaped captive, Patty. The vision of the man nailed to the cross reappeared in his mind. Staring at the yellowing ceiling, he lay contemplating whether the hanging Jesus had answered the girl's prayer—or had Patty's escape been coincidence? He vowed to find out more about the green-jacketed girl so he could best determine the answer.

Once his decision was made, he relaxed and his mind began drifting near sleep. His eyes continued staring at the ceiling until it dissolved, changing into a solemn scene with several people sitting around a table sharing a meal. The man in the middle held a cup and offered it to all present at the table. Each drank from the cup, passing it to the next until at last it was returned to the man in the middle. To his astonishment, the man held the cup out to him. Taking the cup, he lifted it to his lips and tasted the liquid inside. Remarkably, it was blood—the cleanest, sweetest blood he had ever tasted, and he knew from the powerful surge charging through his body he would never need the unfulfilling blood from any human again.

"Judas," the man in the middle said with passion.

"Master, is it I?" asked a male voice sounding strangely

like his own.

"You have spoken," the man answered.

He looked up into the soulful eyes of the man in the middle and knew the materialized vision had spoken audibly to him. He associated the face with the man on the cross. A memory tried to surface but was lost almost as soon as it came. Rubbing his immortal eyes, the dingy ceiling once again came into focus, and the supper scene disappeared.

The vanished scene vaguely reminded him of the famous mural painting created by Leonardo da Vinci, known as *The Last Supper*. He had visited Milan many times and had seen the mural. Although the visionary figures sat in similar clusters, the faces in the vision were different from his memories of the familiar painting. Searching his nearly two-thousand-year-old memory, he recalled that the faces used for the mural were citizens that da Vinci found in Milan, including the Milanese criminal found in the Italian city's jail who was chosen to portray Judas. He was grateful he had learned the names of the disciples pictured in the fifteenth-century mural and mouthed the name of each person represented in the painting, coordinating the position of those pictured in the mural with those in his vision.

At first, he hadn't realized Judas was missing from his vision. On the painted mural, Judas was seated with his elbow on the table in front of Peter. In his vision, he recognized Peter by the knife he held, but the seat in front of him was empty.

Where was Judas? Was the mural wrong? he wondered.

No, his vision had to be false, he rationalized—an imaginary trick triggered by his recent trip to the church where the girl had prayed for Patty, followed by Patty's subsequent escape.

Or, he reckoned, the vision could have stemmed from his body's need for blood. Trying to understand the baffling vision, he searched his body for signs of the inevitable bloodlust that alerted him of the need to renew his internal supply, but after examining himself, he could find no physical evidence of the telltale signs.

Regardless, not wanting to take the chance of disrupting his morning plans he decided to hunt a donor. Tonight, however, he would not be bringing back a captive. His donor's life or death would depend on how willing they were to share his or her blood.

Swinging his legs over the side of the bed, he threw his feet on the floor and kicked an object, making it fly across the small room and smash against the wall. He didn't remember seeing the object before he had lain on the bed.

Retrieving the broken pieces, he reassembled them to form a cup … a cup that looked somewhat familiar and very similar to the one handed him containing the precious blood he drank in the vision. On closer inspection, he was disheartened to discover the inside of the cup was dry to the touch, without the dark red stains of the beloved blood.

Chapter 13

The librarian called early the next morning after Shade and
Charlie had already left on their morning walk. After jotting
down her message, Casper moved aside the front room's curtain
and peered out the window.

Not long before their departure, Charlie had plopped
down on the floor by his leash and remained there until Casper
took it off the hook and held it out for him. The dog bit down on
the leather strap and dragged it up the stairs to Shade's room and
jumped straightaway onto the bed. He dropped the leash just
long enough to lick his master's sleeping face until one eye
opened halfway to look at him. Wagging his tail, he snatched up
the leash to show it to his owner, the canine's way of telling his
human of his plans.

In an attempt to appease the animal, Shade's sleepy eye
stayed open for a second before closing it back in sleep, bringing
a "Woof" from his insistent pet and more wet licks to his face.
Still keeping his eyes closed, he forced a hand out from under
the blanket to grasp the curly hair on Charlie's head and
surprised the dog by throwing the blanket back to uncover his
dressed body.

"Got ya!" Shade teased and jumped to stand by the side
of the bed.

Charlie pranced in a circle, then headed toward the door.

"Hold on … work before play," Shade commented and
took a minute to straighten the bed before going downstairs to
slip on his shoes.

Since being home, Shade made sure he did as much as
he could to help around the house. He didn't want his mother
picking up after him and took measures to show appreciation of
the home she provided for him. Not only did he pick up after
himself, take out the trash, and run the vacuum cleaner, but he
also did his own laundry and, from time to time, cooked dinner.

Due to his lack of cooking skills, often it was soup and grilled cheese, but his mother seemed grateful for the time out of the kitchen and applauded his efforts.

He planned to expand on his meal varieties and tried to watch a couple of cooking shows, but being unfamiliar with many of the food products and utensils, he had a difficult time keeping up with the televised meal preparation. *The Betty Crocker Cookbook,* with everything already written down, was more to his liking. He learned that when he didn't know a food product, such as "Chinese cabbage," he could go to the computer and Google it, bringing up a picture and where to find it in the grocery store. Of course, since he seldom drove, the difficulty was in getting to the store to purchase the items. For the time being, his mom did all of the grocery shopping.

Jogging slowly with Charlie keeping the pace beside him, Shade wondered how his mom would take the news when he asked to borrow the car to go to the city again today. His need to visit the house on the south side to find Patty, or news of her, weighed heavily on his mind. Her choice of lifestyle, he was sure, would in time break her and leave an empty shell of a human being. If she were with Miles, he would have to find a way to talk to her. Besides, he promised Breeze and Susan he would be in touch and didn't want to let his younger sister down any more than he already had in the past two years.

His mother knew he needed to return to the library, but he had hoped the librarian would have called by now in hopes of diminishing her worries and preventing unnecessary suspicions.

Nearing the end of the block, Shade perceived the jog was not enough exercise and wished he could continue the run, but thinking of Charlie, he knew to go any farther might be too much for his older pet. Approaching the house, he was certain of his assessment when Charlie slowed the pace to a walk, refusing to run any farther. Charlie's breathing sounded labored, and Shade let him pick his own speed the rest of the way home. As

soon as they entered the house, he unsnapped the dog's leash and
Charlie made a beeline to his water dish.

"I've got some good news for you," his mom said,
keeping her eyes on Charlie. "He sounds winded. You must have
been running. Good ... exercise is good for him," she said, then
paused. "Maybe I should run with him. Heavens knows we could
both stand to lose a few pounds. Oh, what would the neighbors
say if they saw me running around the block? At my age, they'd
probably think I was hurrying to get home to the bathroom."

Shade chuckled. "What's the news?" he asked.

"The library called and *you* have someone interested in
talking to you about the cemetery. It seems a gentleman, maybe
a teacher from the college, overheard the librarian when she
called the courthouse asking for the name of the cemetery. He
heard her give the court clerk the cemetery location and, after the
call, told her *he knew* the cemetery. She, of course, told him
about you and he offered to meet with you. According to what
she told me, it sounds like he can not only give you the history of
the cemetery, but he also has records of the people buried there.
So how about that? You go shower and I'll fix breakfast, because
your appointment with him is at ten o'clock. I won't need the car
today, so it should work out fine. I hope you didn't have other
plans. I did tell her you would call back if you weren't able to
keep the appointment."

"Wow! You're kidding," he said, pausing to grasp the
unexpected message. "Really?"

"Really," she said. "Now go get ready and make it quick.
I've already started breakfast. At least one of us is making
progress."

Shade stood for a second, frozen to the floor. He
watched his mother walk into the kitchen before he could move
and then, taking two stairs at a time, ran to hop in the shower,
thankful for this turn of events. Maybe his life was beginning to
take a turn in a positive direction.

No, he thought, *it took a turn in a positive direction the day I left the boarded-up house*, and then he frowned when he thought of the dreaded visit he planned later today to the house on the city's south side.

His mom was sitting at the kitchen table drinking a cup of decaffeinated coffee and watching the morning news on the kitchen's small TV when Shade, showered and dressed, reappeared minutes later. His breakfast had already been placed on the table covered with a warming lid.

Charlie lay curled up napping on the woven rug in front of the kitchen's back door that opened to a medium-sized fenced backyard. His snores were periodically heard over the various sounds coming from the television. The news was broadcasting a story about a freak accident involving a car whose driver lost control and smashed through the guardrail on one of the mountainous highways south of the city. Wailing sounds from the sirens of the emergency vehicles arriving on the crash site scene filled the kitchen. Charlie let out a low howl in imitation of the high-pitched wails while his feet ran in midair as he slept.

Upon impact, the airborne car had burst into flames, instantly killing the passenger inside. It had taken several hours for the emergency crews to reach the burning vehicle and secure the scene, making it necessary to close the treacherous section of highway for several hours. "As of now the victim's identify is being withheld until next of kin has been notified," the news anchor finished the story in a compassionate tone.

"That's always been a dangerous section of highway," his mom said, shaking her head, "especially at night."

Following the gory car crash was a curious story of a young female who, "after offering herself to a hungry vampire who refused to drink her blood, cut her own wrist hoping to lure the vampire. A Good Samaritan passing on the street witnessed blood coming from a cloth wrapped around the woman's wrist and called for an ambulance. He states no vampires were in the area at the time of his arrival and believed the unmistakable scent of alcohol coming from the vampire's accommodating victim may have contributed to the woman's erratic behavior. She suffered only minor injuries—and, no, as of yet, she has not turned into a creature of the night," the newscaster finished the story as the camera pulled back to include his female co-anchor.

"I wonder if there were any bats flying overhead," said his co-anchor, struggling not to smile.

"No, Melissa, the eyewitness reported looking up and not even seeing a *pigeon* sitting on one of the overhead ledges," the good-natured newscaster answered in reply.

"Not even *one* pigeon? Now that's a story in itself," the co-anchor Melissa jested before turning to face the camera moving in to focus on her alone.

"Coming up … the heartwarming story of a young girl safely reunited with her family just hours after her abduction. Stay tuned. We'll be right back after this short break," the female anchor said and smiled at the camera while she waited for the commercial break.

Shade, finished with his breakfast, got up from the table and rinsed his plate before placing it in the dishwasher.

"I'm ready to go," he said. "Do you need me to pick up anything on my way home?"

"No, we're good for dinner. Take my cell phone. I don't want you to stop your meeting with the professor, so don't bother calling me until after your meeting with him. Call me, though, if you have any problems," she said, then handed over her cell phone.

"Thanks, Mom, and don't worry. I won't be home late. I'll stop by Breeze's dorm to see if there's any news on the girl that's missing. Any messages for her?" he asked, leaning over to give his mom a quick peck on the cheek.

"No, nothing comes to mind. Wait, yes, tell her to call me sometime this weekend," she said. "Be careful."

"I will. See you later," Shade said and pulled the door shut behind him.

Traffic was miserable once he reached the city limits. At one point, he considered getting off the freeway and traveling backstreets to the library. By the time he neared the closest exit, though, traffic began moving. A few minutes later, he passed a minor accident they had moved to the side of the thoroughfare, and he was at last able to accelerate and speed up to the freeway's speed limit.

He arrived at the library at 9:57 a.m. Not wanting to waste any time, he parked in the nearest space and jumped from the car to hurry inside. He felt mentally stressed, knowing his time was limited, but regardless, he was going to make sure he listened to the teacher's explanation of the unrecorded cemetery and learn as much as he could about the man and the curious symbol on his headstone. That should be enough to please his mom.

Shade thought back to the cemetery when she'd made the request and remembered how he was genuinely sorry he'd kicked one of the old headstones. Nevertheless, he wasn't going to make it up to one old dead guy by getting on more than a first-name basis with some other decaying corpse.

However, he was determined to get enough information to make his mother happy, and then he would head to the house on the south side and find out what he could before he visited Breeze.

If he had any chance of keeping his promise to his mother, he realized he wouldn't have any time to spare. He didn't want to disappoint his mom, so getting home at a proper time was a priority. He had already discovered that her trust in him helped strengthen his resolve to stay on the drug-free path he had begun to relish and to ignore the demons that he admitted continued to tempt him.

Spotting the librarian he had spoken with on his previous

research endeavor, he went to the row of shelved books she disappeared into and found her struggling to reach a book on the top shelf. Reaching up for her, he retrieved the desired book and handed it to her.

"Hi, remember me? I'm Shade Elliott. You're helping me find the name of a cemetery I'm researching. You called earlier this morning and left a message that you've met someone who has information about the cemetery."

"Shade, yes, wonderful news. Can you believe it? The timing couldn't have been more perfect. I believe your appointment was scheduled for ten." Her next words slowed as she turned her wrist to look at her watch and said, "Which is..." After glimpsing the time, she emphasized, "... *now*."

He nodded. "Yeah, sorry, I know I'm cutting it close."

"Let me get your folder. I haven't seen your cemetery's historian yet, but I'm sure he'll be along soon," she said as they headed toward her desk, where she retrieved a folder and handed it to him without stopping to verify its contents. "Oh, here he comes now," she said as a man entered through the glass door of the room's only entrance. "Good luck," she told Shade before waving to the older man who wore a thin black overcoat and strode toward them.

"Hello again," the librarian said, directing a smile at the newcomer. "This is your pupil: Shade, the young man looking for information on the cemetery, which you so graciously offered to share with him." The librarian glanced at Shade and said, "You're welcome to use any of the tables, but please remember to keep your voices down. It's still warm enough outside to use the benches if you feel restricted inside while you talk. I'll leave the two of you alone to share your information. Call me if I can be of any further help," she said, walking away with the same book still clutched in her hand.

Shade's eyes had locked on the man even before the librarian spotted him entering the room through the glass door. A humming noise filled his ears, muting the librarian's polite introduction and commonly known library courtesy. His eyes focused only on the man, oblivious of his surroundings. The unexpected memory of the eerie picture taken at the cemetery flashed in his mind, and he fought the dizziness threatening to physically overtake him. Intuitively he knew with that brief unheard introduction, his life, for some unexplained reason, had changed.

"Hello, Shade, I've been looking forward to meeting you," the older man said in an accent Shade would not have easily identified even if he had been in control of his current shaken mental faculties.

As the man extended his hand, Shade struggled to regain his composure while searching his memory. He had seen this man before, but ...

Where? he wondered.

He hesitated before reaching to shake the man's outreached hand. A light warm tingling sensation vibrated through their handshake when they gripped. The older man seemed not to notice, but Shade jumped slightly before masking his surprise.

Static electricity, he thought but was slow to regain control of his wits. His heart beat a little faster than usual while he mentally strained to force himself to listen to the man's words.

"Shall we take the librarian's suggestion and use one of the benches outside, Shade?" the older man asked, already walking toward the glass door and continuing to talk without waiting for an answer. "Shade," he said thoughtfully, "your name has a double meaning: shady glen or shady character. Which are you?"

Shade, at first taken aback with the man's bold question, glanced sideways at his new acquaintance and, sensing kindness in the man, gave an honest answer to his question: "For a while,

I was the shady character. I'm working on correcting that, however, and hope one day I will be more of a shady glen.

The man nodded. "A fine answer. I believe you're a lot closer to becoming a shady glen than you realize," he said, patting him on the shoulder while they walked to the bench having the most sun.

"May I ask your name? I feel as though I've met or seen you before," Shade said, regaining some control over his previously stupefied senses.

"Are those your pictures of the cemetery?" the man asked. "May I see them?"

"Yes," Shade answered, handing him his folder.

"Most call me Ahasver. American tongues usually have difficulty with the pronunciation," Ahasver said as he looked through the folder. "No, we've never met, although it's possible we've seen one another before. I travel extensively."

"What does ...." Shade fumbled mentally with the pronunciation of the man's name and decided to rephrase his question: "What does your name mean?" he asked.

"Ahasver ... it's a Persian name, taken from the King of Persia, *Ahasverus*." Ahasver then slowly pronounced the ancient king's name: "A-hash-vey-roosh, and it is not my birth name. It was given to me a very long time ago, although I'm not from Persia. Like your name, my name Ahasver has a double meaning: everlasting or wanderer."

"I hope you don't mind me asking, but what country are you from if you're not from Persia ... or I suppose I should say Iran?" Shade asked, knowing even though Iran was called "Persia" for centuries, it was always known to its people as Iran and was the name most often used now to refer to the country. "I can't place your accent," he said.

"No, I don't mind," Ahasver said. "Ask whatever you like. I'm Jewish. I was born in Jerusalem. I was not a good Jewish man, however. I, too, needed to change my life, but unlike you, I didn't know it. I was wealthy and esteemed by my peers, full of myself, until I met a man on the street one day who changed all of that. Now I travel the world working for that man. I guess you can call me a wandering Jew."

"Thus the name Ahasver … meaning the wanderer or, for you, the traveler," Shade said.

"Yes," Ahasver said, holding one of Shade's pictures out for him to see and pointing to the unusual marking. "The 'Chi Rho.' Are you familiar with this symbol?"

"No, but that's the symbol I wanted to ask you about," Shade said.

"This is one of the earliest cruciform symbols used by Christians. It's the monogram of Christ, formed by superimposing the first two letters in the Greek name of Christ, Christós—Chi-rho-iota-sigma-tau-omicron-sigma. See," he said, pointing at the headstone's symbol, "the X and the P." Taking a pen from his pocket, he wrote the Greek name of Christós—Χριστός—on the bottom of the headstone picture. "In the Greek alphabet, X represents the Greek letter chi, and P represents the Greek letter rho, and so forth. Therefore, chi and rho are the first two letters in the Greek spelling of Christ— Christ's monogram. If you translated the Greek letters into English, chi is equivalent to Ch, and rho is equivalent to R."

"Okay … Oh wait! I see now! Wow, yes, I understand," Shade said, looking at the symbol and grasping Ahasver's explanation. "It makes sense to me now. Does that mean the man buried beneath the headstone was saying he was a Christian?" Shade asked.

"Yes, he was, but it also means he was a warrior for Christ," Ahasver replied.

"What? Why?" Shade asked. "Now I'm confused again."

"There is a documented account of Constantine the Great before going into battle seeking divine help from God with an upcoming battle. It was recorded that Constantine looked up to the sky and, in a vision, saw a cross of light with Greek characters attached to it. When translated, it read, 'In this sign, conquer.' At first, Constantine didn't understand the meaning of the vision until the following night when he had a dream. In the dream, Christ explained to him to use the sign against his enemies. The next day, Constantine called his craftsmen and had a labarum built. The labarum consisted of a tall pole with a crossbar. Above the crossbar, a jeweled Chi Rho with a wreath around it was attached at the top of the pole, and a banner with the image of Constantine and his children hung from the crossbar beneath the Chi Rho. He also instructed his soldiers to paint the Chi Rho monogram on their shields. Under this sign, Constantine and his army won their battle. Since then, the Chi Rho has been thought of as a warrior's symbol," Ahasver explained.

"Interesting. I need to make some notes. I don't want to forget any of this," Shade said while writing on the back of the headstone picture Ahasver had given back to him during his explanation.

"The information I've told you can be researched in the library or at home on your computer if you have one, now that you know where to look," Ahasver said.

"When you say he—wait ..." Shade said, deciding to change his original question. "Do you know his name? I can't read it with the moss stain covering the lettering on the stone."

"Yes, that's Brother Benjamin's headstone, but I'll need to have the records faxed to me. I'll get them to you later, now that I know whom you're researching. Will you be needing information on any others buried in the cemetery?" Ahasver asked.

"No, not on any of the others buried there, but I would like information on the cemetery itself: its name and when it came into existence primarily. But first ... " Shade said and glanced down at his watch, noticing time was beginning to slip away but also realizing he was actually interested in the information. "First," he repeated, "when you said the man Benjamin was a warrior, what exactly did you mean? We haven't had any holy wars here in the United States, and we're free to choose our religion without persecution. Did you mean he fought to hold onto his Christian beliefs?" Shade asked, going back to his original question earlier.

"Brother Benjamin had strong Christian beliefs. If not for his beliefs, he would not have been able to survive the hellish battles he fought, but that fits in with the next part of the story. Let me tell you that part first and see if that answers both of your questions."

Ahasver's answer roused Shade's curiosity, and he shifted positions to make himself more comfortable while he listened to Ahasver tell his story.

"The cemetery is hundreds of years old and owned by one of the earliest Christian churches organized, whose members still span the globe. The original church began a hundred years or so after the death of Christ. The founding members dedicated the church and their lives to fighting evil dwelling in this world.

"Once your country was founded, it was necessary for certain members to come to America to prevent the evil ones from escaping unwatched in this new country. Partially as a cover for the transferred members but also to bring Christianity to the new world, it was decided to establish a church to spread the knowledge of Christ to the pioneers of this new forming country. The ground the cemetery sits on was originally the site of a church built by members affiliated with the mother church in the Old World.

"Not long after the church was established, one of the newly accepted members was discovered to be of the evil ones, and in his attempt to avoid capture, he killed the church members. The church was destroyed during the hard-fought battle. However, the loss of the building was of little consequence compared to the loss of the godly lives. For their safety, the later joining members relocated, and the church was never rebuilt.

"The Christian warriors who lost their lives in that battle are buried in the grounds of the cemetery, which is still owned by the church. Since then, the cemetery's existence has been guarded and known only by a select few who have been blessed with the truest love of God ... or those outside few who are chosen by God."

Shade felt a growing sense of disbelief as he listened to Ahasver's story, and he raised a hand to stop the man from continuing. "But that's not possible," Shade said. "My mother and I both know of the cemetery's existence ... and surely neighboring houses, and the county, state, and federal governments all know of its existence."

Ahasver shook his head. "The church came to this country before laws were established, and it carefully placed their own people in high places, ensuring that laws, for their privacy and protection, were written on the early law books," he said. "I believe the law says simply, 'Recording the cemetery is unlawful since it's on private property.' The law has never been and never will be stricken from the books. The church continues to place their people in strategic positions, enabling them to continue their work behind the scenes.

"After the tragedy, the land surrounding the cemetery was bought once an original settler moved or died until the church owned all the land. For those settlers' families who wished to stay after the deeded family member passed on, more than fair amounts of money were offered to buy their property, making it hard for the remaining family members to refuse to sell since land was sold so cheap in early days. I'm sure you noticed the absence of farms or houses in the area," he said. "Remember, the church is here to confine the evil ones, not to hurt the good people of this world. They were, and still are, honest and considerate in their activities. They only wish to remain anonymous and out of the public eye."

"Are you saying this church … vigilante group is still active in today's society? But … we have the police and the military to keep people safe. What could they possibly do in today's world?" Shade asked, shaking his head.

"I know this is difficult for you to understand, let alone believe, but let me finish giving you the details before you come to your conclusions," Ahasver said. "In this world, Shade, there are beasts walking among us. They are not demons, which are without physical bodies, but people who look like you and me. At one time, they were men, known associates of Christ. They were helpers during Christ's ministry on earth, once members of His inner circle who lost their way and whose souls are now damned."

Shade could only blink as Ahasver continued.

"Some blasphemed God's Holy Spirit and were lost for all eternity. One, at least, committed suicide. Others lost their way after the death of Jesus, possibly because of the horrific trials and persecutions they suffered. And there were those who ridiculed Christ when He hung on the cross and were killed during the earth-shattering quakes at the time of His death, before asking His forgiveness for their sin.

"The loyal disciples of Christ continued His teachings, spreading the word of God. Through their steadfast love and obedience, they brought some of the lost back into His fold, but not all of the lost were receptive to His word, and so their teachings fell on deaf ears and hardened hearts. Those privileged members of Christ's inner circle were lost forever to darkness.

"These men, once beloved of Jesus Christ, are important to Satan. He knows how much Jesus loved them. The ruler of darkness resurrected these beloved men of Christ from the depths of hell and freed them to roam the earth. However, they are no longer men but beasts, lost souls and capable of horrendous atrocities. Satan, believing Jesus can do nothing to save them or stop them, uses these beasts to mock Jesus.

"The church, as I said earlier, was in a horrible battle with one of these beasts. The beast killed all but one warrior, Brother Benjamin. However, Benjamin died later from wounds suffered during the battle. Sadly we have lost many of our Christian warriors through the years. It's to be expected. Our most recent loss occurred not long ago, and we have need of his replacement," Ahasver said as looked straight into Shade's eyes while saying the last words.

"How did he die? Another battle with one of those man-beasts?" Shade asked.

"Old age, Shade. He died of old age. You see, we don't battle the beasts often. They can't be killed. We monitor their activities if they should get too high in our world governments and then try to slow them down in their endeavors. We have learned to keep our eyes open and watch for anything out of the ordinary. And of course, we are always vigilant for the beast yet to come," Ahasver answered.

"The warrior who died ... where will you find his replacement?" Although Shade was skeptical of Ahasver's story, for some reason he couldn't quite put his finger on, he was curious to hear the answer.

"He's already been chosen, Shade." Ahasver paused and reached inside a pocket of his overcoat. "Here's my card. Call me in a few days and I'll have the information about Brother Benjamin ready for you. If you need to talk to me before then, you'll find me at the church across the street. I've already written the name and phone number on the back of the card. I look forward to our next meeting, Shade." Ahasver rose from the library bench and extended his hand. "Good-bye for now. I trust the information has been helpful with your research."

"Thank you, sir. I appreciate all of your time and information. The history of the Chi Rho as both a Christian and warrior symbol was fascinating, but to be honest, much of the latter part of the information is … difficult for me to believe. I'll certainly give it some thought," Shade said, returning the older man's handshake.

"Of course, Shade. By the way, one last thing before I leave: the church members privy to the cemetery's existence will be meeting at the cemetery next week. We meet yearly to honor our fallen members and bless the cemetery. Since its inception, we have sprinkled dirt from Golgotha throughout the cemetery— soil that is blessed by the highest saints within the church. In particular the area near the grove of trees where Brother Benjamin is buried. I wouldn't normally invite an outsider because of the consequences, but since you've already been to the cemetery, I think it will be okay. Think about it and let me know if you'd like to come and add your blessing to Brother Benjamin's grave."

Ahasver turned to leave but stopped when Shade asked, "What consequences could face an outsider from visiting the cemetery?"

"The largest part of the cemetery is just sprinkled with the holy blessed soil from Calvary, but up by the grove of trees, well, it's all holy ground. Most people can't walk on holy ground without becoming ill. Even those chosen by God will become dizzy or lightheaded when first standing on the blessed dirt."

Then Ahasver walked toward the sidewalk, waving his hand in a final good-bye. Shade stared at Ahasver's back, remembering how dizzy and lightheaded he'd gotten standing at Brother Benjamin's grave in front of the grove of trees. He was still staring even after Ahasver disappeared from sight.

Chapter 14

The desk clerk looked up with a practiced smile when he greeted the disheveled man crossing the lobby.

"Good morning, sir," the clerk said, then nodded and looked back down after observing the hotel guest's unnerving glare. He didn't lift his head again until he heard the gentle bump of the elevator doors closing to carry the disconcerting guest to his floor.

/////

Entering his hotel room, he surveyed his surroundings, checking to see if anything had been disturbed during his absence. Once satisfied everything was as he left it, he strode to the marble and granite bathroom and adjusted the shower to steaming hot before stripping himself and tossing his clothes in a heap just outside the bathroom door. He would notify the hotel's housekeeping staff to have his dirty laundry cleaned.

He wished he had stopped at the storage facility near the warehouse before returning to the hotel. The storage facility was the reason he had been on the south side of town when the woman Patty approached him for sex. At the time, though, his need for a hot shower and clean clothing seemed more important. From experience, he knew the shower this morning, as in the past, would not wash away the unclean feeling that tormented him. He never felt clean, even after his hot shower left his skin bright red from the near scalding water, as if the dirt and grime on him was just beneath his skin and something that couldn't be washed away.

Lost in thought after his shower, he looked close at his reddened skin as though he was trying to peer beneath its surface. He scratched at his arm and looked up to see his reflection in the mirror above the bathroom vanity. The memory of the previous night's visualization reemerged in his thoughts, haunting him with the question of its meaning.

Why did the Christ man call me "Judas"? he asked himself.

On an impulse, he went into the next room and opened the desk drawer where he'd put his passport before leaving to check on his items stored in the pre-arranged storage facility where he had them shipped prior to coming to America. Knowing already what it said, he lifted the small blue book and opened it anyway. The puzzled face that stared back at him in the bathroom mirror continued to look puzzled when he read the name: *Jude Dam*—the name he had given when he acquired the illegal passport many years ago. His first name ... a shortened version of "Judas." His last name ... "Dam," the "a" pronounced like the "a" in the word father—*dam* being the English spelling for the Hebrew word "blood." The name popped in his head when the forger asked what name he wanted to use on his identification papers. Was it a coincidence?

Jude laid the passport on top of the desk beside the phone. Seeing the phone reminded him to call the front desk and request a rental car instead of his usual taxi.

The clothes he wore were casual but expensive. His work as an antiquities dealer paid well. After all, antiquities were easy to find for a man who lived before they became known as antiquities. Once the realization registered that large amounts of money could be made from the items already familiar to him, he arranged archaeological digs to be performed by locals in the area—locals who quite often became blood donors after the valuables were unearthed. Stashing the coins, statues, vessels, and documents until vast amounts of objects were stored, Jude sold them when he felt the need or desire. Through the years, he had become a wealthy man.

With his fortune always growing, after a while he took his wealth for granted. Nonetheless, he appreciated being financially unrestricted when he wanted to travel and never hesitated using his wealth to intimidate those humans who wanted to pry and whom he wanted kept at a distance.

When the phone rang, it surprised him, then he remembered his call to the front desk requesting the rental car. "The car," he was courteously informed, "is parked for your convenience at the front of the hotel."

Pocketing his passport, Jude reached for his briefcase but stopped short when he realized he had forgotten the hazel-colored contacts. Going back to the vanity, he picked up the small case containing the human visual aids from the countertop and, without looking in the mirror, put the lenses in his eyes, afterward appraising the now human eyes staring back at him from the mirror. Generally he wore only his sunglasses when going out in the daytime, but today was business and he needed the buyer of his expensive items to be able to look him in the eye, thereby creating a sense of trust. The lenses were not only enlarged to cover the sclera, or white area of the eye, but were also specially color treated with lighter specks to create an illusion of trust to his otherwise emotionless pupils. With the edges of the contacts unexposed, the existence of the lenses was never guessed. The only drawback to wearing the deceptive contacts came from his disturbed night vision. With the specially crafted contacts, he was unable to see clear at night and thus wore them only when necessary.

Satisfied with his appearance, he picked up his briefcase, containing papers of authenticity for his current offered antiques and proceeded to the door. He removed the *Do Not Disturb* sign from the outside door handle and tossed it inside the room. Two members of the hotel's housekeeping staff passed him on his way to the elevator. Stopping to give them his room number, he instructed them to have his room and clothing cleaned, handing each of them a large tip. He counted on the more than generous tip to not only ensure a job well done but, more importantly, to ensure the room's contents would remain undisturbed. If not, he would remember their faces.

The desk clerk pushed the car keys to the opposite side of the desk when he saw Jude approaching from the elevator. Feigning a smile, he described the car and pointed toward the entrance of the hotel where the dark blue sedan was waiting.

Jude picked up the keys and looked into the eyes of the middle-aged man. The clerk's initial apprehension was replaced by a look of confidence after witnessing Jude's friendly expression. His smile and words were genuine when he said, "Have a good day, sir," as Jude left the hotel.

Chapter 15

Shade was lost in thought while driving to the south side of the city. His plans to mentally prepare himself during the drive to the undesirable house were thwarted by Ahasver's parting words. He was unable to focus on anything other than the cemetery's curious effect on him and the man's words concerning the "already" chosen warrior. He preferred to know who the "already" chosen warrior was and felt he may need to contact Ahasver earlier than they discussed.

All too soon, the small, dirty-white, faded house came into view. Very conscious of the fact that he was mentally and physically unprepared to enter the drug dealers' domain, he was, at the same time, very aware it was an absolute necessity.

Realizing he couldn't just go in, ask his questions, and be out in a matter of minutes, he parked across the street and called his mom to keep her from worrying—or maybe it was to strengthen his resolve before entering the dreaded house. Regardless, he needed to ask her a question.

"Hi, Mom. The meeting went well," Shade told her, grateful for the diversion. "I learned the history of the cemetery *and* about the man buried beneath the headstone with the strange symbol. And, you're going to like this, I know all about the symbol: what it means and its historical beginning."

"Terrific! It sounds like you've had a successful day so far. Are you still at the library?" she asked.

"No, I thought I would check around and see if anyone has heard anything about the girl missing from the college before I meet Breeze. I'm guessing she's still in class. I'll head over to see her before too much longer," he told his mother, feeling a bit guilty but inwardly acknowledging it wasn't a lie.

"Okay, just be careful. I'm looking forward to hearing all about your discoveries when you get home," his mom answered. "We'll talk more when you get here."

"Mom, wait … When you took the picture of the headstone with the marking, where were you? I mean, how close were you to it … the grave by the trees?" Shade asked.

"How close was I? Let me think … Well, I remember I put the camera on zoom to get a good look at the headstone. For some reason, probably from that hike up the hill, I started feeling weak and a little dizzy. That's when I knew it was definitely time to eat. Anyway, I decided not to go any farther, so I snapped the shot through the zoom lens. Why? Didn't he like my picture?"

"No, he liked it—he liked all of your pictures actually. I was just curious. I'll tell you about it when I get home after I see Breeze," Shade said.

"Okay, be careful. We'll talk at dinner," Mom said and hung up the phone.

Shade flipped the cell phone shut, laid it on the passenger seat, and unfastened his seatbelt, feeling more convinced Ahasver was referring to him when he mentioned the new warrior. The incredulous and foreign idea was beginning to take hold. Knowing he was unworthy of such a title, and full of doubts the strange story was true, he nonetheless frankly admitted to himself that he was roused by the possibility.

He opened the door and stepped out onto the potholed street's pavement. The possibility of being a warrior lifted his spirits in hopes God was with him when he attempted his first endeavor. This was not what he presumed his intended warrior duties would be but, for the time being, chose to ignore that suspected bit of knowledge.

A loud metallic slap jolted him from his thoughts as soon as he was out of the car, and he spun around to face the noise.

"Shade Elliott. Haven't seen you for a while. What brings you to this part of town? You buying, selling … or maybe snitching?"

Two of the house dealers—aka security members—stood inches from him … the bigger one clutching a ball bat perched on top of his shoulder. Although the bat was held in a nonthreatening position, Shade knew the man in possession of the bat was definitely not off to a fun-filled day at the park with his baseball buddies and understood the bat's significance as a silent warning.

He realized his dumb mistake at once. It was never a good idea to sit across from a drug dealer's house and talk on the phone to anybody. He'd been caught off guard because of his preoccupied reasoning and now had to scramble for the right words to explain why he was there.

"If I were going to snitch, don't you think I could have done that without coming here?" Shade said. "No, man, I'm looking for Mile Marker. You seen him around?"

Keeping his fingers mentally crossed, he prayed it was enough to rid them of their suspicions.

"What's you want with the Mile Marker?" asked the bigger one, clenching his fingers around the bat.

"I'm looking for one of his girls," Shade said, forcing his voice to stay casual.

"You can't find no women on yer own? You gotta *buy* your action, rat?" the smaller unarmed guard said.

"What? No! No … nothing like that! And I'm not a rat. I know her from college," Shade said, stretching the truth. In no way did he want to tell these brutes about Breeze's and her roommate's worries. "She's been helping me at school, but she's missing and I've been looking for her. Can you keep that quiet, though? I don't want to get her into trouble with Miles."

"You talking about Patty, right?" the big one said. "She ain't missing no more, we done found her. She's on her way here with the Marker right now. Come on inside."

Shade nodded, and the threesome headed toward the house by way of a well-worn path on the building's right side, leading to a back-door entrance while avoiding the dogs guarding the front door. The dogs, straining at the end of their chains, lurched toward Shade when the men passed near them but were harshly ordered, "Get back!" by both guards.

Away from the view of the street, Shade was pushed roughly against a high, rusted wire fence that separated the house from a warehouse and its parking lot. Obviously not entirely convinced of Shade's reason for being at the house, the guards patted him down, looking for any weapons or, more importantly, taping devices. The weapons would have given him respect. A taping device would have given him a death sentence. Finding nothing, the ruffians relented and, no doubt remembering the Shade of old, gave him the benefit of the doubt. Shade nonetheless stayed vigilant, knowing one slip and he would have firsthand knowledge of the real reason for the ball bat. He remained alert, praying silently he would soon be on his way.

"Makin' sure you ain't hiding nothin'. What's Patty got to do with you?" bat man questioned.

"We got a class together. My grades aren't so hot. She helps me study," Shade lied.

"Yeah, I bet she helps you study. You smart people ain't so smart. I know what she's doing for you," he said and then held out his hand.

Shade looked down to see a couple of Adderall tablets—another popular study aid used to treat ADHD. He realized a quick response was essential. Blurting out "Thanks!" he managed to sound immensely grateful and dug inside his pocket for the money to pay for the pills.

"Forget it. On the house … this time … but it ain't gonna be no habit. Next time you pay full price and leave Patty alone. Miles ain't giving her no help with studyin' no more. Thinks she needs to quit school and start working full time for him. Personally I think he needs to let her go to school, but that's none of my business … and if you tell him I said so you won't be telling him or nobody else nothin'. You got that?"

"Yeah, I got it. I'm not making trouble for you. Why would I want to make trouble for you? You've treated me more than fair," Shade said.

"You still a crackhead? Got some if you want a little while we wait for 'em to show up," bat man said, then slapped him on his back.

Shade knew this was how they hooked many of their customers, and he shook his head. "Thanks, not now, but how about a little weed?" he asked, hoping it would be enough to squash any suspicions.

"Look in the fridge. But remember, next time's not free," the dealer said.

There were several small bags of the herb in the kitchen's refrigerator. Shade chose an almost empty one sitting on the top shelf in the front of the otherwise bare refrigerator. He hesitated picking it up but reconsidered, knowing to walk back empty-handed would refuel the house guard's suspicions. Anxiety set in from the undeniable certainty he would have to smoke the mind-altering substance in view of the dealers. Caught in the trap, in his anxiety he slammed the refrigerator door harder than necessary, accidentally making it rock violently backward.

His mind was busy weighing his nonexistent options, and he didn't hear the living room's window guard announce Miles's arrival seconds before the man entered through the back door with Patty following on his heels.

"What's he doing here?" Miles demanded to know when Shade returned to the front room and sat on the room's chewed-up couch. "I heard he cleaned up. Looks like he's back to his old habits."

"Lookin' for you. Says he knows Patty from school and came to let you know she was missin'," the bat guard told Miles.

Miles turned around and looked at Patty. "You know him?" he asked.

Patty leaned forward unsteadily and looked at the back of Shade's head. She shook her head. "Nooo … Mayybeee … I dunno," she said.

"Well, damn, girl, either you do or you don't," Miles said.

The guard cocked his head and looked from Patty to Shade and back at Miles but kept his mouth shut.

"You got any rolling papers?" Shade said, raising his voice for the guard to hear.

Hearing several footsteps approaching behind him, he turned and was caught by surprise to see the two new arrivals.

"Miles … Patty." He thought quick and faked knowing the girl entering the room with Miles, presuming she was the missing Patty. "I didn't hear you come in. I'm glad to see you're okay, Patty. I was worried about you."

Shade was horrified to see the girl's bruised face and overall condition but kept his concerns to himself. He knew the pimp's reputation for keeping his working girls in line.

"Welll … yeaahh." Patty leaned toward Miles and unsuccessfully whispered in the overall direction of his ear, "I know 'im." As soon as her slurred words were out, she stumbled to the sofa and slumped down beside Shade. "Here," she said and then handed him a small package she picked up from a cardboard box turned upside down to use as the sofa's end table. "Hurrrry and rollll it. I neeed … need a hit." Patty laid her head back on the couch and waited for him to roll the joint.

Shade removed a small rectangular sheet of paper from the package. Holding it in his hand, he emptied the contents of the refrigerated bag onto it. He rolled the paper together with the herb inside, afterward licking the paper to form a bit larger than normal, unfiltered cigarette. The contents of this cigarette, however, were not grown in the local tobacco fields of the USA.

Miles shook his head, displaying his distaste as he observed Shade roll the joint and said, "Just remember, no freebies. You want a piece of that," he said with a brief nod in Patty's direction, "you see me. I don't want you wearing my girls out."

Patty glared in Miles's direction. Even in her hazy state, it was apparent to Shade she grasped Miles's meaning. After the offensive statement, she scooted closer to Shade.

"Come on, Miles. You can light it," Shade offered, reaching the fresh-rolled joint out to him.

"I've got work to do," Miles said and left the room.

Shade could tell by Miles's voice that he was peeved, but when he left the room, Shade knew he was safe in the house, at least for the time being. He would find a way to leave soon but, unbeknownst to anyone, was contemplating on how to get Patty out of the house with him. He thought about being a warrior and was strengthened by the remote possibility, but the addict in him remained unconvinced: *"A few hits of this and you'll get your head back in the real world. Warriors don't exist in this day and age,"* the devious inner voice reasoned.

The possible warrior in him, however, remained vigilant as he held the joint high in the air, joking about its size, waiting for someone to give him a lighter. Using his opposite hand, he traced the sign of the Chi Rho on Patty's shoulder, focusing his inner strength on the upcoming battle.

Oddly, in a house known for its drugs, no one had a lighter. It took several minutes before a pack of matches was found.

/////

The driver looked doubtful but chose to remain silent when she opened the doors to let the two young women off the bus. Outside on the sidewalk, the girls joked with one another as they warmed up with stretching exercises before beginning their run. They were excited about the run on the city's south side and agreed they were ready for the full ten miles, eager to begin the lengthy run. They would walk part of the way if they had to, but because both had finished classes early, they felt this was the day to attempt their ten-mile excursion and find out if they were up to the challenge. Due to the warmth of the afternoon sun, Breeze wore her green jacket wrapped around her waist. Even without the night's lights shining on the reflective material to create the glowing effect, the jacket was easily visible on the streets.

It took only two blocks to reach the warehouse district, where the girls became very aware of the change in their surroundings and began to feel uncomfortable. The sound of barking dogs drew their attention to a small, dingy, white house coming up on their right. Agitated by the approaching young women, the dogs leapt at the rusted wrought-iron fence bordering the sidewalk in front of their house. The closer the women got, the more the large animals clawed at the fence's iron bars in their attempts to gain a foothold and strengthen their efforts to break free of their chains. Frightened the chains might break, the girls crossed to the opposite side of the street.

Keeping her eyes on the large canines, Susan ran into the front fender of a car parked at the street's curb. Nervous giggles erupted into laughter, forcing them to stop for a moment to regain their composure.

Breeze glanced at the parked vehicle and, still in stitches, commented, "My mom has a car like that."

At the nearby storage facility, they had just passed, a garage door slammed, snapping them back to reality and out of their breathless laughing fit. Starting out at a slow pace, they began running, increasing their speed with each step. After just a few feet, Breeze noticed one of her shoes was untied and stopped to retie it. While kneeling on the sidewalk, she glanced back at the barking dogs on the far side of the street, and the license plate of the parked car caught her eye.

She raised an eyebrow and said, "Susan … I think that *is* my mom's car." Then Breeze jogged back to the auto.

"What? Are you sure? Why would your mother be here?

Does she ... Do you know anyone who lives here?" Susan asked and ran back to the car with Breeze.

"No ... No one I know, but I'm pretty sure that's Mom's car," Breeze said and looked up and down the street.

Seeing no one in either direction, she eyed each of the nearby buildings. Nothing looked familiar, and giving up, she looked back at the car.

A cell phone lay on the passenger seat. Checking the door, she discovered it was unlocked and opened it. She picked up the cell phone then looked for the car keys, but they weren't in the ignition. Flipping open the phone, she checked the contact list and read her very own name first on the list. Sure now it was her mother's car, she and Susan climbed inside the vehicle. As they climbed in, both once again checked up and down the sidewalk in anticipation of the mysterious appearance of Casper.

The girls were unaware of the dark blue sedan that pulled from the storage facility and stopped not far from them.

/////

Shade held the fresh rolled joint to his lips, waiting for Patty to light it for him. But, whether it was from too much anticipation of the euphoric effect the marijuana imported from Colombia created or her weakened wrist still in need of healing, she didn't seem able to light the match.

The living-room guard, still peering out the window, jerked his head in Shade's direction when Patty handed him the pack of matches. "You got a couple of hos stealing your car, man. Come on, let's bust their cherries and teach 'em a lesson," he said and headed out the door with the ball-bat guard following close behind.

"What? ... Now?" Shade's disappointment and annoyance was evident in his voice.

Grabbing an empty matchbox, he slid the joint inside the box and thrust it and the pack of matches in his pocket. He followed out the back door, a few steps behind the two guards.

118

Because of the suddenness of the disrupting change in events, Shade forgot about Patty. Glimpsing her unsteady weaving behind the marauding party, he rushed back to grab her hand and pulled her behind him. He clutched her hand tight, trying to keep her with him, but she wobbled all the way as he tried to hurry out the back door, past the excited dogs, and out onto the empty street.

"What are you bitches doing in my buddy's car?" yelled the guard holding the bat as he crossed the street to the car.

/////

Inside the car, the girls were considering whether to call Casper, but since they had her phone, they couldn't make up their minds. Calling the police seemed the best solution; however, they weren't sure Casper was in trouble. Unaware anyone was talking to them, they were stunned to see the intimidating foursome approaching the vehicle and panicked when they realized they were being accused of car theft. Frantic, they raced to lock all four doors.

/////

"This can't be happening!" Shade whispered to himself.

He watched as the bat man glared through the windshield and raised his bat, plainly displaying an unspoken promise to break out the driver's side window.

"Call 9-1-1!" a female voice yelled from inside the car.

"I'm 9-1-1, ho!" bat man raged and began swinging the bat toward the window.

"Wait!" Shade yelled and jumped between the window and the bat. He firmly grabbed the weapon before the blow landed. "That's my car!"

"It's not your car! It's my mother's car!" another female voice yelled through the glass.

The smaller guard standing by the passenger window half-choked on a loud snort.

"Get your lyin', crack-smokin' ass out here, bitch. Does

this man look like your mother?" bat man said.

Grabbing Shade by the shoulder, he swung him around so he was staring directly into the face of ...

Breeze?

"What the ... what are you doing here?" Shade stammered.

Breeze sat motionless, staring back at him for a split second before she answered him.

"We were running. We saw the ca—Wait! What are you doing here?" Breeze asked.

"I ..." Shade said, then swallowed hard.

"What's going on?" Breeze asked. "Is that Patty? Patty, is that you? Are you okay? Where were you? Shade, what are you doing here?"

"You know these bitches?" bat man asked as he lowered the bat but kept both hands on it.

"Yeah, I know 'em," Shade said. "They're just a couple of runner friends of mine."

"What're they doin' here? You hos followin' my boy? You spyin' on him or you spyin' on us?" bat man asked.

"What? No!" Breeze said. "Spying? No, we're not following or spying on anybody! Why would we be spying? We're just running."

"Get 'em outta here!" bat man ordered Shade. Then, looking at Breeze and Susan, he said, "And don't come back. Anybody run in this neighborhood gotta reason ta run. Don't come back 'less you wanna know what that reason is."

"Unlock the door," Shade told Breeze. Once she complied, he opened the door and said, "Get in back."

She got out of the driver's seat and crawled to the back, and Susan, sitting in the passenger seat, did the same.

"Thanks," Shade told the ball bat guard. "And Patty needs to come with us. There are people looking for her. She can come back later."

"I can't let you take Miles's bitch. Now you sound like *you* been smokin' crack, dawg," he said.

Shade knew Breeze had overheard the man's refusal to let Patty go with them when she jumped out of the car. He shook his head and said, "Get back in the car, Br—"

"Patty needs to come with us," Breeze said and looked up at the guard. "Please?"

Bat man's eyebrows jerked together. "Don't be gettin' outta that car! Did you hear me? I said get back in that car!" he ordered, but other than look annoyed and confused, he didn't do anything to stop the small girl when she grabbed Patty by the arm.

"What the devil is all the commotion about?" Miles shouted, coming out of the house at full walking speed and reaching the group when Breeze pulled Patty toward the car.

Without warning, Miles's hand struck out and backhanded Breeze, knocking her backward and causing her to fall in one of the street's many potholes. Hastily getting back up, Breeze grimaced and struggled to stand. Water filled her eyes. She staggered and let out a small groan.

Feeling shock and anger at Miles's abusive actions, Shade reacted with quick strides to defend his sister but was stopped short by the man holding the ball bat in a position usually intended for an out-of-the-park home run. Shade moved quicker than the batter and ducked before the bat struck its intended target. He spun around and ripped the bat from the guard's hands. Dropping down, he swung the bat low, knocking the would-be batter off his feet. The man's head slammed back on the pavement, dazing him. Ridding the guard of his bat for good, Shade flung it across the fence into the warehouse parking lot.

Susan ran to Breeze's side, helping her stand and hobble toward the car. Miles, meanwhile, was clutching Patty's wounded wrist when suddenly his arm was yanked and twisted behind him. His agonized yell alerted the smaller guard, who pulled a gun from under the waistband of his baggy jeans.

The second Patty was free, Breeze pulled away from Susan's supporting arm and hopped and limped as fast as she could to the released woman. Susan ran close behind her and assisted both women. Frozen in place, Patty stood staring wide-eyed at the man now holding Miles hostage. Breeze's eyes followed Patty's shocked gaze and locked eyes with the man who had come to their aid. Her inquisitive look changed to an expression of thanks before she did a double take and squinted as if trying to recognize the dark man as the two girls pulled the paralyzed woman stumbling toward the car.

Relieved that a Good Samaritan had intervened to take care of Miles, Shade turned his attention to the guard who had pulled out a pistol. In one swift movement, Shade kicked the gun-toting guard's hand and knocked the weapon loose. All eyes looked upward at the loaded gun flying high in the air. Coming back down, it was caught by the man holding Miles.

The man thrust the gun against Miles's cheek and glanced at the girls. When they ran toward their vehicle, he aimed the gun at the two guards and started backing toward a nearby car, using Miles as a shield.

Shade ran behind the fleeing girls and jumped into the driver's seat of his mother's car, with all three women piling into the backseat in one swift motion. Even as he started the car, Shade saw that the Good Samaritan had shoved Miles toward the enraged guards, pushing him so hard that Miles landed on his hands and knees. Gunning the car's engine, Shade raced forward and positioned the vehicle between Miles and the Samaritan.

One guard ran to help Miles to his feet while the other guard sprinted back to the house and unchained the dogs. Seeing just one stranger on foot, the dogs took off full speed after him. Shade spun the car at the fearsome animals, but they dodged the sliding vehicle, and the tricky maneuver barely delayed them in their deadly pursuit. They reached the Samaritan just as he yanked open the door of the car he'd been heading toward.

All eyes stayed glued on the colliding threesome; some soon squeezed shut in horror while others opened wider with deep male voices screaming orders for the dogs to attack. Time stopped … but not long enough for the Samaritan to get into the car and close the door. Cornered, he turned and faced the deadly animals. Instead of attacking, for some unknown reason, the dogs yelped and backed up fast. Further disobeying the screaming owners' attack commands, they turned tail and raced off in the opposite direction down the street. Figuring, the Samaritan was safe now, Shade hit the gas.

/////

With the dogs no longer a threat, Jude turned back to his car. Before he got inside, he threw the gun over the car's roof. It flew across the street and kept flying until it was over the warehouse's high fence, landing somewhere in the abandoned building's parking lot. Before the weapon hit the ground, Jude slid into the driver's seat and backed the car into the storage facility's driveway. He waited until the small group in the fleeing car drove past him, then, squealing his tires, Jude sped out after them. Once he knew the occupants in the car ahead of him were safe, he turned the car down a side street.

Jude would have preferred staying to finish the fight. However, more important issues were at stake. Running into the green-jacketed girl was too coincidental. When he first caught the gun, he had fully intended to force the gun into Miles's mouth and pull the trigger. That was until making eye contact with the girl when she rescued Patty. He mentally calculated the cost, knowing at once if she witnessed the deadly act, she would never permit him to get close enough to find the answers to his questions.

Another time, he thought as he turned the car, knowing that unless destiny changed its course, they would meet again.

Whether the destined meeting was predetermined by the cosmos, or, by his own, desire was not mused. His instincts told him the girl had something to do with him. He would let destiny play its hand—and even help her if need be. His mind became consumed with an uncompromising desire to know the role this small, insignificant human played in his existence.

/////

Ahasver had no difficulty deciding which of the two cars to follow. He waited until both cars were a safe distance away before pulling out of his concealed parking space. He eyed the disheveled men—drug dealers, no doubt—and sensed their outrage right before it was confirmed by the obscene gestures and obscenities shouted when he passed them as they stood in the street.

Concerned by the street brawl, Ahasver was glad to see Shade and the girls escape with what appeared to be just minor injuries. Despite his relief, though, he was perplexed by the presence of the antiquities dealer who had come to the rescue.

Chapter 16

Feeling they had driven far enough away from the fight scene, Shade looked for a spot to pull the car over to the curb. They needed to stop and catch their breath. Not only were the girls nearly hysterical but he, also, felt shaken to the core. Expecting their timely liberator to stop behind them, Shade was surprised to look in his rearview mirror and see the heroic man's car turn down a side street.

A Good Samaritan who prefers not to be thanked or recognized, he thought.

Breeze leaned toward the front seat. "What in the world were you doing at that place, Shade?" she asked.

"Looking for Patty. I'll explain later," he replied.

It took several minutes before the group calmed down. Once they determined they were safe and all in one piece, a plan of action became the focus of their discussion. First, Breeze needed her ankle X-rayed, and Patty definitely needed medical attention. Her behavior grew increasingly odd. Her drugged state was obvious, and they blamed much of her behavior on the effects of the drugs, but they were becoming more worried by her bizarre ravings. All they were able to get from her was "A monster, he's a monster," and afterward, she'd bury her face in her hands.

Susan, Breeze, and Shade emphatically agreed with Patty: "Yes, Miles is a monster," they said. The girls put their arms around her and assured her Miles couldn't hurt her anymore, but Patty's response was to look at them and shake her head and repeat her words: "No, no! He's a monster!"

To their dismay, Patty refused to go to the hospital for medical attention, and mention of going to the police just escalated her alarm: "I don't want to go to jail! I can't be locked up. Please don't let them lock me up again. I want to go home. He's coming ... the monster's coming! I want to go home.

Please … Please let me go home!" she cried.

All three gave in to her pleas with the promise of no hospital or police. They managed to explain to her it would be necessary to go back to the college dormitory to get her things and let everyone looking for her know she was safe. She could contact her parents from there and make arrangements for them to pick her up. They would keep her previous whereabouts confidential unless she chose to make it public or they were backed into a corner. The agreement subdued Patty enough for them to at last get back on the road.

The hospital was closer than the girl's dormitory. Shade, concerned for his sister, stopped in front of the emergency room doors but let Susan escort Breeze inside after promising her to come right back. He waited in the car with Patty, who sat motionless with her eyes fixed on the back of the seat. Minutes later, Susan returned with the hospital staff's assurance that Breeze would be in good hands until their return. Susan rejoined Patty in the car's backseat and placed her arm around her shoulders, attempting to comfort her during the short drive to the dormitory.

Unbeknownst to Shade and Patty, Susan called the dorm supervisor when she was inside the hospital with Breeze. Arriving at the dormitory, Susan directed Shade to the back of the building where college personnel were waiting for them. Shade, they decided, could leave to take care of his sister, who they understood had fallen when the girls were running. They insisted that Susan stay with Patty and answer any ensuing questions.

Satisfied there was nothing else he could do, Shade left the dormitory and headed back to the hospital. He found Breeze in the emergency room with an ice pack attached to her ankle, which had swollen considerably. The X-ray, she relayed, had already been done and she should know the results soon.

While they waited, Shade explained his reason for being

at the house without giving her any of the alarming details. Once her questions were answered and his short explanation accepted, they pondered their mother, knowing they needed to call home. The unspoken question was how much did they want to tell her? The two siblings considered the ramifications and came to a mutual decision. Their mom would be horrified if she knew Shade had been to the drug dealer's house even if it had been for a noble purpose and, most likely, saved Patty from a life filled with pain and despair.

Their mother would also be equally horrified to hear Breeze and Susan were running on the city's dangerous south side. Their dilemma was determined to be no dilemma at all. Just one possible solution occurred to them. Mom would have to wait, however, to hear their condensed version until after Breeze was released from the hospital.

Considering the busy atmosphere of the emergency room, the doctor returned with the X-ray results fairly quick. His smile reflected the good news displayed on the large plastic film's two-dimensional image.

The X-ray confirmed no bones were broken. Although she would not be jogging for a few weeks, it was okay to walk on the tender and swollen ankle. Crutches were at her discretion.

"For the first forty-eight hours," the doctor said, "use ice for twenty minutes every three to four hours, and elevate the injured foot at night." Quite possibly from remembering his own college years, the doctor suggested placing books under the foot of her mattress. "I expect you'll be good as new before you know it, but see your family doctor if it doesn't get better in the next few days. Any questions?" the doctor asked before shuffling off to disappear into a room farther down the corridor.

Before going to the dormitory, Breeze, it was decided, would be the one to call their mother: "Hi, Mom. ... Yes, he's with me now. He's getting ready to come home as soon as he drops me off. ... Where are we? Well ... don't get all worried but we're leaving the hospital. ... No, Mom, everything's fine. I just stepped in a pothole and twisted my ankle. Shade was with me and he drove me to the hospital for an X-ray. ... No, it's not broken. ... I just need to put ice on it and take it easy for a few days. ... What? ... Oh, no, I didn't have the insurance card with me, but Shade and I gave them the information. Can you call them and make sure they have everything they need? They already have your name on file. ... Tomorrow? ... Yes, I have an excuse, but I don't want to miss any of my classes. ... Okay, that sounds fine. I'll see you then. Maybe you can drop me off at the library when you leave so I don't have to walk so far. ... All right, I'll tell him. See you tomorrow. I love you. Bye, Mom."

Breeze breathed a sigh of relief and looked over at Shade with a smile that lit up her entire face. "She's going to drop off an ACE bandage tomorrow so I can wrap my ankle ... told you to be careful ... *and* she'll see you when you get home."

"Whew! There is a God! ... Close call," Shade said, then let out a huge breath.

During the rest of the ride back to the dormitory, Shade told Breeze the parts of the city to avoid and made her promise to stay away from those areas.

As soon as they arrived, Susan ran to their car. She filled them in on the details of what had happened during their absence, all the questions asked as well as the answers she and Patty gave.

"Patty told them she was in an accident and wasn't apprehended at all. She must be protecting Miles—that creep," Susan said. "She asked them to call her parents, who it turned out were already in town and have been since she was first reported missing. She left with them about a half hour ago. You should have seen their reunion. It made us cry. She did promise her parents she would make an appointment with their family doctor when they get home. I overheard her mother whisper to her dad that the pain medication was making her too woozy," she said and paused. "Maybe this will give her the chance to get her life back together."

"Did they ask you anything?" Shade said.

"No, not really. They wanted to know how we found her. I just told them we were taking a short break from running and saw her on the street," Susan answered.

"Is that it?" Breeze asked.

"Yes," Susan said. "Oh, wait, no ... I guess somehow I gave them the idea we were running to meet your brother. I'm not sure how they got that idea, but since they had it, I didn't want to confuse them. Besides, we're not running on the south side of town anymore."

"No way!" Breeze said. "Shade briefed me on the rough parts of town, but maybe after my ankle heals, we'll stick to running on campus for now anyway."

"I like that idea. I bet there's still areas here we haven't seen. We'll remedy that," Susan replied.

"All's well that ends well," Shade said then opened the car door. "I'm off."

"Thanks, big brother." Wobbling on one tiptoe, Breeze gave him a kiss on the cheek. "By the way, when did you become a warrior? I never knew you were so capable. I'm impressed."

"I second that. You were incredible! You earned warrior status," Susan said and emulated Breeze's kiss on his opposite cheek.

"Uh ... Today ... I became a ... warrior today. See ya, girls. If I leave now, this warrior just may make it home before curfew," Shade joked and left the girls with Susan supporting Breeze as she hobbled to their dorm.

Oohs and Ahs came from various students along the way, classmates and friends empathizing with each painful step. Shade chuckled, picturing the guys who would be willing to carry Breeze's books to class. Knowing his sister, he didn't think many, if any, would have the chance. Her independence was too valuable to her, and it would take more than a swollen ankle for her to give it up, even if just for a few days.

One thought led to another, and he caught himself wondering what kind of man would someday sweep his sister off her feet. Whoever she chose would be okay with him. At that instant, he decided to make it a point that no matter who it was, he was going to be friends with him as well.

Alone in the car, Shade felt the tension in his body begin easing. He hadn't had time to let his guard all the way down and at last did so, a display of physical or mental strength no longer necessary.

Not until the ride home did Shade became fully aware of the seriousness of the day's situation. It could have ended much worse, possibly with the death of any involved in the fiasco. Shade's outraged reaction at Miles, when he struck Breeze, not only surprised him but scared him as well. He had never been a fighter, preferring to settle his disputes with words. Nevertheless, he knew now when threatened by violence that he was not one to turn and run.

The silence inside the car amplified the chaos of the day. Perhaps he should have turned on the radio to distract his thoughts, but the need to analyze the day's events was foremost on his mind.

How was it possible to have a friendly conversation with someone and minutes later duck a baseball bat coming at your head wielded by the same person with whom you were having said friendly conversation?

Violent men must have a hard time trusting one another, he thought and then decided they weren't the loyal friends he wanted in his life.

If not for his quick reactions, he knew he could be lying dead in the street instead of driving home. What then would have happened to the girls if he and the Samaritan had been unable to defend them? Startled, he realized how fortunate they were.

Closing his eyes for a brief second, he whispered what his heart felt: "Thank you, God."

Chapter 17

Ahasver waited by the church's fax machine for his promised files. The sighting of the antiquities dealer still perplexed him. Although Ahasver was familiar with the dealer who had a reputation for finding some of the world's most beloved treasures, for him to show up in the same vicinity as God's new warrior was disturbing.

Shade could be in danger. To confront *anyone* with the knowledge he was about to share would be foolhardy without factual proof. He hoped the soon-to-be-faxed files would be enough for the boy. It was happening too fast. There hadn't been enough time for Shade to absorb yesterday's incredible story, and yet he was about to tell him another, albeit true, story that would come across as even more incredulous.

The fax jumped to life, and paper began emerging from the machine. He waited until the machine was silent before gathering the freshly printed pages and placing them inside a folder. With his folder in hand, he exited the church and walked the short distance to his car. He couldn't help looking at his reflection in the car's window when he inserted the key in the door lock. He paused briefly, envisioning himself in times past and comparing the changes to his current outward appearance. His clothes were different. His hair was shorter. His skin not so tan since he hadn't spent much time in the sun for a while. Other than those few observations, he couldn't see any other changes.

He ducked to slide into the car's seat but still managed to knock his hat off before sitting down. Using the rearview mirror to replace it properly on his head, he noticed the thickness of his hair before re-covering it with the favorite, despite well-worn, hat. It was past time to replace the hat with a new one, but he wasn't in any hurry. He had time, and there would probably be plenty more hats to get before his days were done.

God stopping the sun for King Hezekiah entered his

thoughts, and Ahasver likened himself to the incident. He wondered if God had stopped time for Hezekiah when he stopped the sun. No, that wouldn't be right. Not only did God stop the sun; he moved it backward by ten degrees. He must have reversed time.

Ahasver's physical aging had not been reversed. He hadn't gotten younger by ten years or even one. At least, he didn't think so. His body, however, had stopped aging. Thus, in that sense, time had stopped for him. The process of aging—his molecular structure, he guessed you could call it—had been stopped, frozen in time. His hair hadn't grown an inch, although he cut it many years ago to blend in with the times. Since then, it had never grown back. He never had to clip his fingernails or toenails. His skin didn't display the age marks that he witnessed on the faces and arms of his aging clergy friends. The observance had not been out of pride but curiosity. Nonetheless, he admitted to himself, he was grateful to live without the aches, pains, and telltale signs of aging.

The sidewalk was busy with the young adults attending the nearby college, traveling to and from classes, the library, or wherever the day's activities took them. He did not envy their youth. He did envy their wisdom. Although his days had been countless, spending numerous years learning, he found that his mind was limited. He had learned much throughout his lifetime and was very well versed and knowledgeable in religious matters, but if he were to choose a different path, he would be hard pressed on career choices. He was suited for his present job. Even the shoes that he was once so adept at making would now present a difficult task, what with the new shoes designed for walking, running, jumping, or who knew what else. His years spent in the shoe business taught him to fit the size of the foot instead of the activity of the wearer.

He was appreciative of the students learning the medical profession, the lawyers learning the laws of the land, the teachers teaching their pupils, the mechanics who kept the cars running, the workers who were there to hand him his food when he stopped at one of the many food places.

No job is too big or too small. We all have a purpose, he thought. *We're like a gigantic puzzle being put together to form a masterpiece.*

Unfortunately careless choices, whether made consciously or due to tragic circumstances, would too often get in the way or disguise the pieces of the puzzle, destroying or delaying the pieces waiting to be put into place.

Is it all part of a plan? he wondered. *Is this what you intended, Lord?*

And he knew all had changed when Satan had fallen from heaven.

Then, in the distance, a rainbow appeared. Ahasver's mood lightened when he saw the symbol of God's promise to mankind, and his nostalgic thoughts gave way to the upcoming mission of enlightening Shade with the knowledge of the true identity of the man the world knew as Jude Dam.

Chapter 18

Finished with her first two classes, Breeze headed back to the
dormitory where she planned to meet her mother for lunch. Her
bruised and swollen ankle ached and slowed her progress. She
was relieved when the dormitory came into sight and tried to
speed up when she spotted her mother at one of the yard's picnic
tables. Her mother, busy smoothing a plastic red and white,
checkered tablecloth on the picnic table, didn't see her coming.

Realizing a scare could be accomplished, Breeze crept
the last few feet until she was able to grab her mother by the arm
and yell a loud, "BOO!"

Her mom was getting a soda in a small cooler and jerked
her arm up. The icy surface of the can slid through her fingers
and flew through the air, landing a few feet away. Laughter
erupted from Breeze and was echoed by her mother once the
initial scare passed.

"You're lucky that soda didn't land on your foot," Mom
said, hugging her daughter, then leaning back to eye her swollen
foot. "How's your ankle today?"

"It hurts!" Breeze reported with a grimace.

"Have you taken anything for the pain?"

"No, I didn't think I would need anything, but it aches
more than I expected."

"Here, take a couple of these. I'll leave the bottle with
you." Removing a small bottle from her purse, her mom shook a
couple of ibuprofen caplets into her hand and held them out to
Breeze. "There's a bottle of water in the cooler," she said and
then pointed toward the cooler on her way to pick up the recently
airborne soda.

"Shade told me your missing dorm mate is back. That's
good to hear," her mom said.

"Yes, everyone is so relieved. She went home with her
parents. I don't know whether she's coming back to school or

not, but at least she's safe."

"Tell me about it while we eat. I've got homemade chicken-salad sandwiches, chips, apple wedges, and a Twinkie for dessert—and don't tell me you're on a diet. You need some calories to put some meat on your skinny ankles so they don't twist so easily," her mom said as she pulled food from the cooler and placed it on the covered table.

"Lunch looks good, Mom, but you know I can't run for a while to work the calories off."

"And? Your problem is? As if you have to worry about calories! Like I said, you need some meat on those skinny little ankles, and it wouldn't hurt to put a few pounds on the rest of you, too."

After satisfying her mother's inquiries about Patty's return to school, their chatter moved on to Breeze's ankle.

"I want to try out for track in the spring, and I'm worried about my ankle," she said.

"Don't worry, it will be good as new in no time. Just take it easy until it has a chance to heal."

Her mom's confidence her ankle would be fine lifted Breeze's spirits and renewed her hopes of qualifying as a walk-on for the college track team. By the time lunch was finished, the ache in Breeze's ankle was forgotten.

"Drop me off at the library, okay, Mom?" Breeze asked once the table was cleared.

"I almost forgot. I brought crutches from home if you think they would help. Want them?"

"Yes! Good idea. I'll give them a try. They should help keep the weight off my foot."

Carrying the small cooler in one hand, her mother offered Breeze her other arm for support as they walked to the car. At the library, her mom hesitated leaving, mentioning Breeze's painful walk home.

"No, Mom, I'll be fine. I have a class in about an hour

and a half. I'll go straight there from the library. The crutches will help, and my ankle doesn't even hurt now since you gave me the pain pills."

"Okay, call me if you need me. Put ice on your ankle when you get home and remember to elevate it tonight when you go to bed. Make sure you wrap it with the ACE bandage tomorrow ... but not too tight."

"I will. Thanks, Mom."

Her backpack once again in place, Breeze positioned the crutches under her arms and tottered to the library entrance. Perchance, another student exited the building and, seeing the crutches, held the door open for her.

Her mom honked the horn and waved out the window as she drove away.

Breeze looked back through the glass doors and saw her mother's car heading toward the street. Going farther inside the library, she felt awkward, but she maneuvered the crutches without getting too frustrated, figuring she wouldn't need them long. Using them with her backpack was troublesome, though, and she struggled to get to a study table, where she at once discarded the burdensome bag.

The paper for her world religions class was due at the end of the week, and she planned to use her time to research before beginning the essay. The library's religions section was empty except for a lone male reading at one of the waist-high pedestals positioned at the end of each aisle. At one time, the pedestals held busts of the mythological gods and goddesses immortalized in the various books housed in that particular section of the library. Unfortunately, due to student pranks during which the busts came up missing only to reappear a short time later in unique places throughout the college, it was decided to remove the busts from their places of honor and shelter them in a safer refuge: a locked display case in the hall outside the study room, the once social gods and goddesses now deemed untouchable.

Being careful to be quiet when she passed the preoccupied man, Breeze touched the shelves for support as she roamed the aisles until she found the books she needed for her research. Carrying the hefty books in one arm, she retraced her steps toward the study table and past the room's only occupant. She glanced up on her way past him and was stunned to find herself looking into the eyes of their previous day's mysterious Samaritan.

"It's you!" she exclaimed.

/////

Jude, fully aware of the girl's entrance earlier, returned her wide-eyed stare. Beneath the colored contacts, his eyes dilated with the craving to taste the blood running through the veins presently so close that he could see the blood pulsing through her neck. His bloodlust had not yet resurfaced, which greatly reinforced his current required self-control. Noticing her use of the shelf for support, her plight was apparent to him. He took the books from her arms and placed them beside his open book atop the pedestal.

"Jude ... Jude Dam," he said. "We appear to be on the same path."

"Yes, it seems we are. Brianna Elliott ... but most people call me Breeze. And I—*we*—owe you a debt of gratitude for saving us from what could have been disastrous yesterday."

"Do you find yourself in those situations often?" Jude asked.

"First time and hopefully my last. We were helping a friend," Breeze said.

"Male or female?"

"Female. The man was my brother. Patty, the girl we were helping, had been missing until yesterday."

"Did you pray for Patty when she was missing?" Jude asked.

"What? Well ... yes ... actually I did. Wait ... that's

right! It was you at the church!" Breeze said, at last recognizing him and connecting the dots. "I remember you. Did you hear my prayer?"

"Yes. Does God always answer your prayers?"

"God always answers the prayers of His believers. It's not always the answer we want. We just have to have faith. This time, He chose you to help with the answer," Breeze said.

"Humph, it's more likely you're the one chosen. The confrontation was just fate's way of an introduction." Pausing, Jude looked back at the book lying on the pedestal. "Do you know this painting?" he asked, nodding toward his open book.

"Of course. That's the painting of *The Last Supper* by Leonardo da Vinci. The original is in Milan, Italy. I'd love to see it in person," she told him with a wistful sigh.

"I've seen it. Do you know the people in it?"

Breeze, still looking at the picture, pointed to the first apostle depicted on the left side of the painting. "This is Bartholomew; some scholars interpret him to be Nathaniel. Not much is known about him. It's thought he was arrested for preaching the gospel in Armenia. Some believe he was crucified, while others believe he was flayed alive with a whip or possibly both," she said, glancing up at Jude as she finished.

"Go on."

Jude's dilated eyes shrank to normal size and he listened, paying rapt attention to her narration of the saints.

"Next to Bartholomew is James the Less, or James the Minor, the son of Alpheus. His death is also uncertain, but some speculate he was clubbed to death.

"Andrew," she continued, "was a fisherman who was at first an apostle for John the Baptist but left John to become an apostle for Jesus. He was Jesus's first disciple. He's said to have died on a cross on which he was tied instead of nailed as Jesus was.

"Peter, Andrew's brother, was also a fisherman. He's

commonly known as Simon called Peter. He was given the Aramaic name 'Cephas' by Jesus. The name 'Cephas' means 'rock' in Hebrew. Peter is derived from the Greek word *petros,* which means 'rock.' He was crucified, but he requested his head be put downward because he felt unworthy to be put to death in the same manner as Jesus."

Breeze stopped and looked at Jude. "Do you want me to go on?" she asked.

"Don't stop!" Jude said—a bit harshly, he knew. Noting Breeze's startled expression, he added, "Please. I find it most interesting."

Breeze paused slightly, then nodded and looked back at the book.

"Judas," Breeze said, "the treasurer. Most often known as the traitor. He betrayed Jesus, causing Him to be arrested and later crucified. Judas, we know, killed himself."

"Killed himself? What? How?" Jude said, again using that same harsh tone and not caring this time.

"He hung himself," Breeze said, and this time, her eyes flashed a warning at Jude.

"Where?" Jude asked in a softer tone.

"A field, which the chief priests later bought. The field, a potter's field, was a place to bury foreigners or strangers. It's also known as *Akeldama,* which is Aramaic for 'field of blood,' and it was located in the Valley of Gehenna. Translated, 'Gehenna' means 'hell.' Jewish folklore tells the story of a gate leading to a lake of fire from there."

"Ah, yes, the lake of fire where the wicked will be cast. One of the portals to hell," Jude said, then nodded.

"Do you want me to finish?" Breeze asked.

"Yes, but let's sit down so you can rest your foot."

Clutching the books in one arm, Jude offered his other arm to help her walk back to the table where her backpack had been left.

Once they were seated, Breeze reopened the book and, finding her place, resumed her narration: "Okay ... let's see. Who's next? John most loved of Jesus. Some believe the person in the painting is Mary Magdalene because of his softer, more feminine looks, but tradition says Leonardo painted John. John, again, was a fisherman. He wrote the Book of Revelation, the last book in the Bible, and thought to have been exiled to the Island of Patmos where he died of natural causes.

"Then, of course, Jesus, the Son of God who preferred to call himself the Son of Man. Fully God ... fully man. First born of a human, the Virgin Mary, who during an angelic visit was planted with God's seed and as a result gave birth to Jesus. His mission on earth was to spread God's word ... to give man hope of eternal life and forgiveness for their sins. He healed the sick and raised the dead. He was betrayed by Judas and arrested by the Sanhedrin and sent to the Romans. Pilate, the governor, washed his hands of it all because he was unable to find any fault with Jesus, and he handed Him back to them for judgment. Due to Jewish laws, they couldn't sentence anyone to death so they badgered Pilate into crucifying Him, telling Pilate that Jesus's blood would be on their and their children's hands. Jesus was beaten and hung on a cross at Golgotha, where He died. Three days later, He rose from the grave and later ascended to heaven, where He now sits at the right hand of God."

"Who did He raise from the dead? Judas?" Jude asked.

"No, Judas hung himself when Jesus was sentenced to be crucified. The Bible tells of three people Jesus raised from the dead: the only son of a widow, the daughter of one of the religious leaders, and his friend Lazarus, who had been dead four days."

"Do you believe it's possible to raise someone from the dead?" Jude asked.

"I believe there are things in this world we don't understand."

"Yes," Jude absently agreed, then prompted Breeze to continue before she grew suspicious of his internal quest. "Thomas is next."

"I thought you didn't know them," Breeze exclaimed.

"I never said that. I asked if you knew who they were," Jude replied. "Who was Thomas?"

Staring at Jude for a long second, Breeze then looked back at the book.

"Thomas, known as Doubting Thomas, because he didn't believe when he heard the news of Jesus's resurrection. It is claimed he died in India by being pierced through with spears by four soldiers.

"Then James the Greater, or Major, was the brother of the apostle John. He was another fisherman. Together James and John were known as the Sons of Thunder because of their great zeal. James was one of the three apostles Jesus picked to witness the Transfiguration. James, the first apostle to die for Christ, was beheaded.

"Four more ... Philip was a follower of John the Baptist but, like Andrew, left John and became a disciple of Jesus. Philip was sentenced to death because he converted the wife of a Roman governor. The proconsul, angered by his wife's conversion to Christianity, sentenced Philip to be tortured, crucified, and then stoned to death.

"Next, Matthew was originally a tax collector. Jesus saw him sitting at a tax booth and said, 'Follow me,' and Matthew did. He is traditionally thought to be the author of the first book of the New Testament. It's believed he was axed to death.

"Thaddeus, also known as Jude or Judas, is a mystery because various books of the Bible list his name differently, although each name is believed to belong to him. Possibly some authors chose another name he was known by to avoid confusion with Judas. And there's no reliable source for his death. Some accounts say he was clubbed to death, others crucified, and still others say he died a natural death. There are also accounts of his body being in a crypt in St. Peter's Basilica, but that's never been proven.

"Last, Simon the Zealot. Not much is known about Simon. One story has him preaching in Egypt, afterward traveling to join Thaddeus of James in Persia. Like Thaddeus, only rumors of his death have ever surfaced. Guesses range from crucifixion to being hacked or sawed to death."

Jude drew his eyebrows together before he asked his next question: "Only Judas betrayed Jesus? All of the rest remained loyal. Why did Judas betray the man?"

"No one knows for sure. One theory is Judas was a Zealot with a big ego. The Zealots were aggressive and wanted to overthrow the Romans. He may have thought Jesus planned to reign on earth and, when he realized differently, began finding fault with Him. Also, Judas likely came from wealthy parents and was a good businessman. He resented Jesus helping the poor, who he felt were beneath him. Most likely, he began doubting Jesus was the Messiah and, feeling superior, thought to bring Him down a notch—especially after being scolded by Jesus when Judas complained about Lazarus's sister Mary pouring the precious ointment on Jesus that Judas thought should have been sold for money to put in the treasury bag he kept. I don't believe he thought Jesus would be hurt, certainly not crucified. Otherwise why would he feel so remorseful that he hung himself? Only Judas knows why he did what he did. Maybe we weren't meant to know. It was between Jesus and Judas."

"Interesting." Rising from his seat, Jude paused to give Breeze a curious expression. "Here's my card. Call me the next time you decide to kick someone's ass."

/////

Jude closed the book with the pictured painting then turned and left Breeze to her studies. Watching his back until he was out of sight, it was Breeze's "Humph" that broke the silence of the room. Attempting to maintain her composure after his abrupt departure, she opened her books but stopped short to read his business card before tucking it in a side pocket of her book bag.

Antiquities ... Rare Items ... appeared in bold lettering above a phone number that looked international. She wasn't sure what to make of the man. *Unnerving ... eccentric ... oddly interesting* were the only words that came to mind.

She glanced at her watch. It was later than she thought. As hard as she tried, she couldn't keep herself focused on her studies. Getting nowhere, she gave up and was surprised to find Susan waiting outside to carry her backpack to class for her. For some reason, she could not bring herself to tell Susan about the unusual, unexpected meeting with the fearless man who was no longer a stranger.

Chapter 19

Knocking on the door felt odd to Ahasver. He couldn't
remember the last time he had been at someone's home. All of
his friends were members of the clergy, and their meetings were
held at churches.

The suit he wore was secondhand and would be obvious
to those living in this upper-middle-class neighborhood. If
someone saw him through a front window, they might guess him
a peddler and at the least close their drapes in an effort to avert
his attempt beforehand to stop at their house. Soliciting door to
door was a thing of the past. Nowadays the law might be called.
He wasn't worried. He never worried about such things when he
was on one of God's missions. Although, that by no means
meant problems didn't occur. The problems that did occur,
nonetheless, worked out in a way resulting in the benefit of the
mission. Even more, the kind of problems that did happen were
those that never would have been found and corrected in time
without the mission.

He clutched a folder in his hand and waited. If Shade
hadn't heard his knock, he was pretty sure he would hear the
barking dog that, from the sound of it, waited mere inches from
him on the opposite side of the door.

It wasn't long before he heard hurried footsteps followed
by a male voice he felt sure was talking to the dog: "Who is it,
Charlie? Why didn't you open the door?" Shade's voice asked.

Ahasver couldn't help chuckling when the door flew
open.

"Mr. Ahasver, I was going to call you!" Shade said.

"Hello, Shade. Please, just call me Ahasver. I know you
didn't plan to see me so soon, but I need to talk to you. I've
brought the information on Brother Benjamin that I promised,
along with some new information too important to wait until
later. May I come inside?"

Shade hesitated, seeming a little unsure, then moved back to allow Ahasver inside. "Sorry… yes, come in," he said, looking a bit apprehensive.

Once Ahasver was through the door and standing beside him, Shade asked, "How did you find me? I don't remember telling you where I lived."

"You didn't. I followed you," Ahasver said.

"*Followed me*? When? … Why? … You couldn't have. *Yesterday*?" Shade questioned.

"No, not to your home yesterday." Ahasver, having followed Shade twice, knew he had some explaining ahead of him. "I was aware of you before our meeting at the library. Yesterday's meeting was my way of an introduction. If it's alright, could we sit down and I'll try to explain?"

"Yes … okay. Come on in. We can sit in here. My mom's out right now, so we'll be alone," Shade replied and led Ahasver into the living room.

The dog Charlie followed on the heels of Ahasver and sat at his feet once their visitor was seated. Ahasver reached down and scratched behind his ears while saying something inaudible to the small animal. Shade gave the animal a dirty look but, instead of calling his pet to him, returned his attention to Ahasver when the man began his extraordinary explanation.

"You may not remember, but we crossed paths at a small diner the day after you visited the cemetery," Ahasver said.

Shade's eyes grew wide. "That's where I've seen you! I knew I'd seen you before we met at the library!"

Ahasver nodded. "And the map that led you to the cemetery was mine, or at least it was in my possession before you found it at the motel," Ahasver said while opening his folder from the back and pulling out the map for Shade to see.

Shade looked dumbfounded when he saw the map. He took it from Ahasver, turning it over and staring at it.

"How did *you* get it?" Shade asked.

"I returned to the motel after I saw you at the diner and picked it up. When I saw you at the diner, I knew you were the one chosen to receive the map and find the holy cemetery. God works in mysterious ways, Shade. It was His voice that told me to leave the map at the motel. I didn't know why at the time." He paused. "I know this is hard for you to believe, but I have no choice but to tell you now so I can warn and prepare you for possible danger. You, Shade, *are* God's new warrior."

Shade shook his head. "Ahasver, I ... I've been thinking about all this warrior stuff since you told me and ... no, please don't say that. You're wrong. Even though I want to believe it, you have to be wrong! God's warriors are in the stories about heaven and angels. They're in books I've read and the stories I heard in Sunday school class when I was growing up. Other than religious men like you, there are no warriors chosen by God on this earth protecting men from ... from ... beasts or Satan or the underworld ... and if there were, God would choose someone with religious convictions. Those Sunday school classes are the one time in my life I was ever close to a church," Shade said. "Yesterday it was fun for me to think I could be a warrior. But I've thought more about it, and you know what? I almost got my brains smashed in by a guy who was just a common criminal. He didn't have superpowers. So how do you suppose I'm going to fight a supernatural beast that can't die? No, Ahasver, I'm not God's chosen warrior."

"But you didn't die, Shade. You fought those street criminals and remained unharmed."

Shade looked at him. "Wait ... You saw the fight?"

Ahasver nodded. "It will take time for you to accept, but don't close the door to things you don't yet understand. You need to be ready when the time comes to confront the enemy. It *will* happen and then you won't be able to deny the truth. You may not believe you're worthy, but for whatever reason, God *has* chosen you, Shade."

"You can believe that, Ahasver, but I need proof. For now, I still don't even know how you *knew* who I was at the diner," Shade said.

"Some people, Shade, have the ability to see, ah, shall we say, the aura around a person. The aura around you is brilliant, shades of color seen radiating only from those who have been touched by the holiness of God—holiness you acquired from walking on God's holy ground at the cemetery. The cemetery, Shade, is sprinkled with dirt blessed with Christ's blood. Ordinary dirt packing the earthly path Jesus walked when He was forced to follow behind the cross upon which He would be crucified, dripping his blood along the way—the un-thought of dirt glorified by soaking up the sacred blood and sweat droplets that fell upon the soil when He was led to his death and while He hung dying on the cross at Calvary. Holy ground blessed, above all, by the precious blood of Christ and later by the prayers of the saints."

Shade was clearly stunned by Ahasver's explanation and paused before he spoke: "That's ... profound. I don't know what to say. Dirt made holy by Jesus's blood ... it's unfathomable but—Wait! I want to show you something."

Jumping out of his chair, Shade left the room, returning moments later.

"This picture, look!" Shade said. "I thought the strange glow of lights was created by my shirt. Could this be what you're talking about?"

Ahasver gazed at the picture with interest, smiling when he looked back up at Shade. "Yes, some of your aura has been captured. I've never seen a picture able to do that. The picture doesn't show the entire brilliance of your aura, but you're able to see a small portion of the colors surrounding you."

Ahasver handed the picture back, grateful for the image, knowing it would make it easier for Shade to accept the supernatural occurrences he was about to share.

"Let's say, although I'm not willing to wholeheartedly believe all of your story, I'm willing to listen." Shade looked at the picture a moment longer, then, laying it aside, returned his attention to Ahasver and waited for the man to continue.

"Fair enough." Believing the door to Shade's mind had been cracked open, Ahasver continued. "Outside the diner after our brief contact, I read your car's license plate to obtain the state and county of your residence. Although I suspected my visit to this country was twofold, it was the first time I became aware of my present mission.

"Before beginning my journey here, I returned to the motel to retrieve the map ... so, of course, didn't follow you here. Our meeting time and place, I trusted, would be revealed when the time was right. My American contacts arranged my stay at the church where I'm currently housed. It's close to the city's college and even closer to the library where I enjoyed feeding the squirrels nesting in the trees while I waited until God brought our paths together again."

"You were the man on the bench at the library!" Shade exclaimed.

"Yes, I followed you home *that* day," Ahasver said.

"Have you been watching me here?" Shade asked.

"No, I just needed to know where to reach you if necessary."

"Okay, let's say I believe you. Why today? What's so important that you had to see me today?"

"Because of yesterday."

"The street fight?"

"Yes. I followed you again yesterday. The years have taught me to listen and follow where I'm led. You looked worried when you glanced at your watch, and my instincts sensed your apprehension had to do with more than just the time. It was too soon for you to confide in me, so out of concern, I followed you."

"You followed me yesterday? To the *south side* of town?" Shade's face flushed, exposing his embarrassment of the prior day's destination and tumultuous events.

"Yes, your warrior status has thrust you into a new arena—an arena, until now, you didn't know existed. It's my responsibility to prepare you," Ahasver said.

"You mean God wants you to protect me from those drug thugs? God may not want me to be around them, but if He wanted to protect me from them, He had plenty of time a couple of years ago. No, that's doesn't fit. Although, I will have to say, I'm a little worried they may want to retaliate," Shade said.

"No, any protection from the rough characters you fought yesterday will have to come from the local authorities. However, the man who came later to assist you is different," Ahasver said, his eyes glued on Shade.

"*The man*? Who do you mean? The Samaritan? The guy who came to our aid?" Shade asked, and his eyebrows crinkled together.

"Yes. He may look like a man, but he's no man, Shade. He's a beast. I'm sure he's one of the lost followers of Jesus from His inner circle that was released from hell by Satan. But I'm not sure which one. I can't identify him. If his name is any clue, then I would guess him to be Judas," Ahasver said, then dwelling on his own words, he stared down at the living room carpet.

"Judas? … Judas who?" Shade asked.

Ahasver looked up and stared into Shade's eyes. "Judas Iscariot, the disciple who betrayed Jesus and afterward hung himself—his dead body left on the ground rotting, only to end up missing later."

Shade sat straight up in his seat. "Ahasver, no one could know what Judas looked like. That was two thousand years ago. There's no one alive that could recognize him. How could you or anyone possibly know what Judas looks or … or … I mean looked like?"

"Looks aren't important, Shade. Jesus rose from the grave after being dead three days, and no one recognized Him. Now this man—other than his name and occupation—no one knows anything about him, *except* we know he has supernatural strength and is ageless," Ahasver said.

"What? ... Ahasver, I'm sorry. I don't mean to discredit or offend you ... and I want you to know I'm grateful. ... You've taught me things," he said and paused. "Like the Chi Rho symbol ... its historical significance ... Constantine the Great ... but ... but ... this ... if not for that man ... I might not be here ... or one of the girls might not have survived. He *rescued* us!"

"That's not his true character. I don't know why he chose to defend you. From what we know about this beast, it's not in his nature to aid or interfere with human activities. He just communicates with people in his business dealings. You must have done something to create an interest. Otherwise he would never care. He's not capable of caring whether you or anyone lives or dies. His only concern is feeding his bloodlust."

"His ... what? Did you say *bloodlust*? What are you talking about? What do you mean *bloodlust*?"

"It means just that. He—this beast—feeds off other people's blood. We stop the beasts when we're able, but as I said before, we don't attempt to capture or subdue them. We keep an eye on them. We're provided with avenues to keep the loss of human life at a minimum, but we're powerless to physically fight Satan's spawn on a daily basis. We would need the archangel Michael and his army of heaven's warriors to fight these beasts that cannot die. We, alone, would over time be annihilated. We can't permit that to happen," Ahasver answered.

"Uh, so you're telling me ... *he's a vampire?*" Shade's voice rose a pitch with the question while the unsaid words, *"Ahasver is off his rocker,"* spoke in a surer and deeper tone through his eyes.

"No ... not in the traditional sense of vampires. Although, the oldest vampires may have come into existence through some of the beasts' sexual exploits. He, though, *is a beast* ... a pawn of Satan. As I said yesterday, this is one of Satan's ways of discrediting and hurting Jesus. Not only does Satan use those once closest to Jesus to wreak havoc, but the fallen angel is, also, taunting God with his depraved mockery of godly power by bringing back these fallen followers of Christ. But Satan creates beasts, not living beings filled with their own life force. They are monstrosities, without a conscience or a soul."

"He sure looks human, Ahasver."

"He's fooled many throughout the centuries and has used countless humans to replenish his body with their lifeblood. Did you see how the dogs backed away from him? Their natural instincts alerted them to danger. Those dogs wouldn't have backed away from an ordinary man no matter how strong he was," Ahasver said.

"Maybe he used pepper spray," Shade said.

"Did you see him spray anything? Where was it? He didn't have time to get anything out of his car. And did the dogs act blinded by anything? Did they paw at their eyes like they burned? Did they even shake their heads? Think, Shade! Why were they afraid of him? Those dogs were trained to attack."

Shade shrugged. "There has to be an explanation. This is too absurd. How can I believe this?"

"I've brought something to help you with your disbelief. Look at these photos. One was taken in 1870 and the other in 1922. Do they look like the man you saw yesterday?"

Ahasver handed Shade the photos from his folder.

Shade stared at the photos and spoke only after a lengthy pause: "Where did you get these? The resemblance is ... well, undeniable. This couldn't be him." Looking confused and shaken, he finally said, "No ... this can't be the same man. It isn't possible. How could it be?"

"These pictures have been in our archives for many years. They were taken at archeological digs this man-beast organized. We knew of him prior to the photographs and have several drawings of him and other similar beasts dating back several centuries. These were faxed to me this morning."

Ahasver watched Shade's face turn ashen.

"Did any of the girls with you know him?" Ahasver asked.

"No. ... No one—wait. Patty kept saying something about a monster, but we thought she was talking about Miles, the boyfriend she was with," Shade said. His voice wavered and didn't sound quite as sure as before.

"Where is she now?" Ahasver asked.

"She left with her parents. They're not from around here. I think they live several hours away," Shade answered.

"If she's the one he's after, he'll follow her. We need to make sure she's okay. Did anyone else know him?"

Shade shook his head. "No ... no one did. The other girls were my sister and her roommate. Neither of them knew him. We wanted to thank him, but he turned on another street when we stopped our car."

"He went to a hotel. I followed him after you and the girls stopped," Ahasver said.

Shade snorted. "You followed him, too! You're pretty good at following people. From now on, *please* don't follow me. If you want to know where I am or where I'm going, ask!"

"I don't need to follow you anymore. The time for secrecy is past. You already know you've been chosen. Now you're one of us, one of God's warriors whose job is to guard and protect humanity from Satan's beasts."

"Uh ... we'll leave that part out for now. Let's get back to Patty for a minute. Okay, if he went back to his hotel ... then he wasn't following Patty. Or he thought he knew where to find her … but that means she's safe because he wouldn't know how to find her at her parents' home. But just in case, I'll have my sister call to make sure she's okay," Shade said.

"There's one more thing, Shade. You can't tell anyone of your warrior status. We work in total secrecy. You can't tell your parents, sister, or wife … when you have one. You don't have one, do you?"

Ahasver waited until Shade shook his head and answered, "No," before he continued.

"If word got out about the man-beasts roaming the earth, panic would pit neighbor against neighbor whenever anything out of the ordinary took place," Ahasver said. "Senseless killings would result. Vigilantes would spring up on every street corner, sure anyone who didn't fit society's accepted pattern of human behavior was a man-beast that needed to be killed."

"Yeah … okay. I see your point. You're right. People would be unable to trust any newcomer—every stranger would pose a threat. I can understand the need for secrecy … but I'm still not sure about any of this," Shade answered. "But for now— *just* for now—let's say I do believe your story and these supernatural beasts are real. If I did, then I would agree with your theory about the world's reaction. For now, that's the best I can do."

"That's fair. I understand your hesitation, but remember … no one can know, Shade—not even your own family," Ahasver replied.

"No one. I understand." Shade nodded.

"I hope you make the decision to join our blessing at the cemetery. Afterward I'll take you to the church and familiarize you with the beasts in this world. For the time being, you just need to concern yourself with the one close at hand."

"Uh … okay."

"Now … how about that call to make sure this girl Patty

is all right?" Ahasver asked.

/////

Finished with their strange discussion, Shade called Breeze to check on Patty. He frowned when an unrecognized voice answered.

"Hi, this is Shade Elliott. I was calling my sister, but I must have the wrong number," he said and then started to hang up.

"Shade, wait! No, this is Susan. I've got Breeze's backpack, and her cell phone was inside it. She's still in class. Do you want me to have her call you back or can I take a message for her?"

"Is everything okay with you girls? Miles and his paid buddies haven't been around have they?" Shade asked.

"No, we haven't seen or heard anything from him," Susan answered.

"Good. Let's hope it stays that way. Would either you or Breeze call Patty just to make sure she's okay? I would feel better knowing she made it home safe and hasn't heard from the guy," Shade asked.

"I'll have to ask our dorm supervisor to call her. I don't have her parents' phone number, and they're not allowed to give it to anyone without consent. Patty destroyed her cell phone and threw it away before she left. Evidently she didn't want Miles calling her, either."

"Okay, that'll be fine. I'd appreciate it if you call me back afterward," Shade said.

"Sure, no problem. I think we'd all like to make sure she's okay. I'll let you know as soon as I hear something," Susan said.

"You girls be careful too. Promise to call me if Miles comes around," Shade said.

"We're being careful, but I promise we'll call if anything happens. Talk to you soon."

"Okay, later ... oh, and hey, Susan ... thanks," Shade said and hung up the phone.

He looked at Ahasver, who nodded. "Thanks for trying, Shade."

"Sure," Shade said.

"And I think I've taken up enough of your time for now, so I'll be going."

Ahasver picked up his folder and pictures off the coffee table. Before putting the two pictures of Jude back inside the folder, he held them up for Shade.

"Remember his face, Shade. He wants something. We need to find out what it is."

Chapter 20

Miles was livid. It was after noon, and Patty hadn't returned.
Fortunately she was still in need of healing, so his lost income
was not foremost on his mind. Shade Elliott and the interfering
girls were. He could spare Patty's absence a few days; however,
he preferred to keep his girls in line. They left when he said.
Once an employee of Miles, anyone who knew him knew not to
get between him and his money.

Shade, he guessed, was getting his freebies while he
could. Miles was sure Patty was with him now. Shade was a
loser. He saw that yesterday when the Shade of old returned to
the house looking for drugs. They always came back. They
would whine and say, "I'm through," and head off to get clean
and sober, and then wouldn't have the balls to follow through.
That's why Miles never used. He never touched any kind of
drug.

He learned by watching his mother. Born an only child
to wealthy parents, his younger years had been privileged. His
father was a well-known attorney whom all the highbrow
criminals sought when caught in their illegal moneymaking
schemes. He himself had yet to call his father concerning any
legal problems. It was easy for him to work untethered. The cops
working on his business side of town knew of his family ties and
left him alone. They wanted no trouble with their higher-ups.
Slipping them a few dollars now and then didn't hurt, either.
From time to time, they even called to schedule an appointment
when one of the veteran cops retired and they wanted to have
more than just a few beers at the local cop bar to help him
celebrate. Although he saved his classier women for the higher
officials with more money to pay, he had yet to hear any
complaints about the girls he provided for the badge-carrying
members of the force who cared enough to ensure the old geezer
retiring could have a last memory of young female

companionship before going home to spend the rest of his life with the woman he promised to be faithful to forty years earlier.

His mother, through no effort of her own, had too much money and too much time to do nothing with it. He wasn't sure when the drugs began. All he knew was whenever he stopped in to visit, she was always high on something. He often wasn't even sure if she knew he was there. His father didn't seem to mind. As a matter of fact, his father would be the first to find a bottle of pills and insist she take one whenever she would voice a desire to stop. The pills were his assurance of having a wife waiting for him when he returned from his usual late nights of work.

He wondered where they got the stuff. It was kind of funny for him to think it was most likely from one of his dealers. *What would dear old Dad think if he knew his supplier was his own son?* he thought. It didn't matter to him. It stopped mattering when his dad became a client of his later business.

When beginning his business venture of satisfying the lusts and perversions of the city's finest, Miles used a voice-distortion device to keep his voice unrecognizable to the callers for whom he scheduled appointments. Now he could well afford to hire someone to schedule his girls. His father never knew when he scheduled the prostitutes for his pleasure, even the last time when he turned down a higher offer so his father could have the virgin being offered. His father hadn't called back since that night, Patty's first night on the job. He would, though.

Patty wanted to sleep with Miles the night she was found. He didn't find her appealing—just considered her an investment. Occasionally, though, he was willing to oblige certain requests in an attempt to appease his more finicky women to ensure their willingness to continue providing their highly sought-after services. He actually considered Patty's request, but it kept crossing his mind that his father had already had sex with her. The resulting mental picture was too disturbing and wouldn't let him get any pleasure even in thought. He didn't think he could even get up for the grotesque act.

He avoided the situation by pretending to enjoy cuddling with Patty in his king-sized bed and telling her he couldn't take the chance of hurting her more, preferring to wait until she was healed. Patty thought he was genuinely glad for her safe return and, at last, cared for her … until morning anyway, when he kicked her out of bed for being on his side.

By his calculations, she needed a week to heal. Then he would schedule her with his cheaper clients until the bruises disappeared, and unless scarring occurred, she would be back earning top dollar within the month. For now, she could do some paperwork during her week of healing. After all, she was in college. Why let her education go to waste?

Calling Patty's new cell phone enraged Miles even more. The phone went straight to voicemail every time. He was in no mood to leave a message for the unexcused absent female. Grabbing his car keys from the glass-top table occupying the luxury apartment's dining room, Miles headed to the door, intending to pick up a couple of buddies and go over to the campus to find the crazy bitch. His buddies would come in handy if he ran into Shade Elliott, whom he expected to pay for the behavior of his unruly girl accomplices for forcing Patty to go with them. Miles's face reddened with anger as he relived being held hostage by the nervy man who had overpowered him. Someone was going to pay for the disrespectful treatment. No one touched the Mile Marker without consequences!

It was a short drive to pick up his buddies—buddies who coveted his position and would turn on him in a heartbeat if the opportunity presented itself. Even so, they were useful to him, and since their brains were wired only for low-watt usage, he wasn't too worried.

Even though he called ahead to tell his comrades what time to expect him, Miles still had to wait for them. Patience wasn't one of his virtues. Actually Miles wasn't sure he had any virtues, but no matter, money normally covered the cost of any necessary kindness.

Preferring not to alienate the men until after his errands were finished, Miles decided to let the slow-moving twosome's lateness slide and was for once jovial when they hopped into the car. A slight change of plans was required, deciding a trip to the south-side house was necessary first to pick up some supplies in case any tongues needed loosened to locate Patty's whereabouts. It was amazing how willing people were to talk when bribed with hallucinogenic drugs. Of course, he made it a point to keep very low-key and talk with only known drug users, which turned out to be at least half of the campus.

When they arrived on campus, their first stop was Patty's dormitory. Several young women were sitting outside studying, gossiping, or sunning themselves. Women who studied bored Miles. Gossiping women were a possibility but often unreliable. Women who were scantily clad, he felt, were the likeliest to be forthcoming with information.

"Hi, I'm a friend of Patty Chandler's, and I heard she's back after missing for a few days. Could you tell me if she's here?" Miles asked, smiling pleasantly at the sunbathers.

"Oh, yes, she's back. Or at least she was back. Whatever … I mean … Yes, she's okay, but she left last night with her parents," one girl answered.

"Yes, she went home already. She's okay, but she did look a little banged up," another added while adjusting the top of her suit.

"I heard she was in a car accident or some kind of accident," a third girl said, apparently not wanting to be left out.

"Is she coming back to school?" Miles asked, still sporting his feigned smile.

"I don't know. I don't think she said."

The girls looked at one another, then began shaking their heads.

"You should ask Susan or Breeze," the first girl said. "They're the ones who found her. Well, I think Breeze's brother was there, too."

Brother? Shade? Miles wondered. *Has to be.*

"Yeah, I bet Susan and Breeze would know more," a girl said.

Then all the girls turned to look at one another and changed their shaking heads to nods.

"Are they here?" Miles asked, perking up with the information.

"No," two girls replied together.

"But they should be back soon. I passed them awhile ago heading to class. The class should be almost over," one said as she noted the time on her watch.

"Yes, I saw them too. Breeze has crutches. She fell in a pothole. You can't miss her," said one of the gossiping girls listening in on the conversation.

"Yeah, so they won't be running today," a sunbather finished.

"Thanks," Miles said, appreciating their openness more than he could tell them.

"Do you want to leave a message for Susan or Breeze?" a girl asked.

"No, it's not necessary. I just wanted to make sure Patty was okay," Miles answered.

"Breeze and Susan should be walking back from toward the library," the gossiping girl told Miles. "If you happen to see two girls and one of them is on crutches, that's gotta be them!"

"I'll remember that. Thanks again."

Miles left, just managing to conceal his rising anger. Patty didn't have his okay to visit her parents. *She'd better not be getting any ideas about staying there,* he thought.

A sudden realization occurred to him that he didn't know anything about Patty. He didn't have a clue where she was from, whether she had been the homecoming queen or the high-school wallflower.

The ungrateful bitch, he thought. *She'd better be coming back or I'm going to have to replace the ho.*

"Hmm, maybe ..." he muttered. "Susan and Breeze ..."

Right away, their names popped into his thoughts.

Who knows? Maybe two nosy, smart little preppie hos can take her place.

It would be easy enough to make some big bucks quick from two top-notch, most likely virginal, and, without question, fit athletic college girls. So what if he had to drug them. Most of his girls were on drugs anyway. It just made them more pliable and uninhibited—fewer complaints when things got a little rough. Anybody came looking for them ... well he would kill them and dump their bodies in an out-of-the-way location. If he were smart, which he had no doubt he was, no one would be the wiser. Of course, Shade might come looking for him, but his habitual drug use would eliminate any real threat, and without proof, what could he do?

Returning to the car, he walked to the passenger side and ordered his complaisant passenger—Jake—to drive. Miles preferred to sit where he would be least noticed and able to watch those passing by. Pointing the newly appointed driver in the library's direction, they pulled out, and Miles soon told Jake to pull to the curb and stop before reaching a church sitting catty-corner to the library a few feet farther down the block.

Sidewalks extending from various educational buildings stretched to connect with the sidewalks located on both sides of the street. Using the rearview and side mirror, Miles was able to watch the students and faculty exiting the buildings from behind, while still able to watch both sides of the street in front of him. As he watched, he filled his clueless buddies in on the latest news, courtesy of the loose-tongued girls outside the dormitory. It wasn't long before the two young women came into view, leaving from one of the academic buildings on the driver's side. They started walking on the campus sidewalk toward the street that connected with the street sidewalk. Although on the opposite side of the street, the girls would pass not far from where they sat watching from the car.

Miles observed the numerous students walking to and from classes and knew the time wasn't right to confront or, what he now admitted to his fellow conspirators, snatch the girls. Nonetheless, he was on peak alert when the girls stopped to talk to one another. After a few words, the girl on crutches unzipped the side of the backpack the other girl carried, and got out a small object that she shoved into her jeans pocket. Finished with their brief exchange, the girl who he now knew must be Susan, continued alone on the sidewalk with the backpack, while the other one on crutches—Breeze, he remembered—crossed the street toward the church.

All at once realizing she would be walking mere inches from the parked car, hormones from his adrenal gland released into Miles blood vessels, stimulating his heart rate and breathing. He lifted his hand to cover his face while he waited with heightened anticipation, mentally preparing himself to do his own dirty work and leap from the car to pull the tiny blondish-haired girl inside.

Breeze hopped along on her crutches, staying on the sidewalk coming toward the waiting men. In spite of taking precautions to keep his face hidden, Miles still managed to keep his eyes glued on each and every slow step forward. When she reached the sidewalk leading to the church, she stopped, adjusted her crutches, then turned and hobbled toward the church's entrance rather than past where Miles sat in the car.

Exhaling a burst of air, Miles thought, *It's just as well.* There were still too many spectators to witness the spur-of-the-moment abduction. He preferred to have his fiendish deeds hidden by the cover of darkness. Waiting for her to come back out gave them more time to combine their expert knowledge and fine-tune their impromptu plan.

Miles, Jake, and good ol' Benny used their time wisely preparing for the injured girl's return by flipping forward one of the two seats in the back, exposing an opening leading to the trunk of the vehicle. It was also decided a change of tactics would be necessary to assure any possible witnesses that the girl was an acquaintance, thereby averting any alarm if someone observed Breeze's unwilling disappearance inside the car. Their devised plan would give the appearance of a lover's spat.

Thankfully for them, Breeze had never seen either of the two men with Miles. Observing her difficulty opening the heavy church doors when she entered, they concluded that one man— Benny—would go sit on the bench near the front of the church. When she came out, he would assist Breeze with the doors when she left the sanctuary and then continue walking and exchanging small talk with her. As they neared the car, Jake would "unwittingly" open the passenger car door, "accidentally" blocking her path. Pretending to be unaware of the approaching twosome, Jake would get out of the car and push the passenger seat forward. For all appearances, it would look like the arriving twosome was expected. Benny would then take Breeze by the arm to help her past the open door. As soon as they were clear of the door, she would be tossed inside the backseat with Benny following PDQ behind her.

Realizing he couldn't use the hallucinogenic drugs to sedate her, Miles searched his car and found a small ziplock baggie in his center console with an assortment of drugs. Sifting through the various pills and tablets, he found a couple of roofies, the drug referred to as the "date rape" drug—a tranquilizer similar to Valium but more than ten times stronger. Once taken, victims had less than ten minutes before the drug knocked them out.

Miles's roofies were the older ones that looked like

aspirin. He preferred them to the newer light greenish-tan oval ones that contain a dye, turning the unsuspecting person's drink blue and alerting them to their spiked beverage.

"Perfect," Miles said, holding a tablet up to look at it before placing both roofies in the empty cup holder next to the bottle containing the hallucinogenic drugs.

A necktie Miles had removed on a previous occasion lay in the form of a noose on the backseat. It would be perfect for gagging the girl, but if necessary, the noose would work fine too. Miles looked through the opening in the backseat into the car's trunk and was rewarded with some rope. He couldn't remember why it was there, but he was sure it was for a good reason. Now he had another reason.

The beauty of the changing leaves to their various autumn colors was lost on the engrossed criminals, but they were nonetheless appreciative of the fall season with its early, fast-approaching dusk and hoped the girl took her time praying to her God.

Chapter 21

Ahasver rose, signifying the end of his visit, and headed to the front door. At the same time, a woman—Shade's mother, he assumed—entered the house via the garage entrance and walked into the foyer. After a brief introduction, Casper insisted that Ahasver stay for a quick bite to eat.

"Dinner," she told them, "is courtesy of our favorite restaurant here in town, where I picked up a pan of their popular homemade vegetarian lasagna on my way home."

Ahasver couldn't remember the last time he had shared a meal with a traditional family. His meals were either eaten alone or with clergy members. Humbled and pleased to be invited, he accepted right away. Not only was he appreciative of the companionship, but he felt twice honored once they were seated and Shade asked him to bless the unanticipated meal. As he bowed his head to begin his prayer, Ahasver noticed Casper glance at Shade with an expression of peace.

"Father, thank You for this meal," Ahasver said. "We thank You for the hands that prepared it and for Your unseen guidance of the hands used for its timely arrival at the table before us. We ask Your blessings on the food, that it will nourish our bodies and minds for Your glory. Lord, I give special thanks to my new acquaintances. Bless them and keep them safe. Watch over their absent family member, Breeze. Protect and guide her. These things I ask in the name of Jesus Christ, Lord and Savior of all. In all things, we give You the praise. Amen."

"Amen," Casper and Shade repeated in unison.

/////

"Vegetarian lasagna," Shade said. "Do I like vegetarian lasagna?"

"It's healthy. And don't complain, we have a guest," his mom answered. "Ahasver, hand me your plate and I'll serve. I hope you're not as picky as my son. Do you like vegetarian

166

lasagna?"

"I'm afraid I don't know, either, but I have no doubt God chose the meal tonight, and if He decided on vegetarian lasagna, then it must be good," Ahasver replied and then cast a curious look at the vegetarian dish.

"Well, let's hope it's good because I don't want to have to disagree with God," Shade said.

"Shade!" his mother said then let out a small gasp.

Ahasver laughed aloud. "It's okay to disagree with God, Shade. The problem comes afterward when you figure out He was right and you wish you would have listened."

All three waited until each one had been served before taking the first bite.

"Mmm, that's really good," Shade said.

His approving opinion on the tasty dish was soon echoed by both of his dinner companions. After that, conversation at the unlikely threesome's table flowed endlessly. Shade told Ahasver about his mother's genealogy pursuits, compelling Ahasver to quiz Casper with endless questions about her quest. Shade's mom seemed downright enchanted with the man who not only showed genuine interest in her, as of yet, unfruitful research but also seemed to be a good influence on her son.

Shade was all ears listening to the chatter. Warm memories surfaced of his father at the dinner table when conversations like these were common. He couldn't help berating himself for not being around the last two years of his dad's life, and remorse for his selfish actions crept into his thoughts.

Hearing his mother's laugh snapped him back to the present. All ears again, he often joined in to give his take on the current topic or add some fun tidbit to the conversation. The change of pace was not just appreciated by their foreign guest, but also a welcome change to both family members.

Soon all three shared in the chore of cleaning the

kitchen. Once satisfied with the job, Ahasver readied himself to leave. The hour was still early, but with the change of seasons, the daylight hours were noticeably shorter and he said he wanted to get back to the church before dark. Shade's mom nodded her head in agreement, acknowledging she didn't care to drive after dark either.

The phone interrupted Ahasver's farewell, and Shade excused himself to answer the untimely call.

/////

While waiting for Shade's return from his phone call, Casper thanked Ahasver for sharing his information on the cemetery and conveyed her hope the research would edge her son toward an interest in the past.

A little embarrassed by her gratitude, Ahasver told her, "The past is too important to be lost. The more young people we can interest in its preservation, the better. Shade's a bright young man. He's full of surprises and asks good questions. I appreciate his interest. The cemetery is special to me. I hope I can share more information with him."

"Yes, I hope so too," Casper said and nodded.

Ahasver made it a point to wait until Shade returned, in case the call revealed news of Patty. Casper used the last of her time alone with Ahasver to extract a promise from him to return for a home-cooked dinner before heading back across the ocean to his homeland.

His time to leave the country was fast approaching. Knowing the importance of putting things in their proper perspective, he assured her that he would tell one of them before his departure. Shade was part of his church warrior family, and frankly Ahasver was glad to be welcome in his mother's home. From this day forward, Shade and his family would be among those foremost on his mind.

Chapter 22

Miles didn't smoke, but if he were a smoker, he thought this would be a good time for a cigarette. It had been almost forty minutes since the girl had gone inside the church. In spite of his impatience, he was appreciative of the gradual darkening shadows growing around him. Observing the overhead streetlights, he backed his car a few feet under the nearest one not working. By the time Breeze and his man reached his car, unless someone knew of their presence, they would be hardly visible.

He now had to strain to see the clown Benny he'd sent to sit on the bench near the entrance of the church. He had already called the idiot to see what the hell he was doing. In the beginning while waiting for the troublesome girl, Benny had sat proper on the bench. Ten minutes later, Miles looked to see him sprawled out on the bench like a hobo finding refuge for the night. Next he'd scoffed when he witnessed the insane fool walk over and start violently kicking the flowers planted not far from where he was supposed to sit. Set on decapitating the plants, the flower killer sent a variety of colored flower heads flying through the air, landing pointlessly a few feet away. Miles, attempting to keep a low profile, thought they would be fortunate to escape without a ticket for vagrancy or destruction of property.

The headlights from a car blinded Miles for a second when he glanced in the rearview mirror at the car's steadfast approach. The car slowed when passing their parked vehicle, and Miles thought at first they had been spotted. The reason for the car's slower speed soon became apparent when it slowed even more to turn into the church's driveway and then disappeared somewhere behind the church. He was on instant alert and glanced to check on his impatient buddy, hoping he was seated on the bench and not engaged in another tangent.

Moments later, he heard a remote clomping of shoes echoing on pavement just before the car's occupant came into view, coming around the corner of the church. Almost invisible in dark clothing, the lone figure blended with the darkening shadows. Walking toward the entrance of the church, the figure stopped to tip his hat at the thin, dark shadow of Benny sitting motionless on the bench outside the door. Miles was surprised to see the shadowy Benny jerk to life and jump to open the door for the man. He was even more surprised when the man backed away from the door to allow another smaller figure to exit the church. Silhouetted by the light shining out the opened door, the man tipped his hat again before disappearing behind the tall wooden doors.

Two pairs of eyes stared from their position in the car. From what they could tell, it appeared the plan was working. The small figure on crutches, at first stopping when approached by Benny, began walking beside the tall, lanky figure sent to propel the girl in their direction.

When he heard a faint girlish chuckle, Miles wondered, *What could that lamebrain have to say to make her laugh?*

Without realizing it, Miles began grinding his teeth each time the muffled whisper of a word reached his ears. Watching the slow progressing twosome stop and belt out a particularly loud laugh caused Miles to look at his car's passenger.

"What could a smart little church mouse and a stupid uneducated thief possibly have in common?" he said.

He wished instead of talking, they'd concentrate a little more on walking. If they ever reached the street, all they had to do was turn down the sidewalk, walk a short distance, and, boom, he had her.

"He's entertaining her so she don't suspect nuthin'. I seen him in action before. He's pretty good with the ladies," Jake said.

"*What* lady? She's a *church* mouse!"

Miles, partly hidden in the shadows, rolled his eyes unseen at the dimwitted Jake beside him and laid his forehead on the top of the steering wheel.

"Church mice are ladies," Jake told him. "I'd like to see you get that smart little church mouse to follow you. Look … see! Here they come."

Lifting his head from the steering wheel, Miles looked up. The church mouse and the thief turned the corner and headed down the sidewalk in the direction of their car.

"I told ya he was good," Jake said.

Miles looked in all directions, and other than a scruffy cat looking ready to leap at a bush behind them, he couldn't see any movement. Again his heart rate sped up and his breathing quickened.

"Get ready," he told Jake.

The monotonous thud of the crutches on the concrete seemed to go on forever, tempting Miles to start the car to pull closer to the twosome and get the job over with.

"Can't he get her to walk a little faster?" Miles said.

Soon, though, the voices were in range enough for Miles to hear bits of conversation.

"… do to your foot?" Benny said to Breeze.

"Oh … sprained … ankle," was the girl's reply.

"You … graceful gal, huh?"

"… wasn't my fault."

"… your foot. How'd you do it without it being your fault? What happened?"

Miles listened closely as the two got close enough for him to make out everything they were saying.

"A guy pushed me and I fell backward into a pothole," Breeze said.

"What'd he push you for?" Benny asked.

"Oh, some people and I were trying to get a friend away from him, and he didn't want to let her go."

"Why didn't she just leave herself? Why'd she need you?"

"He kept her drugged," Breeze said.

"How do you know he kept her drugged?" Benny said. "Couldn't she have been taking drugs on her own?"

"She didn't take drugs before she met him—and besides, he was using her for … other things," Breeze said and sighed.

"Why would he want to keep her drugged? Why would anybody want to do that?" Benny half-whispered.

"Apparently it's the only way he can keep a girl. Sad, huh?" Breeze answered.

"I can keep my girls just fine, you bitch!" Miles yelled from the car window.

The approaching twosome was close to the car, and Miles had waited long enough. Looking to make sure there weren't any witnesses, Miles jumped from the car and strode to kick one crutch from under Breeze's arm, causing her to toddle. He angrily reached to grab her by the arm, but she had already grabbed her remaining crutch. Dodging to avoid Miles grasp, she swung the crutch in his direction, striking him on the shoulder. The unexpected blow brought a string of curses from Miles, each word spat venomously at her. Not waiting to give him a chance to regain his composure, Breeze raised the crutch again and, swinging with all her might, nicked him in the face. Stunned, Miles touched his finger to his face and felt blood.

"What the hell are you waiting for?" Miles screamed at Benny.

"This part wasn't in the plan, Miles," Benny said.

Breeze's head spun in Benny's direction, and realizing what he'd said, he froze with guilt.

"The plan has obviously changed, you moron!" Miles said.

"You're an ass, Miles," Benny said before looking at Breeze. "I'm sorry, but you gotta come with us."

Her terrified eyes darted back and forth between the two men, but she held her ground. She swung her crutch back and forth at them. That's when Jake finally sprang into action. He jumped from the car, threw the passenger seat forward, and ran to pick up the fallen crutch, brandishing it to block the crutch the girl was using for a weapon against Miles and Benny.

At the same time, Benny lunged forward and stretched a skinny arm at Breeze but was at once swatted by the crutch. He grabbed his arm in pain then jumped back to give Jake room. Breeze eyed him and swung her weapon but was stopped with a loud crack when the crutches smacked against one another.

She backed away and attempted a scream but due to her fright could only muster a small squeak: "Help!"

Miles chuckled. "See? I told you she was a church mouse," he said, amused by the frightened squeak. "It's no use. Don't strain your little mouse voice. By the way, have you figured out yet you're going to pay for your little stunt, taking Patty? You're going to find out what she did for me. Although, babe, sorry to say that you're not going to see any of the money."

Miles crept forward, keeping her attention. Jake waited until she raised her crutch and—Wham! He knocked it out of her hand.

"Grab her," Miles told Benny.

Holding Breeze under her arms and wrestling her kicking feet, Miles and Benny carried her to the car. Jake used his crutch to knock one foot down when she braced it against the car door's frame in a desperate attempt to escape from being forced inside. Her eyes widened with understanding when she saw the opening in the backseat that led to the truck.

"Put her down!" a voice from the shadows ordered.

All movement ceased.

"Who's there?" Miles asked, spinning his head in the direction of the voice while his accomplices looked about wildly.

Out of the dark shadows walked … Shade.

"I *said* put her down!" Shade demanded in a louder tone.

Miles scoffed when he saw who it was. "I don't think so! You and your little interfering bitch sister owe me. Fair's fair. You got Patty. I get your sister. You can't have them both, bro."

Moving quickly and hoping to go unnoticed, Miles tried to reach inside the car to open the glove box where his gun was kept. Breeze, though, took advantage when he released his grip, managing to free her foot and kick him. Miles yelped and flinched in pain. His jerking reaction caused him to lose hold altogether. Biting Benny's restraining hand, Breeze kicked and struggled even harder until she broke free and dropped on the ground. She rolled across the yard, distancing herself from the men before jumping up and scrambling toward Shade.

In a flash, Miles reached toward the glove box for the gun. Rapid movement on the opposite side of the car caught his eye, and he froze when thirty or forty people bolted out onto the street, all coming at the vehicle. Porch lights on nearby houses came on. Paralyzed by the fast-approaching mob, Miles remained frozen until Shade moved right in front of him. Shade's fearless posture, combined with the large group circling round the vehicle, startled and confused Miles, and he started backing away from the car—with Benny and Jake right next to him.

Shade reached inside the car, opened the glove box, and pulled out the gun.

"Do something!" Miles yelled at his buddies.

He looked at each of them and saw them holding their hands high above their heads.

"What?" Benny said. "This was *your* idea! *You* deal with it!"

Jake threw the crutch on the ground, confirming his own surrender to the angry-looking mob.

That's when Miles noticed Susan standing beside

Breeze.

"We got it!" Susan said.

Miles's eyes grew wide as he watched Susan hand Breeze a small camera—and from the red light on the front of the camera, it looked like it was still filming.

"We have it all on tape," Breeze said to Miles.

She then limped to the car and, with the overhead lights illuminating the interior, filmed the backseat's opening to the trunk, making sure to include the rope and necktie in the seat. Moving the camera away while she leaned inside to look in the front of the car, she spied the pill bottle in the cup holder and asked Susan to hold the camera while she opened the bottle and then dumped it on the seat to get a picture of the tablets inside.

"If you come near any of us or Patty ever again," Breeze said, "this video will go to the police. The only reason we're not turning it over to them now is because we don't want to create any trouble for Patty. If anything happens to her or any of us, just remember you'll be the last to pay. Now get out of here and don't come back to our part of town."

For several seconds, Miles looked back and forth at the students forming a half circle in front of them. Then, one by one, they began backing away to allow an unblocked path to his partially hidden car. Passing the men and women, Miles defiantly eyed them until he recognized the sunbathers now dressed in jeans and T-shirts. He felt his face redden at the sight of the girls and lowered his eyes, keeping them to the ground until he reached his car.

"What the…?" Miles muttered.

Words had been scribbled on his newer model, high-end vehicle. At first, he thought someone had painted the words *DRUG DEALER* and *PIMP MOBILE* in large red lettering on the car. Closer inspection revealed small red clumps appearing erratically on the various letters in the words, giving the impression they were more likely written with lipstick. Miles's cheeks puffed in and out. Filled with rage, he managed to force himself to swallow the words threatening to come out of his tightly shut lips.

Unsure whether to believe Breeze's words advising them of their release, Miles glanced back for a split second after they reached the car and realized they indeed *weren't* being detained. They hustled to get inside. Miles snapped his fingers and pointed Jake toward the driver's side when all three tried to enter as one from the passenger side.

The crowd began chanting: "Get out! ... Stay out! ... GET OUT! ... STAY OUT!" Louder and louder they shouted.

"Hell with this!" Miles said. "Get us out of here!"

/////

The car sped away, leaving the group to change their chant to cheers while giving one another high-fives. The celebrating group finished congratulating each other and gathered around Breeze, Shade, and Susan, with several members telling Breeze what a fine performance she gave.

"What performance? I was scared half to death!" Breeze said. "It was all thanks to Susan. I didn't have a clue until I came out of class and she filled me in on what was going on." She looked at Shade before continuing. "When you called to ask us to check on Patty, Susan called but couldn't get our supervisor, so she called one of these guys," she said and motioned toward the group.

"Me ... She called me," one of the sunbathers said, waving a hand high in the air.

"Yes," Susan confirmed, "I'm so glad you told me someone was looking for Patty. From your description, I knew it was Miles, but if you hadn't described the car he was driving, we would have never realized it was him parked on the street."

"Yes," Breeze said. "It was easy to spot him when we came out of class. We were so scared, but it was too dangerous to stay together in case they *were* planning to go for us, so we split up and I went to the church. That was, I went *after* we remembered Susan had put my cell phone back in my backpack she was carrying for me!"

"Yes ... close call! We almost forgot!" Susan exclaimed.

The girls rolled their eyes at each other.

"As soon as I saw they weren't paying any attention to me," Susan said, "I hid out of sight and watched until Breeze got inside the church."

"Thank *goodness* we were together. If one of us had been alone, I don't think we would be so fortunate," Breeze said, looking like she was shivering about the possibility.

Susan nodded. "When I saw them stay parked, I knew they were up to no good and called Breeze to tell her to stay put *and* to call you while I went back to get help," she said, turning to look at Shade. "After she called you at home, she called me back, and we stayed on the phone until I got back to the dormitory and then we finished making our plans. I made sure to take a few pictures of the goons with my cell phone before I left and that gave us the idea to video the entire attack."

"Yeah, but what *took* you so long to come out?" Breeze asked Shade.

"We had to make sure we had enough on video," Shade said. "It was dark, and parts of it were just too dim. I'm so sorry, sis. Are you okay?" he asked and then wrapped both arms around her in a bear hug.

"Yes ... Yes, I really am okay," Breeze answered. "But I sure did a lot of praying inside the church waiting on you to get here. I guess if you're going to get in a fix, that's the best place to be. You know, you might have been slow coming out but you made the drive into the city quicker than I thought you would," she told him and then hugged him back after he released her.

Several girls surrounding Breeze and Susan swept the two girls away in their midst.

"Let's go in case any of the neighbors called the police,"

someone said.

Breeze turned back and shouted out to her brother before she disappeared with the crowd: "Are you going home tonight?"

"No … No, I'm spending the night here at the church. They've already got a room for me. I'll see you tomorrow," he called out to her.

"How'd that happen?" she asked.

"I'll tell you later," Shade answered and waved good-bye.

All alone, he picked up his step and headed to the church, mulling over the evening's events. He had planned to confront Miles alone when Breeze first called to tell him about the thugs waiting outside the church for her. Ahasver hadn't left the house yet and was still talking to his mom when he went back to tell his mother that Breeze was on the phone asking him for help. Ahasver offered him a ride … and a place to sleep at the church since it would be well after dark by the time they would be finished. His mother jumped at the invitation.

Knowing Breeze was safe inside the church, Shade had dashed upstairs to his bedroom and threw a change of clothes in his travel bag so his mother wouldn't become suspicious. Before he and Ahasver got out the door, Breeze called back to tell him to meet Susan at their dormitory. Shade, though, didn't want to go along with their plan. But when Breeze had told him they would go ahead with or without him, he knew he couldn't change her mind. He was just glad Ahasver hadn't left already and that his mother didn't mind letting him go to help Breeze "with a project she's working on at school."

Besides, this way, he could do the driving and Ahasver wouldn't be worried if he didn't make it back to the city before dark. On their way, he informed Ahasver of the situation. Ahasver's immediate reaction was to spur him on, and he kept telling Shade to speed up. He chuckled to himself about it now in hindsight, but all the way into the city, he'd kept watching, sure that any minute he would see flashing red lights in his rearview mirror.

Soon Shade saw Ahasver standing outside a side door of the church, looking in the dispersing group's direction.

"Well done ... well done," Ahasver said and patted him on the back when he stopped beside him.

Shade held up Miles's gun for Ahasver to see. "What do I do with this?" he asked.

"Well now ... I don't suppose we should give it back. Let's see ..." Ahasver answered.

He pulled a handkerchief from his pocket and, taking the gun, proceeded to wipe Shade's fingerprints off the grip of the weapon. Using the handkerchief to hold the gun, he placed it and the handkerchief back inside his pocket.

"Follow me," Ahasver said.

He led Shade through the side door into a large inner office. Spotting an older lady working late at the church, Ahasver asked to speak with her privately. She led them to a vacant supply room where Ahasver pulled the handkerchief and gun out of his coat pocket.

"My friend and I are uncertain what we should do with this," Ahasver said.

Without batting an eye, she made it a point to let them know the local police would be more than happy to receive the weapon. She told them that her husband, a retired police officer and an experienced gun handler, would see to it the weapon was turned over to the local authorities anonymously after he found it inside a brown paper bag on their back step with no idea who had left it there.

Clearly relieved to be rid of the gun, Ahasver, still using his handkerchief, put the pistol into her outstretched hand. She removed the clip and checked to make sure the safety was on. Satisfied the weapon was safe, she used Ahasver's handkerchief to wipe off her own prints. Then she reached to a nearby shelf with her free hand to pull a flattened brown paper bag from a plastic bag containing more of the same. Shaking the bag open, she slipped the gun inside and, after giving Ahasver back his handkerchief, carried it with her like an office employee on her way to the lunchroom.

Shade and Ahasver, needless to say, were impressed with her expertise and thanked her twice for her discrete handling of the situation.

Ahasver blew out a long breath. "Busy night, eh?"

Shade just nodded.

"Maybe time for some rest," Ahasver said.

Shade sighed. "That sounds good."

Chapter 23

Normally Jude paid little attention to the battles men engaged in amongst themselves. He had no respect for the lesser humans who placed so little value on life that they waged war on one another.

Even so, Breeze's biblical knowledge might still be useful. Grudgingly he also admitted the girl had earned a certain amount of respect in his eyes. She, it appeared, used her intellectual and physical abilities not only to further her own self but to help her fellow man. Those qualities he rarely observed. Time, he supposed, would after a while break and callous her, curtailing her giving nature until she succumbed to the greed and jealousy he was accustomed to seeing in the men he viewed with disdain in today's world.

When he left the library, he hadn't thought of the girl again but used the time to dissect each of the saints portrayed in the book he had been reading before she'd come into the library's study room and freely given her short descriptions of the men.

He wandered the lawns of the college campus, passing many students who paid little or no attention to his presence among them, as if he were one of their own and belonged in their midst. After walking for some time, he made his way back to his car parked in the library's parking lot. Before getting into the waiting vehicle, he glanced through the trees and looked toward the church farther down on the opposite side of the street—and saw the petite girl hobbling along on her crutches, crossing the street in the church's direction.

Due to his inner turmoil, he had no interest in following the girl. He was still unable to rationalize Judas's betrayal of the man hanging on the cross inside the church and wanted no part of seeing the man today. Even the voiceless saints portrayed in the stained-glass windows rankled him. Once believing their observations of him were indifferent, he now surmised their expressions were more likely looks of accusations, possibly even accusations of cowardice.

Pulling from the library's parking lot, he made it a point to look in the opposite direction of the church, as if the sight of the church or Breeze repulsed him.

Then he noticed a figure standing near the back of one of the educational buildings, appearing to hide. She had her eyes glued on something across the street in front of Jude. Curiosity forced him to look in the direction her eyes were fixed, and he saw three men in a car watching the little Bible scholar turn down the sidewalk toward the church's entrance.

One of the men turned in his direction and looked straight at him when he passed, but no look of recognition passed between the two when their eyes met. However, during the brief glance, Jude was able to recognize one of the men in the car—the one called Miles—and knew why the hidden girl—whom he recognized from the previous day's interlude—stared so intensely in their direction.

"Damn!" Jude uttered.

Passing the parked threesome, he was irked to find he couldn't just drive away and let the situation unfold without his intervention. He had no doubt the girl would be unable to defend herself from the three men apparently planning to attack her. Driving farther down the street, he turned left on a side street to avert suspicion in case the man making eye contact with him was still watching his car.

Finding a place to park, he walked through the college neighborhood, but this time with a different motive on his mind.

Why, he thought, *does this girl matter?*

Somewhere inside, though, he was very aware she did matter, and he could not let the conspiring threesome have her. If anyone were going to have her, it would be him. If her blood would be spilled, he would be the one whose cup would catch the flow and drink it. Not a drop would be wasted on the three know-nothing petty criminals who, because of their ignorance, held no value for the powerful clean life force he sensed was housed inside her body's vessels.

Walking back to the church on a side street leading to the backside of the structure, his purposeful gait appeared casual—the length of his strides deceptively covering more ground than humanly perceived. He hoped the girl planned to stay inside the church for a while, but because of her slow progress, he knew he would still be there in time to prevent her demise if she didn't.

When he reached his destination, he saw one of the men exit the car and walk toward the entrance of the church. Breeze was not in sight, and he assumed with annoyance she was probably inside praying for something she imagined important to her or someone else's life. He found a spot hidden off to the side of the church in the sanctuary's lush bushes, where he could observe out of view while the threesome waited for their prey. Looking up at the stained-glass window nearest him, he sneered at the saint watching from above as if daring him to mock his uncharacteristic heroic endeavor.

He was relieved when the cell phone of the waiting thug rang, apparently a call from someone in the car to admonish the impatient lout from kicking flowers in a bed not far from where Jude himself crouched. Otherwise Jude might have been forced to snap the neck of the encroaching culprit and thus spoil *everyone's* secret plans.

With darkness falling about him, Jude removed his contacts to enable himself to see more clearly in the increasing darkness. He understood the impatience of the hooligan now sitting in the pretense of patience, managing to look like he belonged in the church choir. He wanted to walk away himself, preferring to go on with his evening without any further delay, but couldn't manage to escape the girl's trusting eyes swimming before his face even in the darkness.

Minutes later, headlights entered the church's driveway and disappeared on the opposite side of the structure. Not long after their disappearance, the sound of approaching footsteps grew louder when the apparent owner of the vehicle walked to the front of the church to enter the building. There was a familiarity about the man. Jude's eyebrows drew together as he tried to peer at the man's face. From his position, however, he was unable to get a clear view.

At last, the girl emerged, and the bench-sitter, who had moved into action seconds earlier, began earning his money. Jude listened to the soft-spoken lies the male voice told the girlish figure and shook his head in disbelief when he realized the girl had fallen for them. The two began walking down the sidewalk side by side, chatting as though they were old friends.

Watching and listening, he heard a slight sound of movement to the front and left of his hidden location and saw two figures near the street observing the two approaching from the sidewalk. One figure he recognized as the girl's brother he had fought beside, and the other, the same female hidden earlier behind the school building.

Staring for a minute at the two men in the car, Jude felt sure they were unaware of the two figures behind them hidden in the dark behind a large bush. Jude was at once surprised and glad the situation looked to be under control and might not require his assistance after all. Regardless, he stayed, remembering the fight the day before and knowing his help may yet be necessary. As of now, the odds were still in the favor of the adept criminals.

The two figures walking down the sidewalk seemed to take forever. He was annoyed when the girl's laughter reached his ears, and then it dawned on him she must be in on the apparent trap and was trying to appear unsuspecting of the upcoming ambush.

Once Miles jumped out of the car and kicked the crutch

from under Breeze's arm, the action at last began. The girl fought valiantly, but she was no match for the three large men. At any time, he knew the cat-and-mouse game would be over and the three lowlife scums exposed.

"What is taking so long?" Jude muttered.

He peered through the darkness to determine why the girl's brother hadn't come out and rescued his sister, and then he noticed the girl beside him holding something. The brother was leaning toward her, looking at whatever was in the girl's hands and paying no attention to the scene taking place in front of him. Jude prepared to move in and rescue the girl himself, but then noticed the dim glow given off by the object and realized the girl held a camera. He relaxed a bit and watched with interest as the scene played out. Breeze, once seized, began fighting as though her life depended on it. After the struggle continued longer than he expected, Jude began thinking it actually *might* depend on it.

At last a man's voice spoke: "Put her down!"

Jude's taut muscles relaxed, hearing the girl's brother at last come to life and take charge of the situation.

A side door of the church not far from Jude's camouflaged hideout opened, and the earlier unidentified man walked out into the yard. This time, Jude had a clear view of his face. He had seen this man many times but was stunned by his appearance and questioned why too often he showed up near his own whereabouts, especially now when he was far from home in another country. He was at once on guard and took care to conceal his presence.

A group from out of nowhere began forming in front of the three tricked assailants, and Jude at last, knowing for sure his assistance wasn't needed, was ready to leave. The girl was safe, and he had no desire to be spotted by the familiar stranger. Keeping his eyes on the bothersome man as he watched him move closer to the chaotic scene, he stepped on a twig, snapping it beneath his weight. The man's head jerked round at the breaking sound, but being more concerned with the scuffle still in progress, he quickly turned back to the foiled abduction.

Careful of his footing after his near discovery, Jude left the church grounds the same way he came and, once back on the street, wasted no time getting to his car. Driving to the street corner, he stopped and kept his car running, staying to see the outcome as Miles and his buddies jumped into their car and sped away. In less than a second, he followed them, passing unnoticed by the preoccupied students engaged in congratulating themselves. Knowing he was leaving the city soon—the country actually—Jude resolved tonight to finish the fight he'd prematurely left the day before and rid the girl of this would-be gangster who was determined to see that she met her end.

Chapter 24

Miles was humiliated riding in his car with the offensive, albeit true, words brightly scribbled on its exterior. When they stopped at a red light, he glanced at the driver and passenger in the car sitting next to them and saw an older couple staring back at him after rubber necking to read the lipstick-written words. Their derogatory stares facilitated his unspent anger into boiling over into an insane rage. When he grabbed the door handle to leap from the car and smash their accusing looks right off their faces, the couple made a hasty decision to turn right on red and sped away, leaving Miles with only the opportunity to hold up one of his hands and give them a universally well-known one-fingered gesture while yelling obscenities at their fleeing automobile.

Seething, he snapped at Jake, ordering him to find the nearest car wash. Soon enough, Benny and Jake were washing the large red words off Miles's car while he waited in the comfort of the luxury sedan. After several minutes, Miles heard them grumbling about how "Those preppy college hos must have used that long-lasting lipstick," because it wasn't coming off without a lot of rubbing. It was necessary to wash the car three times before they were satisfied all traces of the red smudges had been blotted from sight.

Once the job was finished, Miles got out of the vehicle and strolled around the car, looking at it as if he were a prospective buyer. His mood lifted when he found none of the red stains on the classy auto's exterior. Happy with the men's cleaning results, he kept his mouth shut and forgave a bright red, foolish-looking smear on Benny's face.

Miles took over the driving again and went to his apartment, intending to pick up another gun he kept inside a safe concealed behind one of his bedroom's cherished erotic paintings—paintings his father would have undoubtedly admired, but his mother would have undoubtedly abhorred.

Neither parent had ever been invited, nor had shown an interest, to see the inside of his pricey, ostentatious apartment.

Upon arrival at their destination, he ordered his buddies to stay in the car while he dashed upstairs to get his gun. His volcanic mood returned and threatened to erupt when he stood waiting for the slow-moving elevator to come down to the ground floor, and after waiting less than a minute, he rushed instead to the stairway and ran up the stairs. By the time he reached his sixth-floor penthouse apartment, he was sure he had developed asthma and wished he would have waited for the slow-moving machine—unsure if he would have reached his apartment quicker, but sure he would have reached it without feeling like his heart was ready to explode.

Huffing and puffing, he unlocked the door to his apartment and went straight to his bedroom, where he swung a large nude painting away from one of the walls, revealing the safe. Still shaky from his footrace up the stairs, he spun the dial of the combination protruding from the safe's door and, shaking, misdialed the lock on his first try. He forced himself to take a few deep breaths and slow his fidgety fingers, then started spinning the dial again. At that precise moment, his cell phone rang out its notifying tune, and one more time, he was ready to erupt.

When the cell phone's screen displayed Jake's name, his response was to mutter "Idiot" and ignore the call. Within seconds, he heard Benny began calling his name from below, causing him to lose his concentration and misdial the combination again. He slammed his hand against the hard metal surface of the safe's front and cursed his decision to bring the two men he generally thought of as imbeciles.

Frustrated by the lamebrain's unending shouts, he raced to the sliding glass doors and hurried out onto the balcony, wishing he had the gun to shoot his loudmouth buddy. Instead he leaned over and saw both men standing outside his car, one preparing another maddening holler, and the other eyeing his cell phone.

Shaking his head with befuddlement, Miles yelled, "What the hell is wrong with you?"

"There's a man!" Benny said. "Just answer your phone!"

At the same time, Jake looked up to see Miles and held his cell phone up as if to show him the look of the object he wanted Miles to answer.

Miles rolled his eyes in exasperation but pulled out his phone when it began playing its alerting call tune again.

"What *is* your problem?" Miles asked. "By now, I'm sure everyone in the neighborhood knows my name and where I live."

"A car passed us when we were parked outside the church," Jake said. "And I saw the man's face. Now he's here! I saw him and … his … his eyes … I … I … They were glowing."

"What? Glowing?" Miles said. "What the hell are you talking about? Stay out of those drugs. I'll be down in a minute. Just wait!"

Miles ran back to the safe and this time managed to open it. He grabbed his gun and as an afterthought grabbed two more for his unarmed comrades outside.

Running back to the balcony, he told them, "I'm on my way down."

"Watch for the man. We'll come up!" Benny yelled in a cupped hoarse whisper.

"No, don't come up here! I'll be down in a minute," he said, then added, "What man?"

"The man with those weird eyes," Jake hollered back.

"There is no man! It's just me, you idiot!" Miles answered.

"No, he's … *Him!*" Benny yelled and pointed while Jake stared and clasped his head between his hands.

Miles glanced to the side where Benny pointed and

asked, "Who?"

"Me," a deep voice said to the rear of Miles.

Before Miles had time to look, he was seized from behind and picked up off the balcony floor. His shoes created a metallic sound when he kicked, striking the metal railing as he rose higher and higher until the railing was no longer within reach of his kicking feet. His terrified eyes looked down at the street, and he saw his goofy buddies with mouths agape, staring strangely at him.

The man held him straight out with both hands. One hand clutched Miles at the back of his neck, supporting his upper torso, and his other hand supported Miles's lower frame by the waistband of his trousers. If not for the man's support, Miles would have appeared to be levitating horizontally in midair.

The whites of Miles eyes dwarfed his pupils as his frantic eyes darted about, not knowing where to look until they at last spotted his attacker. Mindless from fright, Miles still recognized the man who had overpowered him the day before.

"You!" Miles said. "What do you want? ... Money? I have money!"

When the man didn't answer, Miles continued. "Let me go! Who are you?" he shrieked.

"Jude, but you can call me Judas. And what I *want* ... *is* to let you go," and with that, the man called Jude let Miles go.

Miles felt his body roll evenly out of Jude's support. At the instant of release, his body turned in midair and faced the street below, with his hands impossibly reaching ... grabbing ... clawing at the air in an attempt to grab onto something ... anything. They found only air. His mouth and eyes opened even wider, but no scream escaped his lips. Just before impact, his eyes closed ... then he landed ... first on the awning that buckled from the plummeting pounds of added weight ... then slamming with a sickening thud on the sidewalk not far from where his silent buddies gawked. Before it buckled, the awning acted as a trampoline and his body flipped between his first and second landing, propelling him to land on his back. His eyes opened after he bounced off the awning, then closed when his head smacked against the sidewalk's concrete. A small red puddle formed from the blood oozing out beneath him.

/////

Benny and Jake watched in speechless horror and held their breaths as Miles made his way down. Their eyes locked on each of his aerial maneuvers … from his first midair roll … to his reaches … his grabs … to his awkward bounce and graceful flip that determined his landing. They winced in pain when his body hit and groaned afterward at the frightful sight … and then they looked away.

They looked up at the now empty balcony and then at each other. Neither entertained the thought of going to Miles, lying broken at an odd angle on the sidewalk. Other than the initial thud when Miles landed, no other sound came from him.

Without warning, something light brushed against one of their heads and fluttered about before flying over and on top of Miles's still body. Looking up, then back at Miles, then up again, they saw what appeared to be paper raining down from his sixth-floor balcony. No words were spoken as they stared blankly around at the green-tinted paper floating down. Neither was aware of who moved first, but when a fifty-dollar bill dropped into an outstretched hand, it became apparent to them what the paper was. Tentatively at first, but soon forgetting their reservations, they raced back and forth collecting the money— off the sidewalk, in the air, even off Miles's body, accidentally stepping on one of his hands when snatching a hundred-dollar bill floating above where he lay. Grabbing what they could, they stuffed the money in their shirt and pants pockets until they heard distant sirens warning of the impending arrival of cops. Not wanting to stop until all the money was collected, but knowing they couldn't afford to be in the area when the police arrived, they dropped on all fours for the larger piles then forced themselves to leave. They leapt in the car and sped away, never once thinking to check Miles's body, lying deathly still on the sidewalk.

Turning the closest corner, they stopped and watched in silence from their safer location, observing when several of Miles's neighbors ran out and pilfered what little money they could before the police and paramedics arrived.

At last, the silence was broken between the two men: "I don't think he'll be needing them," Benny said, watching the paramedics dash from their vehicle.

"No ... I guess not," Jake agreed. Jake paused and looked down. "I don't think he'll be needing this, either," he said with awed wonder, staring at the heap of green bills he held reverently up to the light.

It didn't occur to either of them to tell the others on Miles's payroll of their employer's demise until later. When it did occur, they tucked the money away and set out for the house on the south side. As they drove, it dawned on them they were riding in a dead man's car, and both men ducked down. Using their not-so-brainless heads, they decided to get rid of the flashy car before the police caught them and thought they had captured Miles's killers, now out joyriding in his luxury vehicle. Making a quick stop at their shared apartment, they picked up some cleaning supplies, then split up with Benny driving his auto and Jake following behind in Miles's car.

Driving to a secluded spot they had used on more than one occasion, they got out the cleaning supplies and once again cleaned Miles's vehicle, this time inside as well as out. They worked feverishly cleaning the car of all fingerprints and shoe marks, cigarette butts ... anything that could lead the police to them. Once they were sure any incriminating evidence had been removed or destroyed, they left the fancy automobile and continued to their previous destination. Neither of them drove a nice car, but they abandoned the sedan without hesitation because both knew of the sure-to-be-found-guilty verdict and prison cell ready for them if they were caught red-handed with the implicating vehicle.

"Who *was* that man?" they asked each other over and over when they finally had time to relive the evening's events. Neither could answer the question.

The unanswered question continued to weigh on their minds when they made a phone call to their associates working at the south side house to inform them of Miles's death. They were unsure whether the news was received with sadness, shock, surprise, or joy. They all agreed, nevertheless, it would be important to display strength throughout this vulnerable twist of events. Otherwise each of them knew an attempt to take over their territory would be forthcoming. After talking for a couple of minutes, Jake heard an angry shout and the cell phone went dead. He slapped the phone shut in the middle of a sentence.

"What was that about?" Benny asked.

"Phone's dead. Probably nothing. You know how he is. He's always making sure everyone stays under his thumb. Now Miles is gone, he's going to be even worse to deal with. I'd like to shove that bat of his right up his ass," Jake answered.

Sirens blared, and Benny glimpsed in the rearview mirror at flashing red lights gaining on them.

"It's not the cops," Benny said. "Lights are too high up off the ground."

Pulling to the side of the road, he stopped for two fire trucks to pass, then sped back into his lane. A short time later, both men realized they were following the speeding emergency vehicles.

"Is it a full moon? There's some weird stuff going on," Jake said.

"Don't know about any moon, but sure as Miles is laying stiff on that sidewalk, there's *definitely* some weirdness about tonight," Benny agreed.

Within minutes, their car stopped for several cops and flashing red lights. The police were stopping all cars attempting to turn on the street where the fire trucks had turned, redirecting traffic with their police cruisers flashing their red and blue lights where they were parked, blocking off the street. The house wasn't far, so instead of driving around to the opposite end of the street, they parked the car to walk past the blockade to the house. It was just a short walk from where they stopped, and they would be there in a matter of minutes. The noise, though, was deafening as another fire truck arrived at the chaotic scene. Benny and Jake were exhilarated by all the commotion. Shouting over the noise to each other, they relived their favorite fire stories from their youth. The bright glow overhead assured them of the fire's close proximity, and all of a sudden, they thanked their lucky stars they got there early enough to get a front-row seat.

Fully charged with insane juvenile-delinquent excitement, they hurried to see what they hoped was an out-of-control fire—but stopped dead in their tracks when they reached the blazing inferno. Both men stared in astonishment and disbelief. Flames shot out of the roof of the south-side house … *their* south-side house! It took an extra spin around to look at the other houses before it truly registered it *was* their house on fire!

Their arrival at the hazardous scene coincided with the last of the firemen jumping down from assigned riding places on their truck. A man's agonized scream coming from the direction of the house rose above the tumultuous noise. Startled by a vague recognition of the screamer's voice, Benny and Jake pushed and elbowed the surrounding gawkers out of the way to get to the front of the small but growing crowd. Horrified, the two tough guys cringed when they saw their earlier phone contact strung up in the middle of the opened front door. Teeter-tottering on tiptoes, he had a noose tight about his neck and was hanging from something unseen above the doorway. Both of his

194

arms were lashed to his beloved bat sticking out on each side from behind the shrieking man. The fibrous hairs of the rope had caught fire, and the burning fibers were falling on the man's head. Benny and Jake edged forward, and the smell of burning hair and flesh assaulted their nostrils before the fire's scorching heat forced them back among the crowd. Unable to help the man, they gawked alongside the neighborhood people watching the fire, waiting as the fire crew assisted their screaming gangster buddy.

A doused fireman ran with his axe toward the front door and shimmied behind the lynched man to chop the remaining portion of the burning rope from above the doorframe. Another fireman followed close behind and threw a thin blanket over the man's scorched body. Once the victim was moved to a safe distance, the paramedics were motioned in to assist with the care of the injured man while more of the firefighters dragged heavy hoses through the street, spraying water onto the building's burning roof. The victim was at once wheeled away on a stretcher and pushed inside the waiting emergency squad vehicle. After the back doors had slammed shut, the emergency transport sprang into action and raced, with sirens blaring, for the nearest hospital.

"Can you imagine being left to burn like that?" a woman asked with a shiver.

"If you ask me, they should let the whole place and everybody in it burn. Good riddance to bad rubbish," another neighbor said.

"Is anyone else in the house?" another voice said to no one in particular.

Benny and Jake silently regarded one another, reading each other's minds: *Two dealers were at the house at all times.*

"Where is he?" Benny whispered.

They urgently searched the crowd for the familiar face but couldn't find the missing dealer.

"And where are the dogs?" Jake whispered to Benny.

They tried to make sense of it all and wondered if the dealers had gotten into a fight.

"There's no way that scrawny guy could have lynched him up unless he was on some powerful drug," Benny said.

"Maybe somebody is making a move and already knows Miles is dead and they're trying to burn us out," Jake said.

"Or maybe *they* killed Miles! So ... who? Who's out to get us?" Benny asked.

"Nobody I know has the balls," Jake answered. The words were spoken matter-of-fact without the slightest hint of arrogance.

The only thing they could determine for sure was someone had it out for them. Maybe another drug dealer wanted their business and was making their move. Why tonight? First the weird man who killed Miles, then this. Did it have something to do with the girl? No, those college kids wouldn't have done anything like this. College kids didn't have the guts or the know-how to stage this kind of scene. There was more to it.

The two looked at the blazing house and the crowd surrounding them. They didn't recognize anyone and couldn't make any sense of the fiery scene. Walking on past the fire's hypnotized crowd and the self-absorbed firemen scrambling on the opposite side of the street, they snuck under the cordoned rope, wanting to see the other side of the smoldering residence. They stared at the house, anticipating something ordinary to happen that would explain the night's extraordinary events.

Jake twisted his head around to look at Benny to offer yet another possibility on the confounding situation, when a slight movement caught his eye. He nudged Benny and jerked a sideways nod, cocking his head instead of pointing with his hand at the warehouse. Pretending to talk, they kept their heads level, but their eyes strained to look up.

Atop the building stood a lone figure. The figure's

shadowy stance gave the impression of a well-built man with arms crossed in front of him and his eyes fixed, staring straight in their direction. In the firelight, his eyes appeared to glow a bright fiery red-orange.

The two streetwise criminals knew what to do. Shoving their way back through the crowd, they forgot all about their buddies … they even forgot about the fire … and they ran straight to their car. In their haste to make a speedy exit, they banged into the vehicles in front and behind them as they bumped back and forth out of the tight parking space, then back onto the street. At the first intersection, they spun around and sped back in the same direction they'd come from.

Both had considered leaving town more than once; however, lack of money had always deterred them. Thanks to Miles, the money they now shared between them would be enough to finance a trip to the other side of the country and then some if they chose.

They stopped at their apartment just long enough to grab what they needed for the trip. If some other drug dealer wanted Miles's drug and prostitution business that bad, then who were they to stop them? It was time to see more of what this country had to offer. They agreed they might even like to try a new line of work. In less than an hour, they were out of the city and on their way to a new future.

Chapter 25

Jude was packed and ready to go home. Returning to the hotel in the wee morning hours, he showered and used the rest of the morning and afternoon to complete last-minute details. Noting the time, he called the front desk to turn in his rental car and order a cab. He also requested that, with the exception of the shoulder bag he carried with him, the hotel make arrangements to have his luggage shipped to his overseas address and was assured they would take care of the process at once ... for an exorbitant fee, of course.

Before catching his evening flight, he had one thing left to do, which involved the girl. Glancing at his watch, he knew she would be finishing her classes and was set on finding her before she got to her college dormitory. He preferred not taking the chance of being recognized by any of her classmates in case one of them had seen him during his prior evening's activities.

He waited until the desk clerk rang to let him know his cab had arrived and then checked out at the front desk on his way out. Preferring his privacy, he climbed into the backseat of the waiting taxicab. The cab driver was quick to strike up a conversation, but other than give his destination, Jude declined to join in the small talk.

/////

The cab driver glanced in his mirror at his rider. Some people liked to talk ... others sat like clams. He made it a habit to talk 'til he figured them out ... like it was his responsibility or something. When his rider sat like a stuffed overdone starched potato, he gave up on the one-sided conversation and didn't pay any more attention to the guy. They weren't going far anyway, so any awkwardness would be short lived and it wouldn't be lived by him—he'd done his part.

Besides, he was used to the uppity ones who thought they were better than the working stiff and didn't want anything to do with his sort. He preferred the weirdos. Just last week, he had a guy all dressed up in a lady's dress, complete with high heels and make up. He didn't look bad for a guy, either. Why, the guy talked a blue streak. Even wanted to lift his dress and show him his slimming polka dot pantyhose, but he didn't want to look. He couldn't help it, though, when he started laughing, and then the dumb mixed-up man-broad got mad and got out ... but not before he paid him. That's what it was all about: the green stuff. He didn't care if the man had three eyes and walked on his hands as long as he paid the fare. And the uppity ones ... well ... come to think of it, they tipped better. He squinted his eyes and nodded his head as if answering an unseen passenger's question and sat noticeably straighter in his seat, deciding to look professional.

Turning on the radio, he found his favorite blues station.
Anybody don't like the blues shouldn't be on the planet, he thought and was carried away to his own planet for the rest of the drive.

//////

Jude spotted the gimpy girl hobbling along on the sidewalk where he suspected she'd be. He ordered the driver to stop and paid him before getting out of the cab, then requested that he return in an hour to take him to the airport. After looking at the wad of green Jude handed him, the cabbie was quick to assure him he'd be waiting at the very spot where they sat.

Breeze looked up when she saw him get out of the cab and head toward her. Her curiosity was evident by the way she cocked her head.

"We meet again," she said when he reached her.

"Not by chance," he answered.

"What do you mean?"

"I came looking for you. You weren't hard to find."

"If I'd known you were looking, I'd have worn camouflage."

"You can't camouflage destiny. She's never fooled," Jude said.

"So why has destiny intertwined our lives?" Breeze asked.

She stopped walking and looked up at Jude.

Jude bent down and picked her up with one arm and walked toward the church. "I haven't figured that out yet," he answered.

"Put me down! What do you think you're doing?" she demanded. She held her crutches firm in her grasp as each of them dangled several inches off the ground.

"You're going to the church and you're too slow. The cab is coming back to pick me up, and I need to finish my business before he gets here," he answered.

He ignored her demand to be released and instead picked up his pace and kept walking toward the church.

Breeze stopped squirming. "How'd you know I was going to the church?" she asked.

"Aren't you?" Jude answered.

"Yes, but you didn't know it."

"Call it destiny."

"Destiny doesn't carry you where you're going."

"Don't underestimate destiny," Jude responded.

He put her down in front of the church doors. Dropping his shoulder bag to his forearm, he unzipped a side pocket. Reaching inside it, he pulled out a puffy sealed envelope.

"This is yours. I'm leaving town and won't see you again," he told her and handed the envelope to Breeze.

Noticeably surprised, Breeze took the envelope and looked up at him. Her surprised expression added a hint of sadness.

"You're leaving?" she asked.

"Yes," Jude answered.

She stared in his eyes then looked down at the envelope

in her hands. "What is it?" she asked and began opening the envelope.

"No!" Jude stopped her before she managed to tear open the envelope. "Not now. Open it after I've gone."

Although her eyes were filled with questions, she nonetheless kept them to herself. Tucking the envelope inside her waistband, she covered it with her loose-fitting T-shirt and grabbed the handholds of her crutches.

"How can I thank you if I don't know what it is?" she asked.

"You want it," Jude said a bit gruffly.

"I do? We've met three times and you already know what I want? Are you psychic?" Breeze asked. She raised her eyebrows at him.

"No … although I have supernatural abilities," Jude replied matter-of-factly.

"I've never met a supernatural person before," Breeze said and chuckled.

"Maybe you have and you never knew it," Jude heard himself telling her, "and I'm not a person; I'm a being." Jude looked straight into Breeze's eyes with the words.

As soon as he finished his odd jest, Breeze's smile changed and her head tipped ever so slight to the right. Her eyes squinted just a little as she held Jude's gaze, looking up at him with an almost imperceptible strangeness as if weighing his words by searching his eyes. Keeping her eyes locked on his, it was only after a lengthy pause that her previous look returned.

"Okay, Mr. Supernatural Being, thank you for the gift," she said.

Jude knew from her expression that something had transpired inside of her and was curious why she wasn't afraid of him. He expected her to dart inside, seeking safety inside the church, and was prepared to open the door for her, but instead she said, "Come inside," without questioning his spur-of-the-moment confession.

Feeling a strange relief, he took a deep breath. "No, I have a cab coming to take me to the airport," he answered.

If he would have been even more honest, he would have admitted he didn't want to go inside and risk running into the man he had seen at the church the night before.

"Your cab isn't here yet. Come inside and let me pray for your journey," she insisted.

"What?" Jude said, stumped by her request.

"You'll see. Come inside. Listen … destiny's calling," Breeze answered and hobbled around to face the church doors.

Knowing it was too soon for the cab to return, Jude let his curiosity get the better of him. The girl's unscathed attitude and fearless reaction to his inhuman divulgence challenged him to enter the holy structure. He seldom backed away from a challenge, and opening the door, he assisted the girl across the threshold. Glimpsing the empty foyer, he followed her inside.

Their footsteps echoed upon the marble entrance until reaching the carpeted aisle of the sanctuary where they walked side by side to the altar. Jude stood mesmerized, looking up at the man hanging on the cross. His memory of standing on the platform and touching His nailed feet, returned vividly in his mind. The thought nearly overwhelmed him, and for a moment, he forgot the girl by his side. Poised to step forward and go up to touch the Christ man again, he felt a slight tug on his left hand. Glancing down to see what had touched him, he saw the girl kneeling by his side at the altar. At first, he couldn't understand why she pulled on his hand and then realized she wanted him to kneel beside her. He had never even remotely considered the idea before. To be on your knees for anybody or anything gave the appearance of weakness. Without waiting for his response, she looked back down and didn't see his eyebrows contort at her monumental request. Even so, he weighed the idea. After great difficulty, knowing he was leaving soon, he relented and permitted the girl this last request.

Bending stiffly, he dropped to one knee and looked at the girl, whose eyes were closed in prayer with her hands held together in front of her face. Once both of his knees touched the floor, he looked up at the man on the cross, and streaks of light began flashing past Jude. He felt as though he were moving at lightning-fast speed and grabbed hold of the altar.

All at once, the lights stopped and he stopped with them … but he wasn't inside the church anymore. He was in a distant land full of sand, heat, and desert. He heard the sound of sheep bleating and men arguing in a busy marketplace …

Soldiers dressed in Roman garb were marching past him, shoving and ridiculing a man less fortunate …

Looking down at himself, he saw the clothes he wore were dusty and wrinkled, and a small bag swung from a thin leather cord tied to a rope about his waist …

A voice near him spoke: "Judas, my friend, where have you been?" and the man slapped him on the back in a friendly gesture. He spun around, and peering into the eyes of the owner of the voice, he found the kindest, brightest, sparkling eyes of the man who he knew now hung on the cross before him. Startled by the shocking revelation, he shot up and, without a word, rushed out of the sanctuary and straight though the heavy wooden doors.

Less than a minute later, the doors opened, and Breeze limped out. "What happened? What's wrong?" she asked.

"Nothing … Nothing … I have to go. It's … time for my cab," he lied to her.

His eyes betrayed his rattled state, and he refused to look at the girl. Instead he watched the street with a grave urgency. Breeze toddled forward and threw her arms around the now bewildered Jude.

At her touch, a light tingling hummed through his body. The sensation was altogether familiar to Jude. Even though not as strong, it reminded him of touching the man's feet on the cross.

The man's energy ... is coming through the girl, he thought, and again felt strangely connected to the girl and, disconcerted, questioned why. In his confusion, he was unable to stop himself and hugged her back. In those few brief seconds, he did not feel the same self-confident brute of the man he had been before entering the church.

/////

The cab driver pulled to the curb in time to see the lengthy hug. Tiny sparks, like those appearing in front of your eyes after you've looked into the bright sun, danced around the pair. He blinked to see more clearly, sure his eyes were playing tricks on him, but the sparks continued to dance in the air around them. Unable to discern just what was happening, he honked his horn, unwilling to give his fare up without a fight.

/////

The sound of the horn made Jude jerk away and out of Breeze's hugging arms. He released his hold on her and took a step backward. For a moment, he stood in silence looking down at her, and she wondered what he was going to say. But then, still without a word, he turned and strode to the cab, stopping to look back only after he opened the back door of the waiting vehicle. A look, possibly of reluctance, but not clearly understood, crossed his face when he lifted a hand and waved good-bye and then disappeared inside the yellow car.

Breeze raised her hand in response to his farewell and watched until the cab was out of sight. She remained a minute more, then reentered the church to finish her prayers.

Returning to the altar, she recalled Jude's words that he had supernatural powers. At first, she was sure he was joking and chuckled. His subsequent words, however—"I'm not a person; I'm a being"—held the ring of truth, and her first memory of him flashed in her mind, recalling her initial fright.

It was here, she thought, and then stared at the altar,

seeing him the first time all over again.

Chilled by the truthful quality in his voice, a soft voice spoke inside her mind, saying, *"Don't be afraid,"* and an instant of unexplained calming warmth spread over her body as though someone had wrapped a warm protective cloak around her. She dismissed his words, chalking them up to his eccentricity. But now she wasn't so sure. She looked up at the man on the cross and felt the calm warmth return. Trusting God, she knelt to pray.

Her primary reason for coming to the church had been to give thanks for their safety during the attack by Miles and his men, but those prayers took a backseat while she prayed for the man who had left on his journey. Sensing that Jude was troubled, she asked for knowledge and guidance for him. Once her heart felt unburdened, she stood and, content, left the church.

She was surprised to hear her name yelled when she walked outside. A car coming up the church driveway stopped near her, and Shade jumped out.

"Hey, sis! I was coming to see you in a few minutes. Are you headed to your dormitory?" he asked.

"Yes, I wondered if you had gone home yet. I thought maybe I needed to have a little talk with you about leaving before you came to see me."

"No, I'm spending another night. I'm going home tomorrow. I've already called Mom to let her know. I want you to meet someone. We've been busy working on a little project," he said, looking pleased about something. Circling behind her, he picked her up and carried her to the waiting car.

"What is it with people picking me up today?" Breeze asked, but this time she gave up on fighting the useless battle before it started and let herself be carried without squirming.

"Sorry, sis, you're too slow, and I don't want to keep Ahasver waiting," Shade answered.

Shade put Breeze down beside the open car window. Glad for a proper introduction, she and Ahasver recognized each other from their brief meeting in the church even before she was back on solid ground and was busy chatting with the older man when she landed beside him. After a few pleasantries, Ahasver left to park in his usual spot in the church lot, and Shade walked Breeze back to her dormitory. The subject of Miles and the previous day's events didn't come up until they were near the building; both paused for a moment to express their eternal gratitude of escaping without injury.

/////

Before Shade and Breeze reached the building, Susan ran from the dormitory's yard to meet them.

"Have you heard about Miles?" she asked.

"No, what? Has he done something to Patty?" Breeze said.

"No! Someone threw him off his balcony! He's in the hospital in critical condition. They don't know if he'll live," Susan said.

"No way! What happened?" Shade asked.

"They think it had something to do with a drug war. Someone wanted him out or wanted to take over his territory. No one knows for sure. It's all over the news! Whoever it was burned down the house where they sell their drugs. I think it's the one we were at. One of the guys working there when it happened was severely burned and is in the hospital too!" Susan said. "They're questioning another guy they found this morning. The news said something about him being locked in a warehouse with some dogs. If those are the dogs we saw, I can't imagine how anybody could have even gotten near them … and then locked them in a warehouse?"

The three joined a group seated on the grass and listened to various details of the incident. Whether it had been an attempt on his life, a drug war, or, as one student had heard, Miles was trying to commit suicide by jumping from his balcony, they examined each theory, attempting to make sense of what had happened. Mixed opinions spread crazily through the student gathering. Most were glad Miles wasn't able to deal drugs but, because of the prior evening's events, were conscience stricken and remorseful upon hearing he was hospitalized with life-threatening injuries. Feelings of guilt, without reason, circulated through the crowd.

Shade even answered a few questions on his own whereabouts after the ruckus. Even though he had not seen Miles after the confrontation, he, too, felt more than a little twang of guilt and was slightly red faced when he told them he had been with a friend after the group dispersed. Indeed, he and Ahasver had sat talking until well past midnight.

The words "What a coincidence" were heard more than once from students reflecting on the odd turn of events. "Karma … it's got to be karma," was also widely agreed upon.

After a lengthy discussion that, without actual facts, amounted to nothing more than rumors and speculation, Shade stood up, ready to head back to the church.

A few of the students watched him with long curious stares, and he knew they were unconvinced of his innocence. He found himself praying Miles lived to identity his would-be assassin, if that was indeed the case. Otherwise the video, instead of assuring them of their safety, could be considered motive.

He pulled Breeze to the side and told her what he was thinking. Breeze listened to her brother, then motioned Susan from the crowd. Once Susan heard their concerns, she ran inside the dormitory to fetch the small video camera.

The threesome didn't particularly care to have the video fall into the wrong hands. Susan handed it to Shade. He slipped the small metallic object into his pocket and leaned down to kiss Susan on the cheek and then gave Breeze a small hug.

The girls watched as he left, passing by a small group still contemplating Miles's attacker. A light tension, created by whispers behind cupped hands, clung to the air—the unheard words like the warning rumbles of an approaching storm and the air slowly filling with its electrical current. A soft breeze tossed strands of hair across the two girls faces as they internalized their observation and realized that accusing eyes have a steady gaze when looking at someone's back.

    With Susan by her side, Breeze walked swifter than she had in two days, while still clutching the handles of her crutches. They hurried to catch Shade and walked with him a ways. Once the dormitory was out of view, they parted, Shade going on to the church and the girls returning to an empty lawn.

Chapter 26

The cab ride was intense. The driver knew something about the man had changed in the hour between dropping him off and returning to pick him up. Regardless, he wasn't in any way ready to strike up another conversation. Still listening to his favorite blues station, he decided to turn off the car's radio so he could listen closer to his silent passenger. He could swear the man wasn't breathing. Now that was weird. Was he holding his breath? He glanced in his rearview mirror to see if the man's chest was rising up and down. While observing his chest, he looked up into the man's face and saw his passenger's eyes staring back at him.

"Stop!" the man ordered.

Holy smokin' crap! He saw me eyeballin' him! he shrieked in his head and almost jumped out of his skin.

He slammed on the brakes and held tight to the steering wheel to keep from flying across it into the windshield. He never did *that* before. Seriously rattled, he scrambled to decide if he should apologize for the rough stop or for looking at the man's chest, but before he could get the first word of his false apology out, the man threw money over the back of the seat and told him, "Wait here. I'll be back," and was gone before he said anything.

Maybe the guy is a weirdo after all, he thought and began counting the money while he waited for him to return. He counted enough to make him willing to wait for, *oh … maybe two or three days*, he thought and smiled. *Yep, I like the weirdos … especially the uppity ones.*

/////

Jude went straight into the bank where he'd ordered the driver to stop. He had been aware when the driver watched him, but he didn't care. Something was on his mind. For almost two thousand years, he had been searching to find the perfect blood. The blood that would make him live forever … was that why he was connected to the girl? Did she have such blood? No … not her. Something had happened to him when he knelt before the altar beside the girl. It had something to do with the Christ man. The blood and the man were connected. He just knew it. Now that the answer was close, he was running away. He, who never ran from anything, was now running without knowing why. He had to know more. He would catch another flight later. First, however, he needed to take care of something before returning to the church.

His gait was sure, and his presence commanded attention when he walked into the bank. He was seated inside the manager's office almost at once. After just one, barely detectable, odd glance, the manager assured him the bank was fully capable and would be most happy to take care of his unusual request. Since they weren't busy and it was near closing time, Jude was assisted by a couple of the bank's officers who pitched in and, working together, acted quick to finalize the legalities so they could close and go home for the day. Within a half hour, Jude was again sitting in the backseat of the yellow cab. Once he pulled the door shut, the driver pulled out in traffic, headed in the direction of the airport.

"Take me back to the church," Jude ordered.

"Sure thing," the cabbie replied.

/////

The cab driver watched his rider for a split second in his mirror. The close-mouthed passenger sat staring out the window. Recognizing the signs, the cabbie knew the man had already zoned him out. Looking back at the street, he did as he was told and headed the cab back to the church.

He wants to go back to the girl and those fire sparky flying things, the cabbie thought, trying to figure out the stiff starched man. *Ah … what the hell!*

He couldn't keep from glancing in his rearview mirror a second time and caught himself looking at the man's chest again.

Yep, his chest was moving up and down just like it should. He returned his eyes to the road and wondered what kind of spell the girl had cast on him.

Just like a woman. Just can't let a man be. Those bloodsuckers just suck the life right out of a man.

He sighed, thinking of the predicament his rider would soon be in. Reaching the church, he pulled to the curb and frowned at the stopped meter.

/////

Jude dropped a wad of cash over the seat as the car stopped and got out of the taxi.

"You want me to wait?" the driver asked.

He looked up at the saints in the windows. Even in the darkness, with his contacts still in place, he knew they were beckoning him.

"No," he told the driver.

"Here's my card. Call me if you need me," the driver replied.

Jude walked toward the church without looking back at the cab driver. "Keep it; I won't be needing you."

When he entered the dimly lit sanctuary, Jude, for the first time, *saw* the beauty surrounding him. Dainty half globes, filled with faint light, were fixed on the walls at the end of each pew on both sides of the massive room. Stained-glass saints watched from high above the platform behind the altar. Angels flying in the stained windows above the saints held their arms outstretched as if to welcome someone into their embrace. In the center of it all, above the platform area, hung the cross, suspended in midair by thick cables fastened to wooden beams on the ceiling. A small brighter light shone down from above, spotlighting the man nailed to the cross.

Walking toward the front of the room, Jude stared up at the man on the cross. Something tugged at his mind. A thought—or was it a memory?—began surfacing ... only to be lost again, hidden just out of the reach of his consciousness. He struggled to make the thought, or memory, resurface but found it was useless.

"Judas," a man's voice spoke.

He looked around to find the owner of the voice and saw he was alone in the room. He recognized the voice and knew it belonged to the man in the vision he'd experienced earlier in the church.

His eyes turned back to look at the Christ man, and he asked, "What is it You want of me?"

The answer was inside of him. It had been all along. He had just needed the girl to help him understand how to find it. Walking to the altar, he stopped for a moment to look up at the man. The tears he was used to seeing were not flowing from his eyes, and he knew this was what the man had wanted. Stepping onto the platform, he walked around the pulpit and stood solidly before the living Christ, reaching up to touch his feet. An electrical current flowed into his hands, giving him an energized feeling of life. He pulled his hand away and felt wetness upon his face. Touching his fingers to his cheek, he felt a droplet of water and understood now it was he who cried.

Kneeling, like he had seen the girl do earlier, he continued to look up at the man above him. Both knees fell at the same time on the carpet, and at once a brilliant kaleidoscope of color streaked in vivid lines around him. His body felt a falling sensation, and he offered no resistance while he fell through the tunnel of lights. As suddenly as it started, it stopped, and he was somewhere else again …

"Judas," his father called from somewhere in the house.

He sat near a window working for his father as his bookkeeper. Excited voices filled the air outside, and he poked his head out the window to see what was going on before he answered yet another of his father's never-ending calls for him. In a field nearby, a man stood on a rock preaching to a crowd.

Climbing through the window to hear more of the man's sermon, his robe caught on the window's wooden frame …

Lights sped past him, and he knew he was back in the tunnel …

He was at a wedding, and people were bellowing for more wine. The man from Galilee gave the host some jugs He had helped fill with water, and the bride's mother began filling everyone's cups … except he was confused because the water looked red. The wedding guests were commenting it was better than the wine they drank earlier …

Lights filled the space around him, zooming at incredible speeds …

He turned toward the voice he heard and found the man in the midst of the crowd. A woman lay at the feet of the Galilean when He spoke his next words, "He that is without sin among you, let him cast the first stone at her." The people in the crowd looked at one another, waiting for the one who would cast their stone and begin the woman's agonizing death. His heart raced when he looked down at the woman weeping on the ground. He felt something hard in his hand and looked to see a rock similar to ones the others held. "No!" he shouted, throwing it down, and ran to stand beside Jesus …

And he was sucked back into the tunnel of lights …

Tagging along, he was with Jesus and some companions at the home of their friend Lazarus. Martha was cleaning up after the extravagant meal she had prepared and fed them. Her sister Mary began rubbing ointment from an alabaster jar on Jesus's feet. They needed money. They could have sold the expensive ointment. Judas was disgusted from the waste. Jesus needed to get off his cloud and realize money doesn't grow on trees—and *why* wasn't He doing something to get rid of the Romans? …

And he was transported with the lights blasting him away to yet another time …

The scene was still vivid in his memory. He had

witnessed an artist's rendition of it not long ago, but instead of the faces painted by the famous artist da Vinci he was surrounded by the faces in his vision at the warehouse. They were gathered around a table. All of Jesus's own chosen followers were there. Jesus passed bread among them and told them it was His body. Judas bit off a chunk, but it tasted like bread to him. He put on a happy expression and by all appearances seemed to be having a good time. Then Jesus passed a cup containing wine and called it His blood. The wine called blood was better than the bread and made him feel warm and good inside. He wanted more, but the others finished it before he could get the cup back in his hands. The rest seemed to cherish the wine, calling it Jesus's precious blood, and he sought to feel as they did. If he just had more money, he could buy some of the wine and say it was His blood at the upcoming Feast of Passover. Then Jesus said something odd: "I tell you the truth, one of you who eats with Me shall betray Me." They all looked at one another and began questioning Him about who would betray Him. "Is it I?" they spoke one by one. And Jesus said, "It is one of the twelve, the one who dips with Me in the dish. The Son of Man will indeed go as it is written of Him, but woe to the man by whom the Son of Man is betrayed! It would be better for that man if he had never been born."

The time tunnel swooped him back up ...

His ears caught the sound of his braying donkey waiting outside the temple while he talked quietly with the chief priests who said they would pay for information on Jesus's whereabouts. They were willing to pay thirty pieces of silver ... and he needed the money. He didn't want to go back to work for his father, and he was tired of being ordered around by the man who had the nerve to call Himself the Son of God but wouldn't rise up and get rid of those idol-worshiping Romans. Besides, the priests only sought to stop Him from spreading more tales about being God's Son and leading *their* flock away from God's true leaders. It would be worth thirty silver coins if he cooperated with these knowledgeable men. He could surely use the money since Jesus seemed to care little for collecting it from the crowds He preached to …

And back inside the tunnel of light he went …

He watched soldiers beat Jesus and then saw Him sentenced to be crucified. What had he done? He ran to the temple to beg for Jesus's life, throwing the money at the priests when they refused to listen …

The lights flashing around him synchronized with those in his head while they sped him away …

He kicked off his sandals to keep his balance on the back of his donkey. The noose hung where he'd tied it to the tree limb. He placed it around his neck. Hanging was too good for him. He couldn't stand the idea of living with what he had done to his friend Jesus … who had never harmed anyone. He should have been the one beaten by those abominable Romans. He jumped up and yelled to scare the donkey from underneath him. His neck was not immediately broken, but after struggling for several seconds, he heard a loud snap and knew what had happened. It was a few minutes before the darkness overtook him and he drifted away. His last vision was of the crows sitting on the branches not far from where he hung …

The tunnel lights changed to molten red. Gone were the brilliant shades of the kaleidoscope …

Jesus held a cup to his parched mouth, but it was slapped from His hand before the water touched his lips. Bending to retrieve the empty cup, Jesus touched His finger to a small droplet of water still inside the vessel and rubbed it across his scorched lips, giving him a small, appreciated kindness. Satan, though, was angered by the gesture.

"Watch and weep, mortal Son of Man!" Satan said. "All of Your precious traitorous companions are mine to do with what I will. Know they will be abominations and walk in darkness, wreaking havoc wherever they roam on earth. They will be a mockery of Your laws and Your human teaching. And know they will kill Your beloved mortal children."

Walking away, Satan's hideous laughter could be heard echoing throughout the prison cells of hell where his captive spirits cowered in the dark corners of their cells ...

Blackness—only blackness in the tunnel ...

Jude gasped for air when his consciousness returned to the present. He was hot and sweaty. His eyes closed as his head tilted back, and he wept openly with remorseful, clear memories of his betrayal of Jesus, repaying his debt by doing the things Satan said, killing His children on earth. He *was* an abomination. Remembering where he was, he looked up at Christ on the cross above him.

"I am sorry. I was vain, selfish, and greedy!" he cried out.

/////

Shade entered the sanctuary to view the heavenly room before going to find Ahasver. He had thought the sanctuary was empty ... until he heard a male voice cry out. Immediately understanding that the humble words were being confessed in prayer, he respectfully turned to leave to allow the burdened man his privacy. Nevertheless, before he was out of earshot, the man began sobbing uncontrollably, and Shade hesitated to leave him. He didn't know enough about God to solve any serious problems or answer any complicated questions about salvation, but maybe what he did know would be enough—and he could call Ahasver if he felt it would benefit the man. Not wanting to disturb the distressed man before he got closer to him, Shade stepped quietly to the platform. He was floored when he recognized the dauntless man who had fearlessly aided them in their first confrontation with Miles. More important, *he* was the man Ahasver spoke of as a beast!

The man's contrite words and heartrending behavior,

though, in no way resembled the fiendish man-beast Ahasver claimed had been created by Satan. Shade was convinced by the man's broken condition that Ahasver had to be mistaken because of this man's nearly identical looks to the man in the old dig photographs.

Stepping upon the platform, Shade went behind the pulpit and walked to the upset man pouring tears. Filled with compassion, he placed an outstretched hand on his shoulder. He felt a sticky dampness on the man's shirt.

"Are you okay? Can I help you?" Shade asked.

When the man didn't respond, Shade knelt on one knee beside him. On closer examination, he realized with horror that blood was oozing slowly from the pores of the kneeling man. He was astounded and knew he needed immediate help. Pulling out his cell phone fast, he called Ahasver and told him to come to the sanctuary.

Startled by a sudden snap, similar to the crackling noise of a burning campfire, Shade swung his head toward some candles lit on a table to the left of him. The candles cast small flickering shadows on the back wall. Darting back and forth together as they gently bounced up and down, the dark shadows touched and created the illusion of intertwining and flickering to join in a sort of dance. For a moment, Shade was mesmerized by the dark rhythmic dance and couldn't pull his eyes away, but his self-control kicked in and he focused again on the man urgently needing medical attention. The crackling noise popped louder, and Shade jerked his head toward the candles again, intending this time to go over and blow them out, sure the church wouldn't want them burning this late in the evening with no one around. Tipping his head back, his eyes widened when his gaze was forced upward to see the top of the shadow.

"What the heck?" he said.

Not at all understanding the dark shadow's sudden growth, his eyes darted back to the burning candles, then returned to the wall. While he stared, the shadow continued to grow until it reached the ceiling and then began growing out instead of up—its form filling like a balloon filling with air. Puzzled by what could be casting a shadow so large, he turned around to inspect the rest of the sanctuary. In the brief time it took him to scan the interior of the room, dark wings sprung out on both sides of the humongous wall shadow.

Glimpsing nothing out of the ordinary within the sanctuary, Shade turned back to the wall and gasped. His first instinct was to run, but he couldn't leave the man. Spots of color began appearing over the blackness of the forming body. Shade recognized scales glowing with various shades of reds, oranges, and yellows as though they had been baked in an oven and were still hot.

He tried to pull the man up from the floor, but because of the oozing blood, his wet arms slid through his hands. The gigantic shadow reached toward the kneeling figure, and Shade jumped in front of the man, firmly standing between him and the thing he now knew was much more than a mere shadow.

The molten creature flapped its extensive wings, creating a powerful wind gust that sent Shade flying through the air and slammed him against the pulpit behind him, shortening his backward flight. Forcing himself back up fast, Shade jumped with a painful grunt and ran back between the thing and the man.

The demon—if that's what it was—glared at him through glowing red pupils set amid dirty mustard-yellow whites. Bending his hot steaming head backward, he swung it back down while thrusting it forward and released a long hot blast of blazing fire at Shade.

Already facing the monstrous demon, Shade had no chance at escape. Without any warning, he did the only thing he could. He raised his arms up in front of his face and dropped on the floor in front of the man. The fire blasted at him with scorching heat, but the shooting flames *stopped* inches in front of him, flaming out in all directions above and beyond him as though he was behind a barrier and the fire couldn't get through.

Clearly angered by the impossible barrier, the demon aimed a blast of fire at the man on the cross. Large splinters of wood sticking from the ceiling's wooden beams burst into tiny flames that sparked and died at once, leaving thin, bright-glowing strings of sizzling light that lit up the ceiling. Lifting his horned head, the demon let out an angry, ear-shattering roar that shook the walls of the church.

Trying to think fast of what he should do, Shade shot up, facing the demon and then it just came to him: "In the name of Christ, begone!" he ordered with his arm outstretched, pointing toward the threatening presence.

"You would challenge Satan himself?" the thing said in a raspy, unearthly voice. "Get out of my way! This man is mine!"

"Not anymore!" Shade said in a deep reverberating voice he didn't recognize as his own.

A hateful growl bubbled up and out of Satan's mouth. Shade remained inflexible, refusing to move from his spot between the penitent man and the hellish demon. If this was his end, so be it.

/////

Ahasver rushed into the sanctuary and stopped in his tracks. His eyes shot upward at the beast filling the back of the sanctuary. Taking in the giant demon, he gasped at the devil's words and believed, without a doubt, he was, in fact, seeing the Prince of Darkness. Then Ahasver looked at Shade. The young man, keeping his arm outstretched toward the hellish monster, cast a giant shadow on the wall. It was the shadow of an enormous warrior holding a flaming sword high, prepared to fight off Satan's attack.

Just then, Satan slashed downward with his sharp claws at Shade. But Shade held fast and raised his free hand. He pushed his palm out with deliberate force toward the giant in a halting gesture. Large, crestless waves, consisting of what might have been nothing more than air, began rolling like a thick transparent gel toward the monstrous winged creature.

Satan slammed back against the wall with an earth-shattering thud after being struck by the thickened airwaves.

"Stay out of this, Michael!" Satan roared, angered by the unexpected blow.

Ahasver froze in place with the startling realization it was the archangel Michael's warrior presence and unyielding stance being manifested in the staunch body and unwavering shadow of Shade.

"Father in heaven, thank You for Your protection," Ahasver whispered.

"Give me the beast. He's mine!" Satan bellowed, fiery sparks shooting from his mouth when he spat the words.

"Begone!" Shade shouted. "Go back to your place of darkness in the pits of hell. In the name of God, I command you to leave God's holy house. You are not welcome here!"

He swung his outreached hand down toward the monster. The demon shrieked in pain as though Shade had physically struck his body. Indeed, the shadow cast on the wall resembled a blazing trail of flames when the burning sword thrust with a powerful swiftness downward, cutting deep into the beast's scaly body.

Howling, Satan lifted high in the air with his mouth open wide, exposing razor-sharp teeth. His volcanic molten body all at once writhed and twitched. Shiny red dots glowed brighter on its rough, scarred scales. Like fleas hopping off their mangy host, engorged red-eyed birdlike demons squirmed to rise and, unfolding bony webbed wings, lifted in flight, flapping madly though the air. Satan seemed to wither and then shrank to half his size when the last parasite demon flew off its master.

The small demons flew with their muscled legs dangling

in the air, circling and lunging at Shade. Keeping his wits about him, Shade spied the church's metal offering plates and grabbed one in each hand to fight the diving devils. He swatted them down one and two at a time, over and over again, stomping on their scaly bodies whenever he got the chance. The demon host swooped to attack and swerved in midair when Shade raised and pointed the palm of his hand.

Forgoing their dive-bomb attack, hell's demons flew to the back of sanctuary to hear Satan roar his commands to them. The beasts did as they were ordered and dove, one at a time, into each other using their strong legs to dig lightning-quick together as one. Satan blasted his hot fire on his shrieking demons, melting their hard scaly bodies. Softened by the fire, the creatures writhed and squirmed and forced their misshapen bodies into place. The blending demons morphed to create a grotesque, queer-eyed twin of their hellish master. Once the unnatural process was complete, the evil prince and his deformed twin creation screeched as one. From outside the church, birds began squawking and crashing into the stained-glass windows, creating a terrifying and deafening noise.

Ahasver ran from the back of the room toward the front. Satan and his demonic beast flew at him. One struck him in the back, embedding his clawed toes and lifting Ahasver off his feet. Carrying the struggling man, the flying monster circled back and flung his captured prey.

Ahasver smashed hard against the end of a long wooden pew. Upon impact, he yelled out in pain, then fell quiet on the carpeted aisle.

Shade dashed to help Ahasver, and the demon beast flew at him. The flying beast overshot him when he dropped and slid on the floor under it to the unmoving man. Shade tried to pull Ahasver under a pew, but before he could drag him far enough, the beast snatched him away. Flying a few feet, it tossed him like a rag doll at the altar and circled back toward Shade even as

Satan did the same.

Shade rolled under the nearest pew when they swooped down at him. The twin demonic beings landed in the aisle and together began hurling away pews. The faster Shade crawled, the quicker the long wood seats were thrown aside, leaving scattered pews lying against or piled in part on top of one another down one side of the church. Nearing the front of the church, Shade ran out of pews to crawl under. When the last wooden seat was tossed aside, light as a feather, he lay under Satan and the beast in plain sight.

From their gaping mouths, slime drooled on Shade when he rolled onto his back. He stared up into their foul-breathed faces and thrust the palm of his hand toward the demonic beast. At once, a thickened airwave slammed the deformed demon hard against the ceiling. Shade rolled to his side to slam the master devil away, but the demonic beast grabbed him by his foot and swung him around and then hurled him against the wall.

Dazed, Shade could only watch as the multi-eyed beast circled the room and headed back. Then Satan blew his blazing fire breath at the demonic beast. The flying freak burst apart in air, and the miniature demon creatures shook out their compressed bodies. Small muscular legs fell, dangling in the air, until they reached their master. Back on familiar turf, the demon parasites dug and squirmed, disguising their shapes and burying themselves deep as they slipped and slithered back into their thick-matted molten host. Satan's scales glowed with dots of red miniature eyes gazing out from their camouflaged positions on the once again gigantic demon prince—the humongous beast now embracing Shade.

A piercing gleam in the monster's red shining eyes matched the fiendish grin on his loathsome face, and more slime drooled onto Shade's captive body. Sparks began shooting out of Satan's red-hot mouth in small, short bursts ... then the fire grew. Already grasping the beast's intentions, Shade threw his arms over his face and again blocked the small fire with the strange invisible shield. Regardless, he couldn't break free of Satan's grip, and the growing fire kept coming.

Ahasver regained consciousness where he was thrown by the altar. He had only to twist around and place his folded hands on the altar to pray.

"We need Your help, Lord! We ask for Your divine intervention. Only You and Your angels have the power to stop Satan!" he said. "What should we do?"

At once, the birds outside stopped screeching and smashing into the windows. Satan spun his head when the noisy racket ceased, and he saw Ahasver at the altar. Enraged, he roared at the older man. Keeping a tight grip on Shade, he leapt in the air and flew at Ahasver, quick to strike out and knock him away from the altar.

But it was too late …

God's holiness filled the sanctuary. The angels in the stained-glass windows above the saints fluttered their wings and flew in place as they sang their heavenly song. The saints below them began praying in a melodic voice, praising and harmonizing with the angelic singing.

Smoke floated in thin, torn clouds on the ceiling where Satan's hot blast had nearly caught the wooden beam on fire, and the scattered white patches drifting from the small glowing splinters at last set off the sprinklers surrounding the cross. He watched the water spray clear as it shot out of the overhead sprinklers … but the clear spray changed to a bright golden glow everywhere the water fell within the circle of light shining on Christ and His cross.

Satan squeezed Shade tight and flew to snatch the penitent man now collapsed on the floor under the cross. The devil reached his clawed hand to reclaim the deathly still man, but shrieked and then jerked his repulsive arm back as a loud noise crackled. Smoke shot up off his arm wherever the golden water touched hell's dark angel. He spun and glared with wise glowing eyes and roared at the praying saints in the windows.

"Your holy water can't keep him," he rasped. "He belongs to me! For now this one pays for your prayers!"

He spat fire at the saints and held Shade pinned to his scaly body. He glared back and forth to include all in the room, then flapped his black bony wings and lifted up into the air, taking Shade back to hell with him.

"Begone! Go back to where you came! I command you in the name of Christ to leave!" Shade's angel warrior voice boomed.

Flames shot, visibly, into the bottom of Satan's chin and exploded out the top of his head. At the same time, Shade's colossal wall shadow revealed the angelic warrior holding the hilt of a sword beneath the demon's chin.

Satan roared and grabbed his head, letting go of Shade when he did.

Shade and his shadow dropped back to the floor, facing the beast. Shade landed with his hands gripped together high over his head. His shadow revealed how he and the warrior kept their tight grip and pulled the flaming sword back through the devil's head.

Satan spread wide his massive wings in midair. His hideous hate-filled eyes fastened on Shade while his hellfire breath spewed molten sparks.

On the floor facing the beast's hovering body, Shade and his shadow released one hand from the hilt of the sword, and together human and shadow held up one hand with palm facing toward Satan, then pushed.

Satan rocked backward, flapped his massive wings in front of his body, and, in the blink of an eye, vaporized behind them, leaving only a large cloud of smoke emanating his reeking odor. The stench remained inside the sanctuary for several minutes.

Shade lowered his hand and looked with utmost caution around the sanctuary. Confident Satan was no longer present in the room, his eyes found the deathly ill man, and he ran, dropping on the wet floor beside him. Catching sight of Ahasver, he beckoned him to the platform. The man's body, still oozing blood, began shriveling up—the blood of his human victims emptying from his body, Shade assumed. His eyes, appearing now as dark pits, peered at Ahasver as the older man knelt beside him.

"I ... didn't know," the man struggled to say. "I'm ... sorry."

"Who are you?" Ahasver asked, wanting to know before the beast slipped away without revealing his true identity.

"Judas ... Judas Iscariot ... I betrayed my ..." His voice strained to talk. "... my friend ... Jesus. I ... I didn't know," he rasped. He weakly lifted his head and reached a bloody hand to touch Shade on the arm. "Thank ... you," he whispered.

His head fell back on the carpet, and his eyelids closed, covering his inhuman eyes. The men continued watching the shriveling Judas but were unable to hear or detect any further signs of life.

Neither Shade nor Ahasver knew how to determine whether he *had* died, since he was thought already to belong to the world of the dead. Unable to fathom that Judas was dead in the earthly sense, Ahasver looked up for a second at the simulated body of Jesus on the cross, then returned his perplexed thoughts back to the unmoving man.

With the blood still oozing from the deathlike body, the man-beast continued to shrink. His body had already shrunk several inches from its original size. Unwilling to take any chances, Ahasver called the church affiliates who already knew of the unnatural beasts and made arrangements for the beast's body to be heavily guarded until it could be transported.

While he was talking on the phone, Ahasver couldn't

help noticing how large the pool of blood was becoming, and he ended the call thinking about the platform's carpeting. He would have some explaining to do, but he wasn't worried about earthly matters that could be remedied without too much trouble. Besides … it didn't look like blood. It was ink black, but he didn't think they'd believe him if he told them his pen had leaked. He'd think of something.

Almost as soon as the thought occurred to Ahasver, particles of the blackened blood began floating up into the air, lifting from the carpet … off the beast … Shade's arm … from wherever the man-beast's blood had been. The small dust-sized particles floated up, swirling through the air, and entered the wounds on the crucified Christ above them. Whether it was through His wrists, feet, or where His side had been pierced, the particles continued swirling and entering the wounds until no traces of the blood were visible. The blood that Judas had drunk from his human victims now became a part of Christ's simulated body.

"Ahasver," Shade said, shocked by the sight of the swirling blood particles as he stood back in awe to look up at Jesus hanging on His cross. "Remember how I told you I didn't believe some of the things you told me … the ones I said were too far-fetched?"

Ahasver looked intently at Shade, expecting he knew the answer to his question but waiting to hear it nonetheless.

"I changed my mind," Shade said.

"I knew you would, son. God has a way of opening our earthly eyes to do His work." Ahasver patted him on the back, proud of his new protégé.

Too small to be visible to the human eye, a bright red molecular-sized particle of blood trickled from the wound of the wrist on Christ's statue, dripping down His alabaster hand to fall on the lips of Judas lying on the floor beneath Him. The man-beast's stirring was not visible as the cleansed blood seeped through a crevice in his lips—the blood that would enable him to live in a state of suspended animation, safe from the bowels of hell and Satan's reversal of death to again roam the earth as one of his beasts. Left to sleep for eternity. The precious invisible drop of Christ's blood enough to keep him alive forever, at last achieving his immortality.

The candles, still burning on the table near Ahasver and Shade, flickered and went out. The sprinklers around the cross reduced their spray to a thin light mist then shut off. The smell of roses filled the sanctuary, replacing the pungent odor left by Satan. Unobservant of the extinguished candles, the two men were at once aware of the velvety flower scent and felt confident that evil was no longer present in the now quiet room.

Shade and Ahasver waited with the body of the beast Judas until near dawn when Ahasver's colleagues joined them. Shade had the impression they already knew who he was.

"Good to see you, Shade," were the closest words he received to an introduction.

He and the warriors all pitched in and returned the battle-torn room to pristine condition. Once the work was finished, they all decided the new warriors flown in would stay with the man-beast's body until the arrival of the truck bringing a pre-constructed vault with a specially designed coffin inside. The body would then be placed inside the burial chamber and transported back to the holy cemetery, where it would be buried with the other beast captured by Brother Benjamin centuries earlier—with God's earthly warriors riding in the back of the enclosed truck with the body.

Preparations for the burial were already made, with immediate plans for interment upon their arrival at the cemetery. Since it was believed the beasts couldn't die, there was confusion about Judas's death. Did his apparent death mean Satan would be able to release him in another form to roam the earth again? Or was Judas only temporarily disabled? They knew for a fact the other captured beast was still alive. Why wasn't Judas—or was he?

After witnessing the beast's blood, enter the wounds of the body of Jesus, Ahasver faithfully believed the beast was in His hands. Still, as a precaution, they would watch Judas for any signs of life as well as alert the others to be vigilant for signs of a new beast. The warriors riding back with Judas's body were notified to stay after his burial until they were confident he was no longer a danger.

Although Ahasver and Shade would be unable to attend the burial of Judas's body, they would nonetheless be at the cemetery's blessing in a matter of days and see his interred body at that ceremony.

Shade decided to get some shut-eye since he had to go home in a couple of hours and appear as though nothing unusual had taken place in the two days in the city with Ahasver.

Charlie, he suspected, would know differently.

Chapter 27

Reliving the battle with the monstrous demon days earlier, Shade raised his hand in a similar halt gesture, still awed by the simple action's previous outcome. The mirror was closer than he realized, and he ended up smacking his reflection. He wiped his handprint from the medicine cabinet's glass and shook his head, trying to fathom just exactly what had happened at the church. All he knew for sure was that he'd fought a demon—Satan himself, it seemed—that wasn't just another character from one of his video games. Plus he had won the battle … and couldn't tell anyone about defeating the devil.

Come to think of it, they would probably think I was still on drugs, he thought and decided he was better off keeping it to himself.

Downstairs he could hear Charlie's toenails clicking on the foyer's tile floor. The clicking stopped, and the dog started barking.

Ahasver must be here, he thought.

He knew his mom was busy preparing dinner, so he hustled downstairs to open the door. After greeting Ahasver, Shade led him through the house to the delicious smelling aromas coming from the kitchen. When they entered, his mom started to apologize for being late with dinner but stopped in mid sentence when Ahasver handed her a pie, and she thanked him for the dessert.

In lieu of the dining room's spacious and formal eating space, Shade opted to set the table in the cozy kitchen instead. The casual dinner was a success, and the threesome's friendship deepened.

The evening, though, was cut short so that Ahasver and Shade could return to the city. It was time for the cemetery's blessing, and they wanted to get an early start in the morning. After the ceremony, Ahasver would be going home. This, then, would be his mother's last meeting with their new foreign friend.

Shade would be coming home by bus and had already purchased the ticket for the return trip. He wrote the bus's scheduled arrival time down and left the note on the table for his mom to pick him up at the city bus terminal.

/////

After the men left, Casper remembered her intuitive feeling about returning to the odd cemetery and realized her intuition must have been for her son. Albeit, the intuitive knowledge persuaded her Shade's return was as it should be.

Snuggling in a cozy blanket, she reached for a book she'd purchased weeks earlier but hadn't found time to read. Curled up on the couch, she was soon caught up in the story. Charlie yawned and stretched out on the floor in front of her.

/////

Shade drove Ahasver's car back to the church, and although the trip wasn't as fast as the last time, they still made it to the church with plenty of time for Ahasver to pack his few clothes and finish any last-minute details before they called it a night.

The next morning, the drive to the cemetery, by no means boring, was long. Shade was glad Ahasver let him drive. His memories of the monotonous ride as his mom's passenger were still too fresh in his mind.

The men made good use of their long hours in the car, discussing a variety of subjects. The times when one or the other grew tired and silence filled the car, however, were not disquieting. Ahasver suggested several classes for Shade to take when he went back to college.

To Shade's surprise, the suggested classes, some of which he had never heard of, sounded compelling. After experiencing the unimaginable, strange, and impossible supernatural event, even the myth and advanced religious courses now seemed exciting learning opportunities to him.

During one of their quiet times, Shade pondered the

possibility of returning to school during the winter quarter instead of waiting until spring. That was *after* he found a job to save some money. He would make it a priority to go job hunting as soon as he got home. Ahasver bravoed the idea when Shade told him of his plans.

Small steps, Shade told himself when he thought of his aspirations to find his way and stand on his own two feet.

He knew his drug cravings were not entirely behind him, but he felt stronger to resist the temptations. Packing for the trip, he had straightened and organized his room and found the Adderall pills and matchbox containing the rolled joint still inside his jeans pocket from the day they rescued Patty. He had forgotten about the drugs, and as soon as he found them, he flushed them down the toilet. A small part of him longed to keep them, but the larger part of him was glad they were gone.

Besides, he had the start of a great support group if his cravings became too much. Between his mother, his sister, and Ahasver—who gave him his international number, specifying, "for help, advice, or just to talk"—he was confident good people were in place. He didn't want to let them down, but more importantly, he felt good about the person he was becoming and didn't want to let *himself* down. His new self-esteem made him feel trustworthy, capable, and ready to get back out into the world.

Stopping at a rest stop after dark, they stretched their legs, and Shade rested his eyes for a few hours. On the evening of their second day, Shade recognized the motel where he and his mother had stayed—the same motel where they'd found the map, leading him full circle on his journey. Tired from the drive, they paid for their rooms and spent the rest of the evening recuperating from their travels. Relieved to be out of the car, Shade wandered the motel grounds, stretching his cramped legs.

Nearing the motel's pool, a man ambled ahead of him with a small boy in tow. The child's eyes were glued on the pool as they passed it. Shade visualized himself in his younger years walking next to his father past a similar pool. When the boy said something inaudible to the man, he was sure the child was asking to go swimming.

"Maybe later," the man said in response to his question, and Shade knew he had guessed right.

/////

At 8:00 a.m., Maria pulled her cart out the office's side door and felt the early morning sun on her back. Due to the cooler weather, she wore a sweater over her housekeeper's uniform. The motel's parking lot was still full, but she saw some of the room doors open as people carried their luggage to their vehicles.

She leaned her head back to enjoy the sun as she strolled to the other end of the cart. She had already gotten the early risers' vacant room numbers and was headed to those rooms. In the short time she'd worked for the motel, she had gotten into a routine, and her days went smoothly since Hank had left on his Las Vegas gambling trip. She hoped she had seen the last of him.

Maria dashed back to reopen the office door and motioned the approaching gentleman in, assuring him the motel's complimentary coffee was brewing inside.

Returning to the cart, she pushed her weight against it, rolling it noisily on the sidewalk. A woman nodded in her direction, and through the glass, Maria saw her join the man inside the office as he fixed his morning coffee. Almost at once, the couple ran back outside, scanning the area and asking anyone within earshot if they had seen a young boy.

Maria's eyes darted around. Catching sight of a small arm waving sporadically in the pool, she flew into action. Yelling to the frantic couple, she ran to the pool and dove in. She pulled the boy's sinking body up to her and swam to the pool wall, keeping his face above the water. She held him until the man pulled him out of the pool. Panicked, the man started shaking the boy. Maria pulled herself out of the water and pulled the boy firmly from him.

Dropping on the concrete beside the child, Maria looked up and said, "Call 9-1-1!"

Maria's mind reverted to the life-saving classes she'd taken so often that she could have been qualified to teach the class. Making herself stay calm, she performed mouth-to-mouth resuscitation until the boy began to gag. She rolled him to his side to make it easier for him to vomit up the pool water he'd swallowed when he was drowning.

Holding on to one another, the couple watched Maria and the boy. When the child gagged and began spewing water, they broke into tears and dropped to the concrete beside him.

A drop of water resembling a teardrop rolled down Maria's cheek and dropped onto the boy, now breathing rapidly but evenly beneath her. She remained with the child and his parents until the paramedics arrived and took over her emergency procedures. By then, the boy was moving about freely, appearing to be well on the road to recovery. Regardless, he was taken to the hospital for further observation and testing.

Maria took a deep breath. She wrapped her arms around herself and watched the emergency crew leave.

"Well done, Maria," said a man standing nearby, moving back to give her space.

Maria's wet hair clung to her face. Running her trembling fingers through its wetness, she said, *"Tenía tanto miedo,"* somewhat blank before catching herself and repeating her words in English: "I was so scared."

Whispering something inaudible, she looked up at the sky and crossed her breast. She could feel her body shaking. She looked at the man who had just spoken to her. It was the man who had let her keep the lottery ticket!

"You come back?" Maria said.

"Yes, but not for long. My friend Shade here and I were

leaving when we saw you at the pool. Are you okay? Is there anything we can do for you?" the man asked.

"No … I'm … I'm okay," she said, looking down at herself. "I just need to change out of these wet clothes," she told him and started toward the office.

The young man Shade took off his jacket and placed it over Maria's shoulders. He took her arm, steadying her when her legs wobbled.

"Ahasver and I both think you were amazing saving the boy," Shade said and held onto her arm.

She gave a little smile. "I'm going to be a nurse," she said. "Someday," she finished through chattering teeth as she pulled Shade's jacket tighter.

Shade and his friend Ahasver escorted her inside the motel's office. She removed the jacket and handed it back to Shade.

"Thank you," Maria said. "I'm sorry I got it wet."

"It's fine. I don't mind," Shade replied.

"Maria, would you like us to stay with you for a while?" Ahasver asked.

"No, I'm okay, but will you say a prayer for the boy?" she said, her voice catching.

"Of course," he told her and then asked them to bow their heads with him. "Father in heaven, we are overjoyed for the life You have spared this morning. We pray the boy is unharmed and will recover with no ill effects. We thank You for using Maria as your tool for Your merciful intervention. Guide her with her abilities and light her path to fulfilling the dreams of healing You've placed inside her. We ask these things in the name of Your Son Jesus. We give You all the praise. Thank You, Holy Father. Amen."

"Thank you. Your prayer keep me safe before, and I know it will help the boy, too." Maria gave Ahasver a quick hug. "Good-bye. I hope I see you again … both of you," she said, glancing at Shade.

Opening a door with a sign attached—*Employees Only*—she disappeared behind it.

/////

Once Maria was gone, Ahasver went to the front desk where the puzzled clerk had been watching the scene. Informing the clerk of Maria's heroism, Ahasver petitioned for her to have some time to herself to recover from the incident. The clerk, seemingly a good man at heart, promised to call his boss to let him know what happened and then vowed Maria would have whatever time she needed.

Ahasver and Shade returned to their packed car. A bird, perched on the motel's eave's spout, chirped at them. Ahasver nodded to it and said, "Good day to you, too." The bird eyed him, then puffed its chest and ruffled its feathers.

Shade headed toward the driver's side, and the two departed for the cemetery.

/////

Wanda, the motel's other housekeeper, hurried to the office after the front-desk clerk called the room she was cleaning and informed her of the events. Finding Maria sitting inside the supply room, Wanda sat down beside the distraught woman and put an arm around her. Maria laid her head down on her shoulder. A half hour later, she was back on the job, insisting that she wanted to finish her day like normal.

Chapter 28

The church leaders and warriors had already gathered at the cemetery by the time Ahasver and Shade arrived. Once the two men showed up, twelve members in all were present: six of the church's holiest leaders, including Ahasver, and six trusted warriors, counting Shade. Five of the men present had crossed the ocean to be at the ceremony. Shade was the only member of the small party present for the first time.

Wondering if more would be coming to the service, Shade asked Ahasver before getting out of the car.

"No," Ahasver said. "Since we keep the cemetery's history secret to keep the beast, or now beasts, undiscovered, few people know about the blessing. Word will be passed down to leaders and warriors on a need-to-know basis. It's the safest way. Come, let's join the others."

Details were being finalized for the rites of the blessing when they joined the small group. The church leaders were pulling robes over their clothing, while the warriors were helping one another with chain-mail body armor. The chain mail looked authentic, and Shade stared in awe while watching the warriors.

"Come on, mon! What are ye waitin' fer?" asked one warrior with a thick Irish brogue.

"Here, Shade, put this armor on," said a warrior whom Shade had met at the church when they came for Judas's body. "And don't mind him. He's still learning to speak English," he said with a wink.

"I be speekin' English afore ye, laddie," the Irishman replied.

Shade, awestruck by the armor, was anxious to feel the weight of the chain mail and at once began putting pulling it over his T-shirt. How medieval knights fought in such heavy gear baffled him when the protective armor was in place. Walking a bit awkwardly to a sport-utility vehicle's side window, he couldn't help admiring himself.

"Is that me?" he asked to no one in particular.

"Nah, it's I. You be the little spot on thee glass beside mae," the Irishman said and ambled up beside Shade and looked at himself.

Soon all the warriors lined up at the SUV, each posing in front of the glass to gaze at their own reflections.

"If you protectors of the earth are finished looking at yourselves, I believe we're ready to proceed with the ceremony," one of the clergymen said.

The Irishman opened the back of the SUV, and each of the warriors, except for Shade, came forward and retrieved their sheathed swords. They fastened them around their waists with the sword hanging from their left side. After the swords were in place, the Irishman reached back inside the SUV and removed a shield and handed it to the warrior nearest him who, seeing it wasn't his own, passed it to the next warrior until each man carried his own shield in his hands … everyone but Shade.

"Ye be too young to have yer own sheld and sword, laddie. Ye gotta wait 'til ye grow a wee bit," he told him.

A procession was formed with two warriors in front, one warrior on each side, and the fifth warrior protecting the group's backside. The church clergy were in the middle of the warriors, with the head of the church in front, three behind him, and Ahasver and Shade following with the remaining church member. Shade was told to stand in the middle of the last row beside Ahasver. He was disappointed not to be allowed to walk with the warriors but kept it to himself.

The holy leader turned to face the group and began reading a psalm of protection from the Bible. When he finished reading the Scripture, he motioned his hand toward the others, and the church clergy fell to their knees.

The group formed two circles: the holy men making up the inner circle with Shade kneeling in their back row, and the warriors, still standing, forming the outer circle, encompassing the holy men. The holy leader began walking ceremoniously through the circle's midst, and the clergymen repositioned themselves to face Shade. The warriors, unsheathing their swords, raised them, touching the tips of the swords together above Shade's head while dropping on one knee behind and beside him, forming a semicircle. Humbled and flabbergasted, Shade knelt.

The holy leader stopped in front of Shade and placed his hand on top of his head. The warriors lowered their swords, two laying the tips of their blades on his right shoulder, two on his left and the fifth warrior touching the tip of his blade to the chain mail at the back of his neck. The holy man, continuing his theme, prayed a prayer of protection with his hand remaining on Shade's head. All present, clergy and warriors, bowed their heads during the prayer.

With the prayer finished, another holy man held out an object in both of his hands to the religious leader. Shade was unable to see what the man had given him. Holding the object up toward heaven as if offering it to God, the holy leader said another short prayer. Before Shade bowed his head, part of a thick silver chain slipped through the holy leader's fingers. Once the prayer was finished, Shade lifted his head and the holy man leaned forward and placed the ample chain over it, lowering it around his neck. Shade had not glimpsed the glistening Chi Rho symbol hanging from the chain's silver metal until it was on his chest, and he was again in awe looking down at the Christian warrior symbol.

"Welcome, chosen warrior of God " the holy man said before backing away a few steps and motioning for all to stand.

The Irishman and all the warriors rose and sheathed their swords. Behind Shade, a sword passed through each warrior's hands until it was handed to the Irish warrior, who then approached and stood facing Shade with the holy man at his back. Both of his large hands held the unsheathed sword horizontally in front of Shade when he gravely spoke: "One drop of human blood upon this sword's blade, and he who owns the sword shall die. Do you take this sword as your own?" the Irishman asked, using perfect English with no trace of an accent.

Shade, grasping the words of the Irishman, hesitated. He held the Irishman's steady gaze. The words "He who lives by the sword, dies by the sword" leapt in his mind, and he understood the meaning. If he used the sword to hurt another human being, he would pay the price. The sword was only to be used against the demons from hell.

"Yes," he said.

The Irishman thrust the sword toward Shade. Gripping the sword's hilt with both hands, Shade pointed it straight up in the air.

"We welcome ye among us, warrior," the Irishman said. "Looks like ye've grown enough a'ready."

The holy leader said a final prayer, and afterward Shade was welcomed and congratulated with hearty slaps on the back by the rest of the warriors.

Soon the welcoming and congratulating voices quieted, and Shade backed away from the group to sheath his sword. Intent on the sword's exposed blade, he didn't notice the warriors gathered around waiting until the sword was sheathed and fastened on his side. At last, a shield was brought forward and handed to him while all eyes watched. Engraved in the protective front of the shield was a winged warrior dressed for battle, holding a shield in one hand and a flaming sword, held high, in the other. At the bottom of the shield were his initials: *S.E.* For a moment, Shade was speechless. The silence was broken when each warrior lifted his shield and, waiting for Shade to do the same, brought them together. The metal shields clanged in unison with a loud battle cry from the brotherhood of warriors.

The procession was reformed. Shade now walked proudly at the rear of the group with the last warrior. He carried his shield with his sword sheathed on his left side, ready to do battle.

The clergy roamed orderly about the cemetery, casting small dust-sized particles of the holy dirt in their sanctified vessels. Hymns of praise filled the air. The warriors watched and waited on guard near the grove of trees where Brother Benjamin was buried. None spoke, paying rapt attention to the proceedings and their surroundings.

Once the clergymen were satisfied the main part of the cemetery had been blessed, they proceeded toward the remaining graves near the grove of trees where the protective warriors waited.

When the church leaders neared their guarded area, the warriors surrounded the grave of the beast that the warrior Benjamin had slain. The Irish warrior knelt and brushed dirt from the head of the grave where the beast's head would be to expose a large earth-colored metal object. Shade watched the warrior find a ridged edge sticking up from the metal, and putting some muscle into his actions, he slid a metal plate back, exposing a glass window.

Shade's curiosity was piqued when he realized he could look through the glass to see the beast. Nevertheless, wanting to remain at attention with the other warriors, he didn't permit himself to lean forward and ended up being unable to see anything.

Another warrior worked at another metal-ridged edge he had uncovered while Shade was looking at the glass. The warrior grabbed hold of the ridge and, in similar fashion, pulled the metal plate back. Holes drilled into the top of the metal vault over the beast's midsection were exposed. One at a time, the godly men moved forward and shook their vessels containing the holy dirt into the holes, pouring sprinkles of dirt on the body inside. The holy leader stood motionless at the foot of the grave with his arms extended out on each side and the palms of his hands facing upward. Although his eyes were closed, he lifted his head toward heaven while offering up prayers for the fallen saint whom Satan had loosed on the earth as a man-beast. When his prayers ended, they backed away from the grave and began singing songs of praise while the warriors recovered the burial vault.

The Irish warrior had already risen from his position at the head of the metal box. Standing at attention, he glanced at Shade and nodded once. At first, Shade didn't grasp his meaning, but all at once, it dawned on him the Irishman wanted him to re-cover the top of the burial box. Springing into action, he knelt and grabbed the ridged metal edge to slide it back in place. Before he closed it, he looked inside the glass window.

Below him lay the body of a man or, as Ahasver would say, a man-beast. From the little he could see, he was a large man with coal-black hair. Shade gasped and jerked backward when the man opened his eyes and looked at him. He was still alive! He reached for his sword, but the Irish warrior stilled his hand before he unsheathed it. With a swift jerk, Shade pushed the metal covering back in place and scooped the dirt back over the box. His hands tingled, and he realized he was touching the holy dirt. This time, however, he didn't feel lightheaded or experience the dizziness he'd felt the first time he was at the cemetery.

Satisfied that the top of the metal vault was covered, he rejoined his fellow warriors. They stood at attention while the holy men sprinkled holy dirt over the beast's grave and said the last "Amen," then they went straight to the grave on the opposite side of the warrior Benjamin and repeated the process.

This time, the Irishman let Shade begin the process of brushing the dirt away to expose the metal box inches beneath the ground. Finding the ridged edge on the top of the burial vault, Shade slid it back. Beneath the glass, mere inches from where he stared down, lay the body of Judas Iscariot. He was sure Judas's eyes were going to open and peer up from his tomb like the other beast. They didn't. To Shade, his body appeared almost pink and less shriveled than the last time he saw it at the church.

He stared at Judas a moment longer and, for an instant, thought he saw his chest rise and fall as though he were breathing. Recalling how his father's lifeless body had given that same illusion in his coffin at the funeral home, he dismissed the movement as a trick of the eye.

Standing, he backed away from the grave and waited for another warrior to brush the dirt from the midsection of the burial vault, but none did. The Bible was read, the songs were sung, and the prayer ended with the amens spoken.

Once the holy men were silent, Ahasver stepped forward and looked through the glass at Judas. No one moved or spoke while he observed. Ahasver's face was emotionless as he stared down at the defunct body. Finished with his observation, he stepped back with the other clergy members.

Glancing at the Irishman, who gave him the signal nod, Shade knelt again and pushed the metal plate back in place. He scooped and brushed the dirt until the metal burial box was again buried beneath the soil.

The holy men ended the cemetery's blessing at the grave of the warrior, Brother Benjamin. No dirt was brushed back to expose his body beneath. The warriors, three on each side of his grave, unsheathed their swords, holding them firmly pointed down by their sides. The holy men sprinkled the holy dirt until the grave was covered and then praised God when their sanctified vessels emptied at the precise time they finished. Still praising God, they pulled flower petals from the deep pockets of their robes and dropped them onto the warrior's sunlit grave. The grave appeared as though the fall sunlight had convinced spring to begin anew on that particular patch of blessed soil. A psalm was read aloud by the holy leader, followed by a song sung by the warriors. Shade listened intently to the words of the song. The ceremony ended with each clergy member echoing "Amen."

"Amen," Shade whispered and stepped in place at the back of the procession to descend the hill and leave the holy cemetery in God's outdoor sanctuary for another year.

The robes were removed, the chain mail put back into the SUV along with the swords and shields.

Ahasver and Shade walked to their car with plans to join the holy men and warriors back at the church headquarters. However, before they got into the vehicle, the holy leader told Ahasver he'd like to talk with him privately and then asked Shade if he would mind riding with the warriors.

Ahasver jerked his head toward Shade when he heard his quick and enthusiastic, "Yes! I mean … no!"

But Ahasver smiled with amusement when he understood that Shade wanted to be with his fellow warriors.

None of the experienced warriors had been in combat with a beast, and Shade was soon bombarded with questions about the battle and the demon they'd heard was Satan himself.

At first Shade, downplayed the fight, not wanting to boast, but after a few minutes, he couldn't contain the excitement in his voice, and forgetting his initial reservations, he gave them a spirited detailed account of the demonic battle.

The men listened to his account and praised his bravery. Afterward they joshed him about how his story would be handed down and retold like the warrior Benjamin's and how he would be honored with a similar grave song.

The possibility reminded them of the warrior song, and they raised their voices in unison to teach Shade the lyrics so he could sing with them the next time they sang it for a fallen brother.

The swords, they assured him, were kept under lock and

key at the church and only used for solemn occasions.

Recalling the Irishman's solemn words, Shade couldn't help asking, "Has anyone ever died from human blood touching their sword's blade?"

Silence filled the SUV.

"Once," a warrior said at last.

"Aye, once, laddie," the Irishman repeated. "We jest left his greeve."

"Brother Benjamin?" Shade asked.

"Aye," confirmed the Irishman.

"Nicked by his own sword when the beast fell into the hole with the holy dirt—the dirt they'd gotten from the foot of Jesus's cross and shipped to America in a small metal box. They brought it to pour around the foot of the cross they were erecting at the new church … where the trees are now. The beast fell backward into the hole they were digging for the cross and couldn't move when the little box fell in with him and the dirt spilled out on top of him. Benjamin nicked himself with his own blade when he slashed at the beast only to find air where the beast had stood only a split second earlier, fighting him," one of the warriors said. His utmost respect for the fallen warrior was obvious in his tone as he gave the details.

"Did you see the little box on top of the beast? It's rusty and hardly visible with the cobwebs all over it, but it's still there," asked the warrior he'd met earlier at the church.

"No," Shade said. "He opened his eyes and looked at me. I was too shocked to look at the rest of him."

"It's there. It's still lying on him," another warrior said. "The only thing that's changed through the centuries is the vault. The vault you saw replaced the original enclosure and was lowered over him a few decades ago. He's still lying on the ground where he fell. No one is going to move him!"

"But that doesn't seem right for Benjamin to die by nicking *himself*," Shade said.

"His death was decided when he took up his sword. God keeps His word, Shade," another warrior answered.

"Aye, and so da we!" the Irish warrior said.

"Aye," was echoed, one at a time, by each warrior.

Shade's "Aye" was the last to be said, and in that instant, he became one with them. The next time the song was sung, all six warriors knew the words.

Chapter 29

The journey was nearly over. Shade hoped he would never see the inside of a bus again. When the bus pulled into the depot, he strained to see the parking lot, looking for his mother's car. He hoped she wasn't late. He needed a shower and a change of clothes.

Even I wouldn't want to sit next to me, he thought.

He chuckled to himself, thinking what his new warrior brothers would say if they saw him now. Most likely they would have approved of his disheveled appearance and manly odor. They were, without a doubt, men with adventurous spirits and cared little to none if the adventure got a little messy, as long as it wasn't boring.

He saw his mother leaning against her car, watching the bus roll into the station. Shade wasted no time and grabbed his bag almost before it touched the ground, heading with relief to the parking lot.

Casper waved a hand when he was close and headed toward the driver's side of the automobile.

"NO, NO, NO!" Shade said. "I've been riding for hours and hours. I can't sit in the passenger seat another minute. *PLEASE* … let me drive!"

She looked amused at his desperation and tossed the keys to him with a chuckle. "You don't sound like you enjoyed riding the bus," she said, then laughed.

"You have *no* idea. If I *ever* come up with an idea like that again, *please* stop me," Shade said.

Using the key fob, Shade popped the car's trunk and threw his bag inside. Unzipping one of the bag's side pockets, he removed an envelope and slammed the trunk shut. Inside the car, he handed the envelope to his mom and started the engine while she turned the envelope over, staring at it in her hand.

"What's this?" she asked.

"A little something Ahasver and I were working on. I wanted you to look at it to see if it was something you would be interested in," he said.

"It's sealed. You want me to open it?" she asked.

"Yeah, it's no big deal. You can open it," he assured her and then looked both ways to make sure no cars were coming before he pulled out onto the street.

His mother turned the envelope over and ripped it open. Shade glanced sideways at her when she removed the paper: a document he knew that she had searched everywhere to find.

"Whaat? ... How? ... Where? Do you *know* what this is?" she said, her eyes growing wide. "It's your grandfather's birth certificate! It has his parents' names and where they were born! How did you get this?" she asked, but didn't let him answer. "Do you know what this means? I can find them! I don't believe it!" she said and began to cry.

Shade, anticipating his mother's reaction, had pulled to the curb and put the car in park.

"Now do you see why I wanted to drive? You're such a crybaby," he said.

His mom reached over and hugged him but sat quickly back in her seat, re-reading and holding the birth certificate against her breast.

"Shade, I can't believe it. I didn't think you were even interested in finding your dad's family. I just can't believe you found it," she said.

"Well ... I can't actually take too much credit. Ahasver and I spent two days looking through all kinds of records when I stayed in the city. We looked and looked for any kind of information on them but came up empty-handed. Ahasver decided to contact his church's historians, and they found the certificate. They surprised us with it when we got to the church headquarters. We were pretty amazed ourselves that they were able to come up with it after we looked so hard."

"You amaze me, Shade. Thank you so much! Maybe we'll find some of Dad's relatives before we go to Europe," she said. "I need to send Ahasver a thank-you note. I don't think I'll *ever* be able to thank either of you enough for finding this."

"Europe? Who's going to Europe? Are you planning a trip to Europe?" he asked.

"Oh, that's right ... you don't know. I've got a surprise of my own, I guess. Well, it's not really my surprise. Maybe I should wait and let Breeze tell you. It's her surprise."

"Mom, don't do this to me. It was a long trip, and I met all the wishy-washy people I care to meet. If you don't tell me, I'll drive you back to the bus station and put you on the first bus with them."

"Well ... I guess Breeze won't mind." His mom paused for a second to think. "You know how Breeze is ... always ready to help. Someone, a man, was at the library with a book open looking at the picture of *The Last Supper* and asked her if she knew it. Well, of course she told him she did and just made a comment she'd like to see it in person. Afterward she took a few minutes to give him a few details about Jesus and the saints. He left when she was done, and she just figured she'd never see him again. *But* ... he came back a few days later, saying he was leaving town and wanted to give her something before he left."

"Wait. How did he know where to find her? Was Breeze at the library again?"

"No. She was walking to the church around the corner from her dormitory. You know ... the one catty-corner to the library. He handed her an envelope and told her not to open it until he left. She took it back to the dormitory, and when she opened it, there were four airline vouchers for tickets to Italy. Can you believe it? And ... I guess he even left money for the trip. I'm not sure how much, though."

"You're kidding! Something has to be wrong. People don't do things like that," Shade said, doubting the vouchers were valid.

"I know. It's odd. I'm going to take a look at the vouchers when I go with her to the bank tomorrow to find out what *they* want," his mom said.

"What do you mean? Is she overdrawn? I didn't even know she had an account," Shade asked as he turned on the freeway.

"She doesn't. She's never been to the bank that wants to see her. She thought I must have opened an account for her when they called her at the dormitory, and then she called me to find out what they wanted. I hope it doesn't have something to do with those tickets and the bank is going to try and make her pay for them."

"Just return them. They can't make her pay for them if she didn't buy them. I wouldn't worry about it. Probably a bank error," Shade said, hoping it *was* a simple bank mistake.

"I know, I know … I'm not going to worry about it. I'll just wait until Breeze and I go to the bank," she said, then paused briefly before continuing. "See what you missed while you were gone?" she said and poked him on his arm.

"I think this is a first … worrying about Breeze instead of me. That's a change," Shade said, mentally comparing his self-assessed inadequacies to his levelheaded sister.

"Oh, I worry about both of you. Parents never stop worrying about their children … no matter how old they get. If I'm still alive when you kids are grandparents, I'll still worry about you."

"Not tonight … No worries tonight, matey," Shade replied, using a not very good Australian accent.

"I'm glad you're home."

"Me, too, Mom."

Shade glanced at his mother and realized just how glad he honestly was to be home. His travels over, at least for now, gave him time to prepare for the future.

Europe? he thought. *Nah.* And dismissed the idea.

Epilogue

Verily I say unto you, There be some standing here, which shall not taste of death, till they see the Son of man coming in his kingdom.
Matthew 16:28

The Wandering Jew
Ahasver's seat was located about halfway between the midsection and the tail of the plane. His window seat was a rare treat. Normally after his USA trips, he was ready to leave and looked forward to traveling back to the Middle East where he was most comfortable. This year, he was leaving with mixed emotions. He had grown fond of Shade and Casper. It had been so many years since his wife and children had passed from this world that he had mostly forgotten what it was like to be a part of a family. Of course, he had his church family, for which he was grateful, and Shade and Casper were certainly not his real family, but it brought back memories—memories that he now had time to reflect upon since the trip back across the ocean would take several hours.

He should sleep, though. God only knew how little of that he got. Nonetheless, his nostalgic thoughts were too vivid in his mind for him to drift off easily.

He didn't often permit his mind to go back to that time … so long ago that now it didn't seem real. But it was. The time that had changed his life in such a way that few people could understand. The time before his name was Ahasver.

His life had been privileged, being born into one of the wealthier Jewish families. He was one of the few Jewish men the high Roman officials permitted into their homes, sought out specifically for his skill. As a result, he was esteemed above the more common Jewish families.

He was the best leather craftsman around. During his

younger years, he worked as an apprentice for his father who taught him his trade. He continued working for his father until his father's death, when he took over the business for his own in his early twenties.

His father had planned to marry him to a girl who held no interest in his eyes. When he refused to marry her, his father relented and let him choose his own bride, but, of course, his father still arranged the marriage. His choice was a young Jewish girl with big, beautiful dark brown eyes and dark brown hair that curled temptingly around her face. Her smile lit up his world. Seven beautiful children—four boys and three girls—were born to them. Life could not have been better.

They lived in Jerusalem among those of similar stature. He owned land on the outskirts of Jerusalem, where he kept the sheep he gave the Jewish priests for their sacrifices and sometimes gave them one when it wasn't the customary time but he felt the need to be purified of a guilty pleasure. He'd acquired the land from his father, land that his father had gotten from his father.

His memory of his first encounter with Jesus was still clear. He was at the temple. Those greedy priests weren't happy with the sheep he'd sent for the sacrifice. They said they were blemished, and they knew he had some perfectly good fat ones that he was keeping for himself instead of offering them to God as he was commanded. He was livid.

"How dare those swine talk to me like that!" he'd muttered to himself that day.

There was no God up in some divine heaven wanting his fat sheep. He knew the priests wanted his fat sheep for themselves. He stormed out of the temple and almost ran into the man who had been calling Himself the Son of God, from the rumors he'd heard. How dare He! He probably wanted his sheep too! Then the crazy man started throwing tables over, and money started rolling everywhere.

Somebody should arrest him! he thought.

Months later, he was on his way home from one of his wealthy Roman clients and cut through the market to buy some figs. A small group of men were talking quietly close to the stand where he was making his purchase. Being a nosy man, he stayed a little longer than necessary to eavesdrop on their conversation.

"If He's supposed to be the Son of God, then when is He going to put those Roman idolaters in their place?" one of the voices raged.

"Judas, there are more things to worry about than the Romans! As long as we stay out of their way, we'll have no problems with them for now," a strong voice replied.

"Peter, you can't be that naive! You of all people! You've never liked the Romans!" the one called Judas said.

"I'm telling you, Jesus is here for more important reasons than to overthrow the Romans!" Peter said and then stormed away from the group.

Hmm, is Jesus out to overthrow our Roman rulers? Could that man Judas be right? Ha! Like I said earlier, someone needs to arrest that man! he thought, sure the man was dangerous … but not convinced that he should tell his Roman benefactors about the conversation, so he kept the eavesdropped conversation to himself.

Ahasver flashed back sadly to about a year or so later when they did arrest Jesus. He was napping and loud voices had awoken him. They were screaming "Crucify Him! Crucify Him!" and he wondered what thief the Pharisees had found in their midst.

Unable to sleep, he decided to dress and see what all the shouting was about. The simple peasants held no interest for him. Nevertheless, he wanted to know what could be going on to gather a crowd so large that they were able to wake him from his slumber.

When he reached the shouting voices, he was surprised to see the governor, Pontius Pilate, seated before them. Jesus was bound and standing in front of the governor. Since the Roman soldiers knew him as an influential man and friend of the Roman heads, he was able to get close to the governor and heard Pilate's wife tell Pilate not to get involved with the "just" man whom the crowd wanted him to crucify. He was confident Pilate knew women were weak. According to what Pilate's wife said, it was some dream she'd had about Jesus that had upset her. After listening for a while, he realized the governor had taken his wife's words to heart, because Pilate, not wanting to order the death of the man, washed his hands and told the Jewish gathering he was innocent of shedding the blood of Jesus, whom he found to be just. If they wanted Him dead, His death would be on them. The chief priests nevertheless convinced the Jewish crowd to tell Pilate that Jesus's blood would be on their own hands and their children's hands, and to release the thief Barabbas and crucify Jesus.

The gathered Jews gave Pilate no choice. Giving in to their demands, Pilate released Barabbas and had Jesus lashed, sending Him afterward to be crucified. Before Jesus was marched to His death, Pilate's soldiers took Jesus—refusing even to defend himself—to Pilate's meeting place outside the governor's own house, where they stripped off His clothes and put a scarlet robe on Him. Somebody made a crown of thorns and put it on His head. It almost fell off, so a soldier picked it up and thrust it back down with such force that the thorns stuck in His head, keeping it from sliding off again. Blood began running down His face. They stuck a reed in His hand like a scepter and bowed their knees before Him in mockery, saying, "Hail, King of the Jews!"

Spitting at their mocked "King of the Jews," they took the reed out of His hand and used it to hit Him over His head. Someone missed when they spit at Jesus and spat their disgusting saliva on him instead. He looked down at his expensive robe and was angered by the disrespectful soldiers and crazed Jewish crowd watching the spectacle. How dare the buffoons spit on his fine clothes! Shoving his way through the crowd, he left before they marched Jesus away to be crucified.

Once he got home, he changed into another robe and handed the soiled one to his wife. He was in the process of telling her what he had witnessed at the governor's house when he heard a multitude of raised voices, sounding like they were getting closer to his residence.

Now what? he thought.

He opened his door to see the loud, rampaging crucifixion mob coming his way.

"They're bringing Him this way through Jerusalem! Can I have no peace today?" he said.

In a matter of minutes, the loud chaotic scene was passing his door. His sons, excited by the cheering voices, wanted to watch when they marched the condemned thieves past their home, and stood outside their door.

"Go outside and keep an eye on the boys," his wife asked him.

"I don't want them outside with those beggars and thieves. And the Pharisees … You know I can't stand those hypocrites," he told her.

"Please?" she asked.

His wife remained beautiful to him until the day she died. Even in her death, he still saw the beautiful young woman he'd married. All she had to do was look at him and he was ready to fulfill anything she asked of him. Soon he was standing outside beside his boys when the so-called Son of God walked by behind the man Simon of Cyrene, whom they'd compelled to carry the cross of Jesus.

He backed his sons against the house to keep them from getting hit by the large wooden cross when it passed near them.

The crowd was jeering and mocking Jesus, who was so close he could see the fresh blood dripping from His wounds. Jesus staggered and fell to His knees right in front of where they stood. He had no patience for the man who had dared to stop in front of his doorway.

"Get up! Move on! You can't stop here!"

God forgive him, he had said that to Christ.

Jesus looked up at him. "A moment. I need but a moment to rest," He said just above a whisper.

"This is not a place of rest. Begone!"

Overwhelming sadness now filled Ahasver's heart with the memory, and a tear rolled down his cheek as he stared out the plane's window and his thoughts returned to that horrific scene.

Looking up at him, Jesus had said, "I warn you, still your tongue, man. For as you say to Me, so shall it be with you."

Then Jesus tried to get up but fell back to the ground. The ground around Him reddened with the blood dripping from his wounds.

A warning? An earnest sounding one, too. Apparently the man believes the words Himself!

His youngest son started toward Jesus, wanting to help Him stand. He grabbed him back. How dare the filthy man issue a warning to him!

"Are You mad? Go! I curse You! You have rested enough on my ground! You could live until the Messiah comes, and Your rest will be no more than what You have had already! Go now! You who have nothing to show for Your life! Pay Your debt with all that You have: Your life!" The words spewed from his mouth with venom.

In that moment, Jesus had looked at him with such sorrow.

Ahasver understood now that what he had mistaken for pain in His eyes had been compassion, knowing already the curse he'd brought upon himself with his own words: the loss, the hardships, the travesties soon to befall him as a result of his hasty and cruel words.

The crowd began poking at Jesus with sticks and laughing cruelly.

"Your place of rest is yonder!" they said, pointing toward the hill where He would be crucified.

A man weeping on the other side of the narrow road came to Him and helped Him to His feet, partially carrying Him until a Roman soldier pushed him away.

Jesus stood and looked back one last time before He continued on to His death. He blinked when blood, or maybe sweat, ran into His eyes. No anger or hatred could be seen in His expression. Looking past the unmistakable pain in His eyes, love seemed to radiate from His gaze.

He had clutched his boys by their robes and pulled them inside the house, closing the door behind him.

It was only minutes before one of his shepherds knocked on his door.

"A man," the shepherd said, "hung himself from a tree on your land. He was one of those men hanging around that Jesus they're taking up the hill to crucify."

Will I ever get any rest today? he wondered with a loud sigh.

He didn't go to the crucifixion. He had better things to do with his time. For instance, complain to those priests for letting that follower of Jesus loose to hang himself on his land. The tree limb had broken, and the man's body had fallen on the ground. The hot sun would surely begin the rank decaying process soon.

The Pharisees knew he had strong ties to the Roman officials and weren't about to let him take his complaint to them—especially after forcing Pontius Pilate to crucify Jesus when Pilate believed the man should have been set free. He went to the chief priests prepared to tell them he wanted the man's body removed and was flabbergasted when they wanted to buy the field from him. They paid him thirty silver coins!

What good luck for a cursed man, he thought.

And he still had plenty of land for his herd of sheep.

That night, there was a tremendous earthquake. His wife, one daughter, and two of his sons were killed when part of the roof caved in on top of them. He later learned the earthquake happened at the time when the man who called Himself the Son of Man had died on the cross. He never completely recovered after the quake took his wife and children. His house was rebuilt, and his two remaining sons and daughters grew up to maturity and married. One son was blessed with children, but the other had none and died a widower. Both daughters married, but one was stoned for adultery—growing up without a mother surely had an effect on her morality. The other daughter died giving birth to her first child; the baby, a boy, died not long after.

The son having children—his grandchildren—was the young son who had attempted to help Jesus to His feet. Remembering the words Jesus had spoke to his father, he blamed his father for the deaths of his mother and siblings, and after growing up and having a family of his own, he began his own leather-crafting business.

The shepherds came to see him again the day after the earthquake to tell him his sheep had spooked during the quake and had run over a cliff. They were all dead. They gathered their bodies and dumped them where Judas had hung himself on the land that he'd sold to the chief priests for a potter's field, sure that he wouldn't want their bodies left to rot on his land. Since the priests owned the field, they hadn't bothered with Judas's body. It continued to lie beneath the tree where it had fallen. He last saw it when he went to see the carcasses of his dead sheep, making sure the shepherds hadn't lied to him about their deaths. Judas's body was partly buried under one of the beasts. His belly had burst open, and his bowels were exposed with flies and maggots crawling on him. The smell was horrible, making him appreciate the shepherds' removal of the dead animals from his land. The ground around the death scene was covered with blood. He left almost as soon as he got there.

The Roman officials he once served, accounting for his wealthy income, died of old age, and the younger ones replacing them called upon his son to make their leather whips, knife casings, sandals, bridles, harnesses, or whatever leather goods they desired.

Without an income, he couldn't pay his taxes, and Caesar took his house and land. Homeless, he wandered about Jerusalem trying to make sense of what had happened to his life. Accustomed to wealth, he just naturally exhibited his highborn ways to those who saw him on the street, and they mocked him as they did Jesus when they'd dressed Him like a king. Over time, he was given the nickname of the Persian King Ahasverus, whose name meant "wanderer" or "everlasting," befitting for a man with his constant traveling lifestyle and his highborn attitude. Due to his unkempt appearance, they didn't think him worthy of the king's full name and shortened it to Ahasver. He kept the name as a constant reminder of his past.

He never aged. He heard his son had became a Christian, but he was afraid to see him, unable to withstand the possibility of his eyes peering at him accusingly when he saw his ageless body. His son would know that the curse, issued from pride by his own mouth, had truly been put upon him—cursing himself to remain alive until the return of the Messiah while his beautiful wife, the mother of his children, lay buried in her grave for many years.

Some years later, he heard talk of an old leather master who had died peacefully in his sleep, and he knew they spoke of his son. He didn't know if he had any descendants still living, since he had severed all family ties years earlier.

There was no rest for him anywhere he stopped. Hearing

the gossip and rumors of his cursed life before he got there, no one permitted him to remain in their area long. He was forced to wander and only able to sleep for brief periods at any given time.

Amazingly he still had the thirty silver coins. Whenever he would try to use them to purchase an item—often paying generously for shelter, food, clothing ... once, even a donkey to ride on—either the money bag would come up missing, causing him to believe he had been robbed, or something horrid would befall the taker of the money. All at once believing the stories of his curse to be true, they would become angry and return the silver coins, accusing him of tricking them into taking the money, afterward praying to be forgiven for associating with the cursed man in hopes their life returned to normal.

Yes, he still had the money, but he no longer kept it with him. What good would it do him? It was stored in a vault at the mother church in the Middle East, where he was most often. Years after his family and all those he knew had been long gone ... after he'd asked Jesus for forgiveness ... he met a church leader, a holy man, and told him his story. The man took pity on him—or was it the love of Christ that overflowed his heart? Whichever ... he'd befriended him. Since then, he had grown in Christ and remained close to the church. The holy man who took him in, of course, was long gone, as were the many holy men serving God after him, but each passed his story on to the next before leaving this world.

And so it was even unto this day.

He hadn't told Shade his life's story ... only what he needed to know. When Shade grew older and noticed that Ahasver's appearance never changed, he would share his story. As he had told Shade about the holy cemetery—the fewer who know, the better—Shade would be told on a need-to-know basis.

His mind began drifting into sleep until the plane bounced from turbulence, causing him to jerk awake. Immediately understanding what had happened, he closed his eyes and was soon fast asleep, glad for a few minutes of rest. It wouldn't last long. It never did ... but for over two thousand years, it was always enough.

/////

Maria lifted the letter and held it tight against her breast. She was going to school! She was unsure how she had been chosen for the scholarship, but remembering Ahasver's prayer, she believed God had seen fit to "light her path" and help her on her way to fulfilling her dream of becoming a nurse, a healer.

Brady, the motel's new desk clerk, brought up the university's website on the office computer, and he, Wanda, and Maria read all they could about the school. The university's nursing program was rated one of the best in the United States. No matter how long Maria would have saved for her schooling, she would never have been able to save enough to go to such a high-rated school. Again she thanked her benefactor ... whoever that might be.

Wanda volunteered to drive her to the bus station. Their new friend Brady stood outside the office, waving good-bye when they drove away.

Before Maria stepped on the bus, she gave Wanda a last hug. Tears filled the eyes of the older, kind-hearted housekeeper, causing Maria's own eyes to fill. She promised to write to Wanda when she was settled in her new school.

Placing her foot on the bottom step, Maria couldn't help but grin, knowing her dream of becoming a nurse was on its way to becoming reality.

La prueba, she thought, *los sueños ... que realmente se pueden hacer realidad.*

Continuing up the steps, she corrected herself and thought the words in English.

Proof, she again mused, *dreams ... they really can come true.*

www.ingramcontent.com/pod-product-compliance
Lightning Source LLC
Chambersburg PA
CBHW072226190626
46809CB00017B/685